He had no intention of kissing her, but as he stared down at her and saw the tremble of her full lower lip, he leaned down and covered her mouth with his.

She hesitated a moment and then returned the kiss, opening her mouth to his as her arms wound tightly around his neck. It might have been wonderful if he hadn't tasted such desperation in her kiss.

It lasted only a moment and then he reluctantly stepped back from her. He wished he could hold her forever, that somehow he could unhear what she'd just told him about herself, about her past.

Cowboy Café: The heart of a small town, the soul of a hero...

Dear Reader,

It's always with a bit of sadness that I come to an end of a series, and I especially hate to say goodbye to all the people of Grady Gulch, Oklahoma, and the Cowboy Café.

There's nothing better than small towns that enjoy a sense of community pride, places where neighbors help neighbors without any expectation of repayment. My heroine, Mary Mathis, lands in Grady Gulch with secrets that threaten both herself and her son, secrets that she hopes nobody ever learns. Sheriff Cameron Evans is a man on a mission, wanting to discover everything he can about the lovely Mary who owns and operates the Cowboy Café. But when her secrets explode, death and destruction follow and Mary must learn to trust the very man who could destroy her.

I hope you enjoy this last book in the Cowboy Café series. Who knows, maybe someday in the future we'll come back to visit.

Happy reading!

Carla Cassidy

CARLA CASSIDY

Confessing to the Cowboy

HARLEQUIN® ROMANTIC SUSPENSE

Recycling programs
for this product may
not exist in your area.

ISBN-13: 978-0-373-27825-1

CONFESSING TO THE COWBOY

Copyright © 2013 by Carla Bracale

Printed in U.S.A.

Books by Carla Cassidy

Harlequin Romantic Suspense

Silhouette Romantic Suspense

Other titles by this author available in ebook format.

CARLA CASSIDY

is an award-winning author who has written more than one hundred books for Harlequin Books. In 1995 she won Best Silhouette Romance from *RT Book Reviews* for *Anything for Danny*. In 1998 she also won a Career Achievement Award for Best Innovative Series from *RT Book Reviews*.

Carla believes the only thing better than curling up with a good book to read is sitting down at the computer with a good story to write. She's looking forward to writing many more books and bringing hours of pleasure to readers.

To the friends who help me through the insanity of my life. You all know who you are...thanks for being there for me!

Chapter 1

Sheriff Cameron Evans was tired of finding women dead in their beds. He stood in the doorway of Dorothy Blake's small bedroom and took in the tragic scene before him. It was definitely a bad start to a new week.

A light breeze fluttered the blue-flowered curtains hanging at the open window, blowing in the cold November early morning air.

Dorothy was clad in a pale pink nightgown and covered by a blue bedspread. Blood stained the spread around her neck but without that telltale sign it would appear that Dorothy slept peacefully. Her eyes were closed and her features showed no sign of stress.

Cameron tightened his hands into fists as two of his men wearing paper booties moved in to collect any evidence that might lead to a clue to the killer. He had little hope that they'd find anything. Two previous deaths in the same manner had yielded nothing. The murderer was smart and meticulous in his efficiency. Get in, slit the throat of a sleeping woman and then get out, leaving nothing behind for law enforcement to work with.

The window appeared to be intact, suggesting that it had been unlocked and had provided easy access. Cameron's frustration grew as he thought of the town hall meeting where he'd cautioned all women living alone to make sure their windows and doors were locked at all times. Apparently there had been some at the meeting who weren't paying attention.

"Where's the kid?" Cameron asked. He'd been told before he'd arrived on scene that the body had been discovered by a teenage kid.

"In the kitchen with the dog," Deputy Adam Benson said from behind Cameron. "He's pretty freaked out."

"I can imagine," Cameron replied. He moved past Adam and headed down the hallway to the kitchen. There was nothing more he could do in the bedroom. His team was well trained and the coroner stood by to move in after the crime-scene team had taken their photos and done their work. In the meantime he had to speak to Jeffrey Lawrence, the young man who had found Dorothy an hour earlier.

Dorothy's kitchen was painted a cheerful bright yellow, with white and yellow gingham curtains hanging at the window. Despite the day's chill the sunshine streamed into the windows with welcome heat that battled with the cold air drifting down the hallway from the bedroom.

Jeff Lawrence sat at the small, wooden kitchen table, his blue eyes red-rimmed as he hugged a wiggly, small furry mutt close to his chest.

"I can't get the picture of her out of my head," he said as he swallowed hard in an obvious effort not to cry. "It's like burned in my brain…all that blood and the smell."

"I'm sorry you had to experience that. What were you doing here so early in the morning?" Cameron took the seat opposite the young man at the table.

"It's my job…to walk Twinkie every morning before I go to school. I'm a senior and trying to save up some extra money for college." Twinkie whined at the sound of her name and licked the underside of Jeff's pointy chin.

"How long have you had this arrangement with Dorothy?"

"Since the beginning of summer. She and my mom are good friends and that's how I know…knew Dorothy." His eyes welled up with tears once again. "My mom is going to be so upset about all of this."

Cameron waited a minute for the kid to get himself back under control and then continued, "How did you enter the house this morning?"

"I have my own key. Sometimes Dorothy worked the night shift at the Cowboy Café and she'd sleep in late in the mornings. If she didn't answer when I knocked, then I used my key to come in and usually found Twinkie on the foot of her bed. Whenever Twinkie saw me she'd jump down and we'd go for our morning walk."

"Is that what happened this morning?"

Jeff's head bobbed like one of those big-headed dolls people put on their dashboards or desks. "Everything was the same as usual. I knocked on the door and when Dorothy didn't answer I went ahead and let myself in. I walked down the hallway to her bedroom and Twinkie was curled up at her feet, just like usual. But this morning Twinkie didn't jump off the bed when she saw me. She just whined and whined and I thought maybe she was hurt. So, I walked over to her and that's when I noticed the blood…and the smell. I didn't touch Dorothy, I knew she was dead. I just grabbed Twinkie and left the room and then called 911."

"You did the right thing," Cameron replied. There was no way Jeff was involved in the crime, at least not at the moment. The kid had the green cast of somebody on the verge of puking. He petted the dog as if the silky fur were the only thing holding him together.

"What's going to happen to Twinkie? Dorothy doesn't have any family, and I can't take her. We already have a big dog, Zeus, who would eat this little girl for lunch." Jeff looked distraught. "Twinkie is a great dog, friendly and well trained. I mean, I'm sorry about Dorothy, but you need to find a good home for Twinkie." Jeff looked at him pleadingly.

Great, Cameron thought. Not only did he have another murder to try to solve, he also had the faith of a softhearted kid depending on him to find a tragically orphaned mutt a good home.

"Gather up all her doggie stuff, and I'll see what I can do," Cameron said. "Then go home. We'll probably have more questions for you later, but right now I'd prefer you not talk to anyone about this crime except with your parents."

Jeff nodded and got up from the table. As he began to gather up all things Twinkie, Cameron went back down the hallway where he met the coroner, who told him what he already suspected.

Time of death was between one and three in the morning, cause of death was a quick, clean slice across the throat. Dorothy's hearing aids were on the night-stand. She'd never heard her screen being removed and the unlocked window sliding open. She'd never heard her killer's approach.

"It's just like the other two," Deputy Benson said. "Three women killed in their beds, their throats cut."

"And all three worked as waitresses at the Cow-boy Café," Cameron added. He frowned, thinking of how this latest murder would affect Mary Mathis, the owner of the café.

He couldn't help the way his heart softened as he thought of her. He'd had a thing for Mary since she'd taken over ownership of the café five years before and for the three years prior when she'd worked as a wait-ress there…unfortunately it was an unrequited thing.

He couldn't think about that now. He had plenty of other tasks ahead of him to find this killer who was tormenting his town.

Throughout the afternoon, his men canvassed the neighborhood to find anyone who had witnessed any-thing unusual, but Grady Gulch was a typical small Oklahoma town where most people were in their beds and sleeping in the wee hours of the morning.

Twinkie spent part of the day either snoozing on the rug in the living room or being walked by one of the deputies on scene. Cameron had already decided he'd take the pooch home with him for now and in his spare time try to find her a good home.

As Cameron attended to his duties overseeing the crime scene and directing his deputies, he couldn't help but think of the other two victims. Candy Bailey had been a young woman killed in her bed in a small cottage behind the Cowboy Café. Shirley Cook had been a middle-aged woman murdered in her bed in her home.

Now Dorothy, sixty-four years old and looking to retire and putter in her garden after years of waiting on other people, was instead murdered while she slept.

He tamped down the unexpected rage that threatened to build inside him, a rage directed at the killer, who moved like a shadow in the night, who sought out the vulnerable and killed them without remorse and left no clues behind.

Who was this person? A native of Grady Gulch or one of the new members of town who had brought with them a dark soul and an evil directed at the waitresses of the popular café?

Before the night was over he needed to have a sit-down with Mary. It was something he dreaded, first telling her that another of her waitresses had been killed, although by the time he got to her she probably would have already heard. But he wanted to pick her brain as to why somebody might be targeting these women who worked for her.

The fact that the first two murdered women had

worked at the café he might have written off as a strange coincidence, but three dead waitresses made a definite pattern that had to be explored. A serial killer, just what he needed, some creep who had chosen this place—his town—to play out some murderous fantasy or whatever darkness was in his mind.

He stepped outside on the front porch and looked around the neighborhood. It was late afternoon and everything that could be done here had been done.

Despite the grimness of the situation he couldn't help the small smile that curved his lips as he watched Adam Benson holding Twinkie's leash and heading toward him up the sidewalk.

Cameron had a feeling when Adam joined the force a month ago he hadn't considered that one of his official duties would be walking a dainty little dog named Twinkie.

The Benson family had been to hell and back in the past two years. Adam's sister Cherry had been killed in a car accident, his eldest brother Sam had tried to kill a woman and remained in jail awaiting trial on attempted murder charges. Adam's youngest brother Nick had left town soon after Cherry's death, leaving Adam alone to deal with the family ranch and emotional baggage that had sent Adam into the bottom of a bottle for a brief period of time.

Nick had come home and reunited with his girlfriend, Courtney, and their child, Garrett, and Adam had moved into a rented room upstairs in a house owned by a wheelchair-bound woman who he'd eventually fallen in love with.

The Benson men, except Sam, who remained in jail charged with attempted murder, had found love and were in the process of building lives with the women who had captured their hearts.

Adam had shown himself to have all the qualities of a good lawman when Melanie Brooks, his handicapped girlfriend, had been kidnapped by one of his own deputies. That man was in jail and Cameron had offered Adam a job on his team. In the month that he'd been working for Cameron, Cameron had never questioned his decision to hire Adam. He'd proven himself to be intelligent, hard-working and detail meticulous.

"As I recall this wasn't in my job description," Adam said good-naturedly as he approached where Cameron stood. "Have you figured out what you're going to do with the little pup?"

Cameron released a sigh as he looked at the tiny dog that appeared to be smiling up at him. "I suppose I'll take her to my place for now until I can find a suitable home for her, unless..."

"Oh, no," Adam quickly protested. "Melanie would kill me. We're in the middle of planning a wedding and we've already decided that pets are out of the question for us." He handed Cameron the leash as if he couldn't get rid of it fast enough.

"Guess I'll run her by my place and then head to the café. I need to talk to Mary. There's got to be a reason this guy is killing her waitresses."

"And if we can figure out the 'why,' maybe we can identify the 'who,'" Adam replied.

"Exactly," Cameron said. "For now I want you to

find out the names of all of Dorothy's friends and set up interviews. I'll be back in the office later this evening to check on progress." He leaned down and picked up Twinkie in his arms. The friendly little beast snuggled against him as if she were already home.

Minutes later Cameron was in his car and headed to his place. Home was a comfortable ranch house on five acres of land. He had a couple of horses, but no cattle. The horses were strictly for riding and not for business.

It was a nice place but also a lonely place for Cameron who at thirty-five had assumed by now it would be filled with a wife and a couple of kids.

Unfortunately the minute he'd seen Mary Mathis in the café, he'd also seen her in his mind as the woman who belonged in his home. Equally as unfortunate, Mary had made it clear that she didn't belong in his home, on a date or in any other space with him beyond friendship.

By now Mary probably would have heard that she'd lost another waitress. The grapevine in Grady Gulch was strong and healthy and it had been hours since Dorothy's body had been discovered.

A frustrating part about these crimes was that Cameron didn't know how to anticipate who might be next. He didn't know what to do to keep other women safe.

After the last murder he'd held a press conference and warned women who lived alone to make sure they kept their doors and windows closed and locked, to be aware of their surroundings and if they felt threatened at all to call 911.

He had a feeling that nobody in town had taken his

warnings seriously. Candy Bailey had been a young woman and initially her boyfriend, Kevin Naperson, had looked good for the murder. Cameron still had his eye on the young man, but couldn't tie him to Shirley Cook's murder.

If Cameron was perfectly honest with himself he'd admit that he had no viable suspects for any of the murders. He had a couple persons of interest, but nobody who popped to the top of the pathetic list.

Several tall trees stood sentry on either side of his house and a nice-sized pond glittered in the not-so-far distance. The barn was located behind the house and the entire back acreage was fenced to keep the three horses where they belonged.

Once he was in the house it didn't take him long to set up space for Twinkie in the laundry room. The dog not only had her own little wardrobe, but also food and water bowls and a tiny four-poster bed that appeared to have never been slept in.

With the dog settled, Cameron left the house once again and headed toward the Cowboy Café and a talk with Mary. As always when he drove toward the café, myriad emotions filled his head.

The café was *the* place in town to go for friendly conversation and a warm and inviting atmosphere. The food was terrific and the prices were appealing. Mary had managed to turn a restaurant into a home away from home for many of the people in the small town.

She'd also managed to twist his heart in a million ways without doing a thing but talking to him and looking at him with her bright blue eyes. But he couldn't go there now. At this moment he couldn't think about Mary, except in the capacity as a piece of a puzzle to solve a series of crimes. This visit to the café was all business.

The first thing he did as he entered the large, popular eating establishment was add his hat onto one of the hooks along the entranceway. The second thing he did was gaze toward the counter, where the pretty blonde usually stood.

She wasn't there. A quick glance around told him she was no place in the front of the café. In her place, behind the counter, Rusty Albright stood surveying the surroundings like a bouncer ready to pounce.

Rusty was a big man with ice-blue eyes and a smashed, crooked nose that told a story Cameron had never heard. He was Mary's cook and right-hand man when it came to running the place.

"Rusty," he said with a nod of his head. "Is Mary around?"

Rusty shook his head. "She's been gone since this morning. Matt's school had a take-a-parent-to-school day and so she's been with him all day." He shook his head. "Had to eat one of those nasty school lunches and everything."

Cameron glanced at his wristwatch. It was almost four. School let out at three forty-five so if they came right back, they should be here anytime.

"I heard we lost Dorothy." Rusty frowned. "Any leads?" He asked the question without enthusiasm, as if knowing what Cameron would reply.

"Not yet. It's early in the investigation. Do you know if Mary has heard about Dorothy?"

"Doubtful, but you can ask her yourself." He nodded toward the door. "She and Matt just walked in."

Cameron turned around to see Mary and her ten-year-old son Matt entering the café. The beautiful smile that curved her lips, the sparkle that lit her eyes let him know that she hadn't heard the latest news and he hated the fact that he would be the one to snatch away her smile, to darken her eyes with pain.

"Hey, Sheriff Evans," Matt greeted with a friendly grin.

"Hey, yourself," Cameron replied affectionately. He'd told Matt a dozen times that he could call him Cameron, but Mary had insisted her son use Cameron's official title. "I just heard that your mom spent the day at school with you. That must have been weird."

Mary laughed, the sound twisting softness around Cameron's heart. "I think *embarrassing* would be first on the page if we were listing adjectives."

"Nah, you didn't embarrass me," Matt replied. "At least you didn't call me honey pie like Billy Morton's mom did." Matt stifled a snicker.

"True, although I did consider calling you honey pooh bear a couple of times."

Matt looked horrified at the very thought, and Mary laughed.

"You wouldn't do that to me," Matt said.

"Probably not," Mary agreed.

At that moment Jimmy Rosario flew through the front door. "Mom, Jimmy's here," Matt said, stating the obvious. "We're going to play some catch in the back, okay?"

"You have one hour and then it's dinner and home-work time," Mary replied. "And stay away from the cabins." Her intense love for her son shone from her eyes as she watched him and his best friend disappear out the door.

She turned back to Cameron and must have seen something in his features that stole some of the light from her eyes. "What are you doing here at this time of the day?"

Normally Cameron came by at the end of the night, just before the restaurant closed to have a cup of cof-fee and share some friendly talk with her. Aware that the restaurant was filling quickly for the dinner rush, he was reluctant to share his information with her here in the middle of the gathering crowd.

"Can we go someplace private to talk?"

She gazed up at him for a long moment, biting her full lower lip in a gesture of anxiety. With a quick bob of her head she gestured for him to follow her through the kitchen and to the doorway that led to her and Matt's living quarters behind kitchen.

He walked into a large living room that not only had a sofa, chairs and a television, but also had a small table and chairs in one corner. In all the years he'd known her, he'd never been in these rooms in the back of the café. As far as he knew, few people were invited into this private space that she and her son called home.

"Nice place," he observed. The blue overstuffed sofa looked broken in and inviting, and the entertainment center held a television with the latest video game system and an array of paperback novels.

"Thanks. There are two bedrooms. Matt's is there," she pointed at a doorway to the left of the room. "And mine is there," she said, this time pointing in the opposite direction of the living room. "We also have a full bath. The only thing we don't have is a kitchen, but of course we have the café kitchen at our disposal any time we want anything."

She stopped talking and tucked a tendril of her shoulder-length, light blond hair behind one ear. "But, you aren't here to talk about my living arrangements. Something has happened." She said the words as a statement, not as a question.

He nodded and fought against the release of a deep, weary sigh. "There's been another one."

Mary didn't just sit on the sofa, she crumpled into it, her legs unable to hold her upright as the horror of his words echoed in her head.

There's been another one. She couldn't wrap her mind around the fact that somebody else she'd considered her café family had been murdered. If it wasn't one of her waitresses from the café, then Cameron wouldn't be here now.

"Who?" The word whispered out of her on an edge of dread.

"Dorothy Blake."

Pain shattered through Mary and her vision blurred with tears as she thought of the older woman who'd always come in with a bright smile, who despite enjoying her job was looking forward to retirement and planting a big vegetable garden beside her stupendous flower garden in her backyard.

Lowering her face into her hands as she realized she had no control over her tears, she was vaguely aware of Cameron standing next to the sofa, awkwardly shifting his weight from one foot to the other.

Overwhelmed by the pain of loss, Mary began to weep in earnest. It wasn't just the tragic death of Dorothy that caused her heart to swell with agony, but also the recent loss of two other waitresses, both of them murdered, as well.

She wasn't sure how long she cried before she felt the weight of Cameron sitting down beside her, smelled the familiar spicy scent of his cologne, and in the very depths of her soul she wanted to throw herself into his arms, feel his strength surrounding her. For just a minute, for just an agonizing second, she wanted to be wrapped in his arms and feel his heart beating against her own.

But she couldn't do that. She wouldn't do that. Instead she drew a deep shuddery breath and sat back, summoning the inner strength that had gotten her through most of her entire life.

"Why? Why is somebody killing the women who work for me?" she asked miserably. Once again she caught her lower lip and reached up to twist a strand of her hair.

Cameron frowned, the gesture doing nothing to detract from his handsomeness. His face was all angles and planes that radiated strength. His warm hazel eyes were now deeper in hues of brown than usual. "I don't know. But I can tell you that two dead waitresses was a coincidence, three is a definite pattern. There's no question in my mind now that we have a serial killer targeting your waitresses."

"But that's crazy. What on earth could these women have done wrong that would warrant their deaths? Serve cold coffee?" A faint hysterical laughter attempted to escape her lips, but was instantly swallowed as she gazed at Cameron for answers.

"I wish I could tell you why, and I definitely wish I could tell you who." His jaw clenched tight and, for a moment, his eyes were cold and hard. "I'm just hoping Dorothy's murder can give us something, anything that might provide a lead. This guy has been so damned careful and so damned lucky." Frustration drifted from him in waves.

Mary dropped her hand from her hair and instead placed it on him, able to feel the muscles in his forearm beneath the long-sleeved khaki shirt he wore. "You'll get him. You're an intelligent man, Cameron. You do your job well and you have good men working for you. It's just a matter of time before you have him in custody."

He smiled at her, that sexy uplift of his lips that warmed her like no other man's had ever done. "There are days I feel like I should be digging ditches instead."

"You know you love what you do, and hopefully you'll catch this madman before another woman dies." She stood from the sofa, finding his nearness slightly overwhelming. Escape. She needed to escape from him before she followed through on her impulse and leaned into him.

"And now I've got a dinner rush to attend to," she said, attempting to focus on business and not on how much she wanted Cameron's arms around her, not on the horror of Dorothy's horrendous death.

"I intend to warn your waitresses again about locking up doors and windows, about safety issues before I leave the café. You might also tell them the same thing. Each and every one of them is a potential victim until I get this guy behind bars."

"I'll remind them." Her heart pounded at the knowledge that simply by working for her, women she cared about were placing their lives in potential danger.

As the two of them reentered the main café area, Mary got to work helping expedite orders as Rusty went back to the kitchen to cook with his helper, Junior Lempke.

The dinner rush was always busy, but with the news of Dorothy's murder making the rounds, the restaurant was unusually full. Mary worked, always conscious of Cameron's tall, commanding presence as he pulled each waitress aside and spoke to each of them for a couple of minutes.

When he finally left, she focused solely on what needed to be done to keep the people in her café happy and well fed. At six o'clock Matt and Jimmy came in and sat at a small table for two near the counter. It was the usual place where Matt ate and most nights Jimmy was with him.

Mary had a feeling Liza Rosario wasn't much of a

cook, but she often had Matt over for playdates with her son. Jimmy was a bright, nice boy who was Matt's best friend and Mary didn't mind feeding the kid dinner each evening as she suspected dinner at home would be something frozen and heated or from a box.

If the boys had their way, they'd order burgers and fries every night, but Mary always ordered for them, insisting they eat real meals with real vegetables. Tonight was meatloaf, green beans and applesauce, along with two huge glasses of milk.

The evening rush seemed to last forever. Just when she thought things were starting to slow down, more people would arrive. It was always this way when tragedy struck…friends and neighbors gathered here to find solace or laughter or just simple conversation and connection.

Jimmy eventually went home and Matt went back to their living quarters to work on his homework before his bath and bedtime. Mary kept her mind emptied of everything but the basic minute-to-minute things she needed to do to keep the café running.

At ten o'clock she locked the door and turned the sign hanging there from Open to Closed. She'd tucked Matt into bed an hour before and normally this was the time that Cameron would show up for a quick cup of coffee before he headed home.

She didn't expect him tonight. He had a murder to solve. Dorothy's murder. Her heart crunched with pain as Rusty stepped up next to her. "Kitchen is clean, grill is ready for the morning. You want me to help you clean up out here?"

"No thanks. I'll take care of it." She'd sent the waitresses home at closing time rather than have them stick around to clean their stations and sweep and mop the floors, which was part of their usual jobs.

"Are you sure you're okay?" Rusty's tough-guy features didn't change, but his gruff voice was softer than usual.

Mary smiled at him with genuine affection. "I'm fine, or at least I will be fine. Cleaning up will help me decompress a little bit. Go home, Rusty." Home for the big man was one of the cabins that Mary rented out located directly behind the café.

Three of the cabins were currently vacant. In one of them Candy Bailey, a young waitress, had been murdered. The other one had also been rented to another waitress who had moved out right after Candy's murder. The third had been empty for a long time and the fourth was Rusty's place.

"If you need me just call. You know I can be here in two minutes," Rusty said.

She nodded. "Thanks. Really, I'll be fine."

Minutes later as she swept up the floor between the tables, her thoughts returned to the murders. She'd managed to keep her mind fairly numb until the café had closed and she was alone, but now the horror reached out to chill her to the bone.

Three murdered women. Three dead waitresses. Had each of the women somehow offended the killer when serving him? Was he somebody who visited the café regularly? She couldn't imagine any of her customers being capable of such a thing. But she also knew how a pleasant face, a friendly smile could hide the soul of a monster.

She switched the broom for a mop and continued cleaning the floor while her head raced with thoughts. If the killer was a customer, then Cameron had a huge pool of potential suspects to investigate. Almost everyone in the small town of Grady Gulch, Oklahoma, came in to eat at one time or another. Many were regulars, others were occasional diners. There was also the possibility that the killer didn't ever eat here at all.

Three waitresses…friends…women she had considered part of her extended family were now gone. Why? What would drive somebody to kill them? A piercing ache shot through her as she finished up the floor and began to wash down tables and chairs.

Did somebody have a grudge against the café? Against her personally? She couldn't imagine either. The café was popular, and she and Matt had worked hard over the past eight years to fit in and become a part of the close-knit community.

This couldn't be about her past. Her heart iced over at the very thought. No, that was impossible. This couldn't be about her and the man she'd once married.

She emptied her mind of everything as she focused on finishing the chores. When the café was ready for opening the next morning she walked through the kitchen toward the door that led to her living quarters.

The navy blue ginger jar lamp set on the end table by the sofa created a soft glow of light around the living room. The first thing she did was move to stand in Matt's bedroom doorway.

As she gazed at her sleeping son, her heart expanded with love, and for a moment all thoughts of murder left her mind. Matt was a well-adjusted, good boy, who rarely needed a stern word or a disapproving look.

Sometimes she worried that he was too accommodating, that in his eagerness to please he'd make mistakes and trust the wrong people. But they were normal motherly concerns and she had bigger worries plaguing her mind.

She walked through the living room and into the bathroom, needing a quick shower before going to bed. As she stood beneath the warm spray of water, her thoughts turned to Cameron.

In another lifetime, he might have been the man she'd invite into her heart, but she was living in this lifetime and had decided long ago that nobody, especially no man, would ever be allowed too close.

She couldn't let any man close to her, there were too many secrets in her past, too much of herself she'd never be able to tell anyone. She feared that if she tried to have a relationship she'd slip up, make a mistake and all would be lost.

Still, there were times when she was in her bed alone that she longed for strong arms to reach out to her, when she wished for an intimacy that she'd never really experienced before with any man.

There were also times she wished she had somebody to talk to about Matt, someone to brag to when he did something amazing and to commiserate with when things went wrong.

Each time she tried to imagine who that man might

have been, an image of Cameron filled her mind. Over the past several years he'd made it a habit to stop in at the café right at closing time.

He'd drink the last cup of coffee in the pot and they'd sit and talk. She'd been there for him when his younger brother had died two years ago in a tragic farming accident and his grief had not only shattered his heart, but also made him the sole child of his older parents.

He'd been there for her when Candy Bailey had been found murdered in one of the cabins she rented behind the café. They'd gone through bad times together and had also shared a lot of laughter.

She knew he was romantically interested in her, and although she enjoyed their evening conversations, she never allowed him to believe their relationship would be anything other than friendship.

The cost of developing anything meaningful with Cameron was too high. She might mess up, accidently share too much with him. He was a sheriff and as far as she knew, there was no statute of limitations on murder.

Chapter 2

Cameron sat in his office alone and sipped a cup of strong coffee, hoping for an adrenaline rush that would get him through the day. It was just after seven in the morning and he hadn't gone to bed the night before until well after midnight.

He'd just collapsed onto the king-size bed when he heard a faint scratching on a door down the hallway and remembered he was now, at least temporarily, a pet owner.

He'd jumped out of bed and opened the laundry room door. Twinkie exploded out and raced to the front door, obviously in desperate need of a potty break.

Cameron opened the door, and watched the little mutt as she sniffed the grassy area until she found a place she liked. When she'd finished her business she came back inside and looked up at Cameron expectantly.

"Good girl," Cameron had said, and Twinkie's tail had wagged in response, then she raced straight to Cameron's bedroom and placed her front paws on the edge of the mattress.

"Oh, no, little girl. That's my bed." Cameron got the four-poster bed from the laundry room and set it next to his. "This is Twinkie's bed."

The dog had looked at it as if she'd never seen it before in her life. Cameron ignored her, got into bed and turned out the bedside lamp. The whine began low in Twinkie's throat as her front paws tap-danced on the side of the mattress.

After fifteen minutes of trying to be firm, Cameron had given in and pulled the pup on top of his bed. Twinkie immediately curled up at Cameron's feet, her body warmth radiating through the blanket.

A spoiled tiny dog wasn't exactly what he thought about when he considered bedmates, but for now the furry dog was all he had.

He'd awakened at dawn after a night filled with haunting visions of dead women, each of them pleading for justice. His nightmares had been a strobe-light event with the dead reaching out to him.

Now here he sat in his office, sipping coffee and waiting for it to be time for the staff meeting he'd called with all his deputies that would occur in another twenty minutes.

While the coffee sent a jolt of caffeine-driven adrenaline through him, it did nothing to make his thoughts any more clear as to solving these crimes. He didn't expect his team to have anything to report to him to answer either of those questions. He reared back in his chair and released a sigh of weary frustration.

At some point today he needed to get out to his parents' place. It had been a full week since he'd been there and he knew there would be things that needed to be done. Since his brother, Bobby's, death, Cameron had been trying to help them around the ranch to fill in the shoes of the child they had lost.

The relationship between him and his father had become strained long ago when Cameron had decided to run for sheriff instead of staying home to help with the family ranch. With Bobby's death the relationship had only become more difficult.

He sat for another fifteen minutes, then swallowed the last of his coffee and stood. Now wasn't the time to think about family dynamics or anything else that didn't pertain to murder. It was time to meet with his team and see if they could figure out how to stop this killer before he struck again.

Minutes later he stood at the head of a long table in the conference room, six deputies seated on each side of the table. They were an even dozen, all good men who made up the law in Grady Gulch and the surrounding area. Thankfully they were in charge of a small county.

"Morning, gentlemen," he said. "Let's get down to business."

For the next hour the men reported what had been done so far in the investigation into Dorothy's murder. The neighborhood had been canvassed, friends had been interviewed and, just as he'd suspected, they had little to report.

Her neighbors had heard nothing throughout the night, friends indicated that they couldn't imagine Dorothy having any enemies. *Yada-yada-yada,* Cameron thought. It was the same song, just a different victim.

No forensic evidence had been left behind, no fingerprints to process, no dropped glove or footprints to cast, this killer was definitely smart enough to cover his tracks well.

"There's no question now that this killer is targeting the waitresses at the Cowboy Café," Cameron said when the others were finished with their meager reports. "That's the only connection that's obvious between the victims." He instantly thought of Mary and wondered if she was in danger, as well.

In her capacity as owner of the café she rarely worked the floor, but she did work behind the counter often and could be considered a waitress.

"Adam, I want you to check and cross-check the personal lives of these women and see if there's anyplace else they connect besides their work at the café. Maybe they go to the same hairdresser or use the same gym. I want to know anyplace these women's lives might intersect besides the café."

"Ben," Cameron said, directly his attention to Deputy Ben Temple, who he considered his right-hand man. "I want you to spend the next couple of days hanging out at the café. See if you notice anyone acting strange, if you see anyone who appears to be focused in on a particular waitress. The rest of you divide up and I want every friend and every neighbor or acquaintance from the previous victims reinterviewed."

It was work that had already been done, but Cameron was grateful and proud that nobody on the team complained. Half the men he dismissed to go home and sleep, the other half who worked the day shift he dismissed to begin their work.

Once the meeting was finished, Cameron went back into his office and pulled on his jacket and his hat. He knew that it was important for him to be seen around town this morning, to assure the public that he and his men were working overtime to catch the evil that was at work in their town.

It wasn't something he was particularly looking forward to doing. People would want answers, and unfortunately he had none to give. He believed it was important to delegate the investigation work to his deputies, but he'd learn what they discovered every step of the way. He was a puzzle guy, he liked to gather pieces, and then attempt to put together the puzzle that would eventually solve the crime.

The last murder that had occurred in Grady Gulch had been two years before, when Jeff Davie had shot his wife, Cheryl, in a domestic dispute. It had been an open-and-shut case as Jeff had confessed to his crime.

Cameron had never had anything like this to take care of before…the murder of three women. He wanted to believe he and his team were up to the task, but if things got too dicey he'd have to request help from the FBI, thus undermining he and his team's ability in the face of the people in town.

As he stepped outside, the blustery air half stole his breath away. Only early November and already he could smell winter in the air. Thankfully the cold wind had chased most people off the streets.

He walked alone down Main, waving into shop windows as he passed. Why now? Why in the last three months had the murders begun to occur? There had to be a trigger of some kind, either that or the murderer had moved here in the past couple of months. There had been several new families and single men who had moved to Grady Gulch in the past year or so. Cameron made a mental note to check each of them thoroughly.

What he'd like to do was head to the café and check on Mary. When he'd told her about Dorothy the night before and she'd fallen onto the sofa and began to weep, there had been nothing Cameron wanted to do more than pull her up into his arms, hold her tight against him in an effort to comfort.

But he wasn't sure that she'd welcome his touch, his closeness. She definitely gave him mixed messages. Although she'd told him a dozen times that she didn't need or want a man in her life, occasionally he caught a whisper of longing in her eyes as she looked at him, a yearning that made him want to believe her eyes and not her lush lips.

He steeled himself as George Wilton walked out of the hardware store and nearly bowled him over. Wearing a thick, long black coat and a hat with huge ear muffs that flapped against his gray whisker-grizzled cheeks, he looked prepared for the snowstorm of the century.

"Heard Dorothy Blake was murdered last night," he said with a scowl, which wasn't unusual. George always found something to scowl about.

"Heard right," Cameron replied.

"Craziness, that's what's taken over this town. You gonna find this creep before he kills all the waitresses from the café?"

"That's my plan, George."

"Yeah, well, my plan is to marry some twenty-three-year-old hottie who thinks I hung the moon, but that ain't happening anytime soon. Hope your plan works out better than mine. You know I take most of my meals at the café. What will I do, where will I eat if this creep manages to kill all the waitresses and Mary has to close down?"

Leave it to George to think about his own creature comforts rather than the loss of the three women. "Mary isn't going to close down the café and we're going to catch whoever is responsible for these crimes," Cameron said with a confidence that didn't quite make it into his heart.

George's scowl deepened. "Well, you'd better hurry up about it," he said as he moved past Cameron and headed in the opposite direction down the sidewalk.

Hurry up about it. How Cameron wished he could do just that. Snap his fingers, speak an ancient incantation, wiggle his nose and magically have the guilty party behind bars. But he knew from experience that it was going to take hours of pounding pavements, talking to people and seeking any minute detail that might have been overlooked that could break the case wide open.

As the day passed, Cameron found himself unable to get Mary out of his head. Outside of the families of the dead women, Mary would be the person most touched by their deaths. Not only because they worked for her, but because she considered the people who worked at the café her extended family.

In one of their late-night talks she'd told him she had no family, that Matt's father had been killed in a car accident when Matt had been just a baby. She and her husband had both been only children of parents who had passed away. In her isolated grief over her husband's death she'd taken Matt and left her hometown in California and wandered until the wind had blown her into Grady Gulch.

Somebody was killing the waitresses at the café. Was it possible that it wasn't some enemy that the women shared, but rather somebody trying to hurt Mary? Maybe he was making too big a leap, but it was a possibility that had to be considered, along with a dozen others.

The day passed far too quickly, with far too many questions remaining unanswered. A noon meeting with his men yielded nothing worthwhile and a quick stop at his parents' ranch reminded him that he'd never be the son his father had wanted, that the son he'd loved was gone and he wasn't even a pale substitute in his eyes.

The weight of discouragement and frustration pressed heavily on his shoulders as he stopped by the house to let Twinkie out of the laundry room. The little dog danced with excitement at the sight of him and licked the underside of his jaw when Cameron picked her up his arms. Cameron suddenly understood why people had pets.

Twinkie didn't care that he had no clues to the three murders, didn't care that he couldn't be the son his parents wanted. All Twinkie needed from him was food and water and love, and the love was returned unconditionally.

If only people were more like dogs, he thought as he watched the little pooch leaping through the grass like a tiny gazelle in the yard. He called the dog's name, and she came running back to Cameron and followed him back through the front door.

He started to lock Twinkie back up in the laundry room and then changed his mind and decided to give her the run of the house. He almost felt guilty leaving the little pooch alone again, but his day was far from over.

Twinkie needed a home where somebody could spend time with her, he thought as he headed toward the café. She was definitely a social butterfly and would thrive where there were people to appreciate her friendly nature.

It was late, almost ten, and he knew that on Wednesday nights ten was closing time at the café. Mary would probably be waiting for him with a last cup of coffee ready to pour. She'd have questions he couldn't answer and he had questions for her, as well.

With three Cowboy Café waitresses dead, he couldn't help but believe in the possibility that Mary was somehow in the center of the storm.

* * *

Minutes before ten, with the café empty and Mary ready to call it a night, Cameron walked in the front door. He flipped the sign on the door to Closed and then hung his hat on a hook.

She hadn't been sure he'd make his usual stop given the fact that he had a fresh murder to investigate, but she couldn't help the way her heart beat just a little more rapidly at the sight of his handsome face. And she couldn't help but recognize her beating heart was a combination of pleasure and a faint edge of dread as she studied his grim features.

"Bad day?" she asked.

"Bad life," he replied and sat on one of the stools at the counter.

She turned to pour him a cup of coffee and tried to ignore his spicy cologne scent that always shot a hint of warmth through her. It wasn't a particularly unusual fragrance. She'd smelled it on other men, but it didn't affect her in the same way when worn by anyone else.

"No leads?" she asked as she placed the cup of strong hot brew in front of him.

"Nothing to brag about. Dorothy's sister is flying in sometime tomorrow from back East."

Mary looked at him in surprise. "I didn't know Dorothy had a sister. She never mentioned having any family."

Cameron took a sip of his coffee, his hazel eyes more brown than green. "Younger sister. Apparently the two weren't close, so I doubt that she'll have any information that would be helpful to the case."

The weary lines that creased his forehead did nothing to take away from his sexy features. Mary had been drawn to him since the first day she'd met him, like a moth to a flame that would quickly burn her to death.

"Did you talk to Winneta Baker? She and Dorothy were close friends," she said, trying to stay focused on the conversation rather than her desire to stroke her hand across his brow to somehow ease those lines of stress.

He nodded and raked a hand through his thick hat-tousled dark brown hair. "Adam spoke with her. She provided the only information that might prove to be a clue. Apparently the night before her murder Dorothy saw somebody skulking around in her yard."

Mary leaned forward, her heart beginning a new rapid beat. "Casing the place?"

"Possibly. Unfortunately Dorothy couldn't tell who it was in the dark. All she told Winneta was that she thought it was a big man."

"Gee, that narrows the suspect pool," Mary said wryly. "You-all grow them big here in Grady Gulch. At least half the men around here would be considered big."

He took another drink of his coffee, his eyes narrowed above the cup as he looked at her. Something in that gaze clenched a knot in her stomach.

He doesn't know, she told herself. *He can't know. I covered my tracks too well. It's been too many years.* Still the intensity of his gaze made her feel as if he could see right through her, straight through to her soul and all the secrets she'd kept there for so long.

He lowered the cup once again, his gaze still holding hers. "I think we have to talk about the possibility that somehow these murders are related to you."

A gasp escaped Mary. Even though in her darkest nightmares she'd worried that somehow she was a part of the madness that had been taking place, that somehow she was responsible for the deaths of the three women, hearing her fears spoken aloud by him horrified her.

"Me? You mean the café. It's obvious the murders are tied to the café," she replied.

"No, I mean you personally." He leaned forward, as if aware of the impact his words had on her, as if he wanted to somehow touch her, to reassure her that everything was going to be all right. "We have to consider it, Mary," he said softly.

"I know." She pulled up a stool on the opposite side of the counter and sat. "I'd already considered the possibility when Shirley Cook was murdered. Now, with Dorothy's murder, the possibility that somebody is killing my waitresses in an attempt to hurt me *and* the café is even stronger." She was aware of the slight tremble of her voice.

"Has somebody given you any trouble over the last couple of months? Have you fired somebody who might have a grudge against you? Have you sensed any ill feelings coming from any of your customers or friends or even the people you're working with now? Has anyone expressed interest in buying the café?" He was all lawman now, the questions firing from him like bullets from a gun.

She held up a hand to stop the questions as her brain felt as if it might explode. "Trust me, I've racked my brain all day, Cameron, trying to come up with a name, the face of anybody who would want to hurt me, but I've come up completely empty. Since I've owned this place nobody has ever mentioned anything about wanting to buy the café and I haven't had problems with anyone." The only person who'd ever wanted to hurt her was gone forever. She'd seen to that personally.

There was no way she could believe this attack on the waitresses had anything to do with the life she'd lived before the one she'd built here in Grady Gulch. There was no reason for her to tell him anything about the horrors she'd suffered in that previous lifetime, the sins that she'd committed to protect all that she held dear. It was history and that particular part of her history couldn't ever hurt her again unless somehow Cameron discovered what she'd done.

Cameron sighed, the lines across his forehead cutting deeper than usual. "I figured that would be your answer. I've tried and tried to think about who might hold a grudge against you, but I can't think of anyone, either. As far as I know you've only made friends here in town, no enemies that I'm aware of."

Before he could say anything more, the back door of the café opened and Junior Lempke came running in. "Junior!" Mary said in stunned surprise. She'd given the mentally challenged man a key to the back door six months before, but he'd never used it before.

"Mary, Mary." He raced toward her, his moon-shaped face radiating happiness. "Look, look what I have." He held out a cell phone. "Mom got it for me as a surprise. It's just for me."

"That's wonderful, Junior," Mary replied. Junior was thirty-two years old but had the capabilities of a twelve-year-old. A lack of oxygen at birth had resulted in his diminished capacities. Mary had hired him as a busboy over a year ago and now had him doing some of the prep work and cooking.

"Sheriff Cameron, it's my very own phone," Junior said as he turned his attention from Mary. "My mom programmed it for me. If I punch one I call home. If I punch two I call Mary." He flashed her a bright smile. "And if I punch three I call 911."

"That's great, Junior. Your mother must think you're very responsible," Cameron said with a smile at him.

"I am responsible. I am, aren't I, Mary?"

"You're one of the most responsible workers I've ever had," Mary agreed with a gentle smile.

Junior nodded, obviously satisfied and proud of her answer. "Okay, I've got to go back home now. I'll lock up behind me because I'm responsible." Without waiting for replies, Junior turned and headed back to the kitchen door he'd come through.

Mary found herself smiling after him. She'd taken a chance on hiring him and discovered that people had underestimated his abilities and his need to feel productive. She turned back to look at Cameron, whose eyes were narrowed in thought.

"Wonder what Junior does at night. I know his mother pretty much lets him come and go as he pleases."

Mary turned back to look at him in surprise. "Surely

you don't think Junior is capable of such crimes. He doesn't have the cunning, he doesn't have the mental capacity to make plans and assure escape without detection. Besides, Junior loves me and he loves the women who work here."

"What about Rusty?"

"What about him?" Mary realized her tone had become slightly defensive. "You know Rusty has worked for me for years. Yes, he has a temper, but he also has a strong protective streak when it comes to the waitresses."

"But what do you know about his past?" Cameron persisted.

"Enough. I know he lost his wife and child in a house fire years ago. I know that he drifted from place to place, eaten up by grief and drinking too much for a long time and he finally wound up here working for me. Cameron, you're looking at the wrong people."

"I have to look at everyone," he replied. "I've got to either dismiss them completely as suspects or put them on my list of potential suspects."

"You have a list of potential suspects?" she asked hopefully.

His lips curved up in a slow, rueful smile. "I'm working on it. Right now I have a list with every man in town on it and I'm trying to weed it down."

"Maybe it's a woman," Mary said.

Cameron stared at her in surprise and leaned against the back of the stool. "To be honest, we hadn't even considered the possibility."

"But there have been no sexual overtones to the murders, so a woman could have been responsible, right?"

Once again Cameron worried a hand through his hair, and for just a moment Mary wondered what that brown richness would feel like beneath her fingertips.

"Thanks, you just put all the members of town over twelve years old on my potential suspect list."

She smiled sympathetically. "Sorry, it was just a thought."

"Unfortunately it's a viable thought. Even though Dorothy told Winneta she saw a large man outside her house the night before her murder, it could have been a big woman or a normal-sized person casting a large shadow in the moonlight." He raised his cup and drained the last of the coffee. "Walk me to the door?"

She nodded. In another lifetime she would have walked with him to her bedroom. They would have made beautiful love that would banish all thoughts of murders and evil. But in this lifetime she walked him to the front door of the café.

He grabbed his hat from the hook and set it on his head, looking every inch an intelligent, sexy man. Instead of reaching for the door, he placed his hands on her shoulders, his eyes lightening to a more golden-green hue.

She wanted to fall into that light, an illumination that whispered of desire and safety and all the things she dreamed about at night. But she knew it was a false light, a mirage that would disappear if he knew about her past.

"I'm worried about you," he said softly.

"About me?"

His hands slid down her arms and then back up again to her shoulders. "You might be the owner of this café, but that makes you the head waitress and somebody is killing waitresses and we don't know if that somebody might consider you the ultimate prize."

His words shot a shuddering chill down her body. Until Dorothy's murder nobody had been sure what was driving the murderer. Now they could make an educated guess that whoever it was had a thing for waitresses.

"But I'm different," she said, her voice a faint whisper. "I'm different than the other waitresses who have been killed. I don't live alone and I have Matt."

"And we don't know how this killer might escalate." He raised a hand to her cheek and she found the impulse to lean into him and instead took a step back, away from his touch. He dropped his hand and instead shoved both of his hands into his coat pockets. "I'm just saying you need to be careful, Mary."

"I promise I will be. Doors and windows firmly locked and I'll sleep with one eye open," she said in an effort to lighten what had suddenly become a tense tone.

"I'm not kidding. Life wouldn't be the same for me without you in it." He frowned as if irritated with himself. "Grady Gulch wouldn't be the same without your famous apple pie. Lock up after me," he said.

"Always," she replied.

When he'd stepped out the door she carefully locked it, then turned out all the lights except the dim security ones over the long counter and went back to her living quarters. Her cheek still burned from his touch and the desire she'd had to lean into him.

She stopped at Matt's bedroom door, surprised to find him still awake. "Hey, buddy, why aren't you asleep?" She eased down on the edge of his bed as he sat up, his blond hair tousled with the beginnings of a bed head.

"I heard what Sheriff Evans said and I just want you to know that I'll never let anyone hurt you." His voice held all the vehemence a ten-year-old could hold. "I'll protect you always."

Mary's heart squeezed tight and she reached out and shoved a strand of his pale blond hair off his forehead. "Thanks, but that's not your job. That's the sheriff's business. Your job is just to be my favorite son."

He eyed her with a small smile. "Mom, I'm your only son."

"Well, then, that makes your job easy." She rose from the bed and kissed him on the forehead. "Don't worry, Matt. Sheriff Evans is a good sheriff and he's going to get the bad guy and nothing bad is going to happen to me."

"You promise?" Matt asked, this time his voice filled with youthful concern.

"I promise," she replied firmly. "Now, get to sleep. I don't want you snoozing through math class in the morning. If you can't go back to sleep right away, then think about what you want to do for your birthday on Saturday."

Matt's tension wafted away as a smile touched his lips. "My birthday…yeah, I'll think about that," he said and then dutifully closed his eyes. Within minutes he'd fallen asleep, hopefully to dreams of birthday cake and colorful balloons, and Mary moved away from his door and fell onto the sofa in the living room.

The left side of her head suffered a faint pounding that spoke of the beginnings of a headache. Three dead women...not just employees, but also friends.

She'd scarcely had time to grieve for Dorothy as the café had buzzed with business all day. Weddings and deaths brought people out of their isolation and into the café to talk with friends and neighbors.

Now, in the quiet of the room, she still couldn't find the grief that Dorothy deserved. Instead the only emotion she could tap into was a simmering anxiety that bordered on terror.

Was Cameron right? Were these murders really about somebody trying to get to her? Was somebody toying with her?

Destroying the people she loved, the business she'd built before finally killing her?

Why? And who? She'd never gotten any negative vibes from anyone who had entered the café, the people she visited with day after day.

But Mary knew better than most that monsters could wear smiling faces. They were chameleons who could blend into any setting, who appeared like ordinary human beings. They could be charming and make you believe any of their lies.

Oh, yes, Mary knew very well about monsters. A little over thirteen years ago she'd married one...and then she'd killed him.

Chapter 3

"I think we need to look at all the newcomers to town," Cameron said as he faced his men the next morning.

"How new of newcomers?" Deputy Larry Brooks asked.

Cameron frowned thoughtfully. "Let's say anyone who has moved to town within the last year or so. I also want somebody checking into anyone Mary Mathis does business with, vendors and services she utilizes and people who repair the café equipment."

"You have a premonition or something that she's our next victim?" Deputy John Mills asked as he moved a toothpick from one side of his mouth to the other.

"No, but I think we can all agree that these murders revolve around the café and that's where our investigation should stay focused," Cameron replied.

What he didn't need to focus on was how soft her cheek had been when he'd touched it the night before, how he believed he'd seen desire flame up sharp and hot in the depths of her blue eyes. Wishful thinking, he mused as he also remembered how quickly she'd stepped back from him.

He dismissed these wayward thoughts and once again gazed at the men who worked for him. "Brent, I want you to check to see if any murders like these have occurred any place else in Oklahoma. If you find nothing, then expand the search to include Texas and Kansas. This killer is just too good for Candy Bailey to have been his first. Someplace he's honed his craft and if we can find where, then maybe we can identify who."

"Unless he's a local," Adam Benson said.

There was a moment of silence. Nobody wanted to believe that a killer walked among them, that somebody who had been born and raised in the small town was a cold-blooded murderer.

"Damn, but I hate this case," Ben Temple said as he twirled a pen between his fingers as he broke the momentary silence.

"We also can't rule out a female killer," Cameron said. The room exploded as the deputies talked about the pros and cons of the possibility of a woman perp.

"I just don't want to think about any woman I know being capable of doing something like this to another woman," Adam said. "But I can't forget it was a woman who tried to kill Courtney Chambers and take my brother's baby from her."

"And I don't like the idea of one of our own home-grown men involved in this," Brent said. "We're a close-knit community. I know most every single man by name, have talked to them over a cup of coffee or been to their houses."

By eight o'clock everyone had their assignments and had dispersed from the room. Only Adam remained behind. "You look exhausted and the day has barely begun," he observed with a critical gaze at Cameron.

"I'm all right, just couldn't sleep much last night."

"I don't think any of us are going to get a lot of sleep until this creep is behind bars."

Cameron nodded. "How's Melanie?"

Softness swept over Adam's features. "She's terrific. Her dance costume business is really starting to take off and she's keeping busy with it. I'm trying to talk her into a Christmas wedding."

"That's great," Cameron replied, truly pleased for the couple who had been to hell and back. Melanie had been a successful dancer in New York when idiopathic neuropathy and foot drop had landed her permanently in a wheelchair. Adam had moved into her upstairs apartment and the two had fallen in love.

Before their love could be fully realized Melanie had been kidnapped and left in a field to die. The perpetrator had been Deputy Jim Collins, one of Cameron's best men, and Cameron would forever feel more than a bit of guilt for not seeing how sick Jim was, sick enough that he'd harbored an obsession that had turned into a sick rage against Melanie.

"What worries me is that our perp is somebody like Jim, somebody who wears the face of a friend or neighbor and easily hides the evil in his soul," Cameron said thoughtfully.

Adam stood and clapped him on the shoulder. "Stop beating yourself up about Jim. He didn't just fool you, he had us all fooled. We're going to find this creep, Cameron. We're all committed to finding him so we can give you back your quiet, beautiful town." With these words he left the conference room.

Cameron remained seated, working over in his mind the duties he'd given his deputies, making sure that everything that had to be done was being done.

A million possibilities roared through his head. Could it be another waitress who was killing women she didn't like working with? Was it perhaps a man who hated the fact that his wife worked at the café? Or was somebody trying to destroy the café itself?

Certainly Mary had already felt the effects of the first two murders. Several of her regular waitresses had quit working based on fear. Now, with Dorothy's murder, he had a feeling she would lose more waitresses.

How long could she keep the café open with a dwindling staff? And why would anyone want the popular place that was the hub of the small town closed down?

Nothing about these murders made sense. No matter how he twisted what little facts he knew around in his head, there was no easy explanation to find, no answers haunting the edges of his consciousness.

Frustration drove him up from the table. Nothing would get accomplished by him sitting here thinking. He needed to do something in order to advance the investigation.

And he needed to find a home for Twinkie.

She was getting under his skin with her tiny kisses and happy dances. Whenever he sat anywhere in the house she managed to get into his lap and curl up with a contented sigh. He'd actually dressed her in a little furry leopard print dress this morning, worried that she might get too cold in the drafty old farm house where he lived.

He should have a bulldog or a German shepherd, if he was going to have a dog. Not some designer diva who already thought she owned not just his house, but him, as well.

With a change in the direction of his thoughts, he decided to head to the café for breakfast and to check out the crowd. While he ate a couple of eggs sunny-side up he might see somebody who piqued his interest as a potential suspect or find out something Mary had thought about while they'd been apart.

When he arrived at the café the breakfast rush was in full swing. The parking lot was almost full and most of the table space was taken. Cameron rarely sat at a table, preferring a stool at the counter where Mary served the customers.

Cameron moved to an empty stool and smiled at Mary, who looked tired and slightly overwhelmed by the amount of people inside.

A glance around the place let him know only three regular waitresses were working the large floor. Normally there were five or six during this time of the morning.

Mary greeted him with a cup of coffee and a forced

smile. "We don't usually see you here at this time of the day," she said.

"You're going to be seeing me a lot around here," he replied. Her eyes were red-rimmed, as if she'd already been weeping that morning.

"Casing the joint?" Her smile didn't quite reach the center of her eyes.

"Casing the customers," he replied. "Are you doing okay?"

She nodded, the artificial light overhead sparkled in her pale blond hair, accentuated by the black Cowboy Café T-shirt that clung to her full breasts and emphasized her small waist. "Fine, although three of my waitresses called in sick this morning and I have a feeling their illness is going to be permanent."

"They'll come back once we solve the crime," he said with an optimism he didn't quite feel. His town would be scarred after this. People would talk for years to come about the reign of terror when good women working at the café had been killed. He hated that, he hated that already the killer had left a lasting mark on Cameron's hometown.

"You want some breakfast?" Mary asked.

"Absolutely, give me the Cowboy special with the eggs sunny-side up." He watched as she walked away to place the order with the kitchen, unable to help but notice the sway of her shapely hips in the tight jeans.

He whirled around on the stool. He was here on business, not to appreciate the sexy shape of Mary Mathis. He'd already spent almost eight years lusting after Mary.

Several of the diners nodded in greeting as their gazes met his. Familiar faces, friendly faces, and yet one of them might be the killer. The thought brought a knot of anxiety into the pit of his stomach, making the idea of breakfast far less appealing. ·

Mary returned to where he sat, as usual the countertop between them. "So, I'm guessing there's nothing new."

"The mayor got me out of bed this morning with a call for action," he said, grimacing as he remembered the early-morning phone call. "Dorothy's sister is flying into Oklahoma City late this afternoon and is renting a car and meeting me at the office around six. I've got everyone on the team working different angles, but there's really nothing new. I still have three dead women and no real leads."

"It will all come together, Cameron. You're an intelligent man and have a great team. I know you're going to catch this guy." Her voice rang with an optimism he couldn't quite find in himself at the moment.

"Hopefully sooner than later," he replied. "Hey, you want a dog?"

She frowned. "A dog?"

"I'm not sure how it happened but I seem to have gained temporary custody of Dorothy's dog."

She stared at him for a long moment and then laughed. "You have Twinkie?" She laughed again, the sound warming him despite the fact that he had a feeling he was the object of her amusement.

"Sorry," she said, finally getting herself under control. "It's just that Dorothy used to carry that dog everywhere with her. She always had her dressed to the nines and looking more like a fashion accessory than a real dog."

He scowled. "She's in a leopard-print dress today. I was afraid my place was so drafty she'd get cold. I need to find her a good home."

Mary grinned again, as if imagining the dog traipsing around his house in her leopard finery. "Sorry, no dog for us. I don't have time for a dog, but I'll ask around for you. I know how sweet Twinkie is so you shouldn't have a problem finding somebody to take her off your hands."

"Thanks, I'd appreciate it. A dog named Twinkie just doesn't seem right for me. If I was going to get myself a dog it would be a big one named Bruiser."

A light of laughter lingered in her eyes. "Ah, that male ego, it gets in the way all the time."

"Order up," Rusty yelled from the pass window.

"That's probably your breakfast," she said as she hurried away. She returned in a jiffy with a large platter and set it in front of him.

"Later I want to pick your brain about some of the regulars who come in here, especially anyone who has started coming in on a regular basis over the last year or so." He reached for his fork, although his appetite had fled the moment he'd thought about what lay ahead of him.

What he'd like to do was sit and eat his breakfast and fantasize about the woman who'd served him. He'd like to believe that someday Mary would let him into her life, into her heart. But he didn't have time for silly fantasies.

He knew a lot of cowboys came in here and flirted with her and he suspected there were times she flirted back, but she'd always made it clear that she had no interest in any romantic relationship.

Apparently the death of her husband in a car accident had tainted her for seeking any other relationship with another man. Her husband must have been something special.

As he began to eat his breakfast, his thoughts shot in other directions. He needed to get out to the family ranch and see his parents, he had to find a home for Twinkie and most of all he had a serial killer to catch before he killed again.

Mary was far too conscious of Cameron as she went about her business serving other customers, and he lingered over his meal. When he'd finished eating, he gestured for a second cup of coffee, and then twirled around on the stool and eyed the rest of the customers.

Although she was too far away and he faced away from her, she knew that his eyes were more brown than green and narrowed in deep concentration. He wasn't the local law casually enjoying a cup of coffee and visiting with other customers. He was a predator on the hunt for another predator.

As the rush began to slow down, Mary wiped down the counter and thought of the past couple of months. She'd lost two good waitresses to romance and love.

Lizzy Wiles had blown into town and had worked at the café for several months before she'd fallen in love with local rancher Daniel Jefferson. The two had married a month ago and Lizzy was now a full-time rancher's wife.

Courtney Chambers had been another waitress who had left her job when her boyfriend, Nick Benson, had returned to Grady Gulch to discover that when he'd left almost two years prior Courtney had been pregnant with his child. The two had worked out their past issues, rediscovered their love for each other and had also gotten married. Courtney was now enjoying the luxury of being a stay-at-home mother and there was a rumor that she was pregnant again.

Mary missed the two women, who had been hard workers and friends. And now she was missing three more waitresses, all killed by the same person.

She hadn't been surprised when several of the waitresses had called in sick that morning. It had become frighteningly obvious since Dorothy's murder that working as a waitress at the Cowboy Café was dangerous.

How long would it be before all the waitresses quit? For the past five years, since she'd taken over ownership of the café, business had boomed. She'd never had trouble covering the expenses and had actually put away a substantial amount of money for Matt's college.

But she was aware of the fact that everything could change in the blink of an eye. She'd always been suspect of her good luck after she'd fled her home in California. The first couple of months on the road had been difficult, but once she'd landed in Grady Gulch magical things had fallen into place.

Somewhere in the very depths of her heart she'd always feared it was all too good to be true, that when she least expected it, it would all disappear. It would be taken away from her as penance.

"Whew, busy morning." Lynette Shivers, one of the waitresses, stepped up next to Mary. "Hopefully we'll get a little breathing room before lunch."

Mary smiled gratefully at the young woman. "I'm just glad you and the other two are here. I wouldn't have blamed any of you for deciding not to work here anymore."

"No creep is going to scare me away from my job," Lynette said with a burst of bravado. "I like working here and I'm not about to quit."

"I just want you all to stay safe," Mary replied.

"I am staying safe. So far these murders have only happened to women who live alone. Regina Maxwell moved in with me last week, so I'm not by myself in that house and we check and double-check the windows and doors all the time to make sure they're locked tight."

"That's good to hear," Mary replied. Regina Maxwell was another of the waitresses who was working that day. Regina was only twenty-four, a bit flighty and often talked too much to the customers, but she was also a favorite among the diners.

"Besides, Denver Walton invited me out on a date for this weekend," Lynette said with a special smile lighting her green eyes. "I'm hoping he'll come in at some time today to firm up the plans."

Mary wanted to warn the young waitress that Denver wasn't a good bet for any kind of a long-term relationship, but she didn't have the heart to dispel the happiness in Lynette's eyes at the moment. There would be time later to warn her about giving away her heart too easily to a man like Denver Walton.

The two women got back to work preparing for the lunch rush to come. Joe Lina, the mailman, arrived with a pile of mail for Mary. "I've got a fistful of things for you today," he said as he set the pile on the counter.

"Catalogs and bills," Mary replied. "That's all I ever get."

"My wife gets dozens of catalogs in the mail. She says looking through them is her favorite hobby. Sometimes she finds something she wants to order and usually has to send it back for some reason or another, but mostly she just looks."

"Most of the catalogs I get are advertising new restaurant equipment that I either can't afford or don't want or need. But it is fun to thumb through them," Mary agreed.

Joe waved a goodbye and Mary carried her mail to the coffee table in her living room and then returned to the café.

Lunchtime came and went and it was about three when Mary poured herself a cup of coffee and sank down on a stool behind the counter to rest her feet for a few minutes.

Deputy Ben Temple was the only customer in the place at the moment. He sat at a table for two against the far wall, a cup of coffee at his elbow and the morning newspaper spread out in front of him. He'd been there through breakfast and lunch and she knew he'd probably be there through dinner, as well. In fact, she had a feeling that he'd be a permanent fixture in the café until the murderer was behind bars.

He'd not only watched every person who walked through the café door, he'd also interviewed each of the three waitresses working that day, asking if they had anyone in their lives who didn't appreciate the fact that they were waitressing. Apparently he hadn't gotten any shocking answers from anyone, for he remained seated and hadn't used his cell phone to contact anyone.

She sipped her coffee and thought about the customers she considered regulars. Joe Lina rarely missed a meal here, but despite his unpleasant nature there was no way she could believe the old man capable of killing anyone.

Although the theory was that Candy Bailey's killer had walked in through the front door either invited or not invited, the killer had gotten to the other two women by climbing through windows. In Shirley Cook's case, the window had been unlocked. She wasn't sure if that had been the case with Dorothy.

Whoever it was had to be agile and move with an almost inhuman stealth. George Wilton was definitely on her "no way" list.

As the dinner rush began around five she wasn't surprised to see Cameron walk back through the door. She also wasn't surprised at how her wayward heart leaped at the sight of him.

Sometimes in the evenings when they sat alone and talked, she found herself wondering what those lips of his would feel like against her own, how they would feel trailing a slow path of kisses along her jawline and down the length of her neck. She found herself wondering what it would be to wake up in the morning and have his big, strong body curled around hers.

As he hung up his hat and then walked toward her, his eyes glimmered with a warmth that threatened to pull her in, but she steeled herself against it…against him.

"Coffee?" she asked as he slid into his usual stool.

He shook his head. "No thanks, I'm all coffeed out." He shrugged off his thick jacket and hung it on the back of his stool. "I think we're in for an early winter. The wind is blowing so cold and I swear I smell snow in the air."

"Then how about a cup of hot cocoa instead?" she asked. He looked tired, dispirited and her need to comfort him was strong. The only way she knew to do that was through food or drink. She didn't dare attempt any other way to give him comfort.

"Actually, a cup of cocoa sounds great, along with a little inside information."

She eyed him curiously. She served his cocoa, pulled up a stool on the opposite side of the counter and watched as he drew the cup to his mouth, took a sip and then quickly licked his upper lip for any errant chocolate residue.

"Inside information?" she prompted him, not wanting to focus on his sinfully sexy lips.

He glanced around, obviously grateful that the café was just beginning to get busy and nobody had yet to sit on the stools on either side of him.

"A little earlier Adam and I worked up a list of some of the newer members of the community and a few of the locals that bounced around in our heads. I'd just like to get your general impression of them."

She nodded, eager to help but unsure that she could. "Okay, but you understand I only have a limited time with most of the people who come in here to eat, and most of the time they are on their best behavior."

"Understood, but it's possible you know more about your customers than you realize." He took another sip of his cocoa and then leaned forward. "Thomas Manning," he said.

She frowned as she thought of the middle-aged man who came in every couple of days for dinner. "I don't know much about him at all. He always comes in alone, he brings a book with him and reads while he eats."

"Doesn't visit much with anyone?" Cameron asked.

"Not really. He pretty much keeps to himself, but he's always pleasant to anyone who speaks to him and none of the waitresses have ever complained about him."

"John and Jeff Taylor."

Mary couldn't help the smile that curved her lips when she thought of the two young twins. "I know they were raised by their mother someplace back East after their mother and father divorced when they were five years old. When their father, Jonathon Taylor, died, he left them his ranch just outside of town." She shrugged. "They seem like nice young men trying to fit into a lifestyle that's a bit alien to them. Jeff is quieter than John, but both of them seem like good people."

She watched him take another sip of his cocoa, aware of the growing crowd of people filling the café. "I'm assuming Brandon Williams isn't on your list of suspects." Brandon had moved to Grady Gulch about six months before. He was a big veteran confined to a motorized scooter. Scars marred his face and he was missing facial hair and was bald, yet his pleasant personality made him a favorite among the waitresses.

"Physically Williams is a write-off, as are several other men in town. The man or woman we're seeking is physically fit and filled with some crazy compulsion to kill waitresses. So far we haven't found any other solid connection between the three women other than the fact that they all worked here for you."

"So, you're fairly sure it's somebody who has a personal grudge against me or the café," Mary said, fighting off a new shiver that threatened to stalk up her back.

"Trust me, that's something uppermost in my mind." His eyes turned the soft golden green that made her want to both fall toward him and run away from him at the same time. "I need a list from you of every vendor, repair company or anyone else you have contact with for the café business."

"There aren't many, but I can have it for you by tomorrow," she replied.

At that moment Rusty called to her from the kitchen. "This is really a bad time to have a long discussion," she said as she got up from her stool. "The dinner rush is heating up. Will you be stopping by later tonight?"

He frowned. "Doubtful. I've got a meeting with

Mayor Davidson at eight and I don't know how long I'll be with Dorothy's sister."

"Dell giving you a hard time?" she asked as she thought of the young mayor who had been elected two years before.

"He's been okay until this last one, but he's more than a little frantic right now. I just wish I had some information to let him know we're on top of this." He got up and grabbed his jacket. "Go on," he said as Rusty called for her again. "I'll catch up with you sometime tomorrow."

Mary watched him shrug on his jacket, grab his hat and then disappear out the door. As she hurried to the kitchen her thoughts remained on Cameron. The weight of the safety of the entire town rested on his broad shoulders and this wasn't the first time he'd faced difficulties as sheriff of the small town.

In the past couple of months he'd had to deal with the kidnapping of a baby and the disappearance of Adam Benson's girlfriend. In that particular case he'd had to arrest one of his own. Along with the bigger crimes came the smaller ones that all towns suffered. Domestic abuse, robberies and bar fights had already kept Cameron's team of deputies pretty busy, now with these murders they all had to be stretched to their very limits.

She knew there were a dozen women in town who would love to be Cameron's rock, the one he came home to every night after a long, hard day. But he'd never looked at any of them. For the past eight years that she'd been in town she'd never heard any gossip about him and any woman.

Several of the waitresses teased her and told her that it was obvious Cameron was crazy about her and was just waiting for her to give him a signal that she was open to him. She hoped that wasn't the case, for he would wait forever. She didn't want Cameron to live the rest of his life alone—that was a choice she had made for herself, but would never choose for anyone else.

As always, the dinner rush pushed all thoughts out of her head as she focused all her concentration on running a successful café.

By the time the café closed and all the cleanup was finished, Mary was tired. Despite her aching feet and overall exhaustion it always took her a little while to wind down before going to sleep.

After checking that Matt was sleeping peacefully, she took a long, hot shower and then pulled on the oversize Cowboy Café T-shirt that she used as nightwear. Finally she sank down on the sofa, the pile of mail in a stack on the coffee table.

The first thing she did was separate the stack into three piles—catalogs, bills and advertising trash. She frowned as she picked up what was obviously a card envelope in her favorite lavender color. It was addressed to the Cowboy Café. Curious, she opened it and pulled out a glittery card that read Happy Anniversary.

She frowned in confusion. She opened it to discover a traditional anniversary verse printed inside and no signature. Why would anyone send such a card to the café? Had the café originally opened its doors on November 10?

As the day's date reverberated around in her head, she gasped and the card fell from her hands to the floor.

Her heart beat with a frantic rhythm that threatened darkness at the edges of her consciousness. She bent over, with her head nearly in her lap and tried to regulate her breathing as images from the past crashed through her brain.

It had to be a coincidence, she thought as she finally raised her head. Her heartbeat slowed from an explosive rapidity to one of simmering panic.

Coincidence, her brain repeated, desperate to believe it so. After all, the card hadn't been addressed to her personally, but rather to the café.

It couldn't have anything to do with her or her past. She leaned over and picked up the envelope from the coffee table. The postmark was from right here in Grady Gulch.

"Nobody knows," she whispered, her voice making the words sound more like a mantra, a prayer rather than a statement of fact.

With a new panicked wildness she ripped both the envelope and the card into tiny little pieces and carried them to the trash can in her bedroom.

She sat on the edge of the bed and clasped her trembling hands together. Who had sent the card and what could it possibly mean?

Over the past eight years had she mentioned anything that personal to anyone? She didn't think so, but how could anyone in Grady Gulch know that thirteen years ago on November 10 she'd married a monster named Jason McKnight. Who in town might know about her past? Who in Grady Gulch might know what she had done?

He wished he could have been there when she'd opened up the card. He wished he could have seen the stunned horror wash across her pretty features as she realized what it was, what it meant.

Everyone in town loved Mary Mathis…everyone but him. He hated her. Everyone thought she was good and kind, but she wasn't. She was a selfish bitch who only pretended there was goodness in her heart.

The Waitress Waster, that's who he considered himself to be, a cheesy name for a serial killer, but he'd claimed it as his own. He only wished he'd been present each time that Mary had learned that one of her precious waitresses had been killed.

He'd wanted to see her grief in the dimming of the brightness of her blue eyes, in the tremble of her lush lower lip. By now she had to realize that the murders were all related and that they were all aimed at the place she called home, at her personally.

He hoped her heart beat with frantic fear each time she got into bed to sleep. He hoped she feared everyone around her, unsure where danger might arise.

Foreplay, that's what the dead waitresses had been to him…a prelude to the big event and of course the big event was the destruction of the café and all that Mary loved, the final big event would be the utter destruction of Mary Mathis.

Chapter 4

Dorothy Blake's funeral took place on Friday morning at eleven o'clock. The weather provided an appropriate setting for the somber affair with gray low-hanging clouds, blustery wind and frigid temperatures. It was as if nature wasn't any happier about the event than the people attending.

Cameron tugged his jacket collar up closer against his neck as he perused the crowd…and it was a big one. It appeared as if nearly everyone in the small town had turned out despite the nasty, wintry day. It didn't help that the Grady Gulch cemetery was on a rise, with few trees to break the wind gusts.

His men were all stationed around the area, also keeping an eye on the people attending. They were looking for somebody who shouldn't be here, somebody expressing inappropriate actions or emotions, anything suspicious that might make them take a second look.

Serial killers often attended the funerals of their victims or returned to the cemetery alone afterward to relive the kill in his mind. They also sometimes worked their way into the center of the investigation, secretly enjoying their role as volunteer avenger in a death they'd committed.

Cameron had already assigned Deputy Brooks to do surveillance on the three grave sites of the victims during the night and Deputy John Mills would take the daytime hours.

He saw Mary standing next to Lynette Shivers in the middle of the crowd. She always closed down the café during funerals and then reopened for anyone who might need food and the comfort of friends afterward.

Mary was dressed in a pair of black dress slacks and a black winter coat. Although her features were stoic, she had an arm around Lynette, who was openly weeping.

He directed his gaze to Sarah Blake, Dorothy's younger sister. She stood with her back stiff, her eyes dry as the minister began the service. Cameron had found her to be a sour woman who'd had little nice to say about her older sister. All Sarah had wanted was to get the funeral over with as quickly as possible so she could get back to her own life.

She was leaving town the minute the service was over. Good riddance, Cameron thought wryly. She'd had nothing to offer to help in any way, had confessed that the two sisters had fallen out years ago and had maintained only phone contact once a year at Christmastime since the falling-out.

Cameron couldn't help but think of his brother, Bobby, and his heart ached with loss. Bobby had been two years younger than Cameron and the brothers had been close. Bobby was one of those people who could light up a room, who, no matter what your mood, could make you laugh.

Bobby had loved the ranch work but had understood that the ranch wasn't Cameron's calling. Ten years ago when Cameron had decided to run for sheriff, Bobby had been his biggest supporter. Cameron couldn't imagine anything driving a wedge between him and his brother. Only death had been a powerful enough force to rob Cameron of that precious relationship.

He forced his concentration back to the crowd, this time trying to discern who wasn't in attendance. Who wasn't here was just as important as who was as far as he was concerned.

One person notably missing from the crowd was Thomas Manning, the loner who had moved to town months ago. Cameron frowned trying to remember if the man had attended any of the funerals of the victims. He didn't think so. It might mean something, it might mean nothing.

A sigh of frustration escaped Cameron's lips. A break, they just needed some kind of a damned break. They'd spent the past two days chasing down all the businesses that helped keep the café running smoothly. Nothing had come from any of those interviews.

As Ben Temple sidled up next to him, he gave his

deputy a grim nod. "Nothing suspicious that I can see so far. What about you?"

"Nada," Ben replied. "Other than the fact that Dorothy's sister appears eager to dash, nobody looks out of the ordinary." Ben raised his collar as a cold gust of wind swept through where they stood.

"You know, I thought of something last night. A couple of months ago I was in the café when Denver Walton asked Mary for a job and she turned him down." Ben kept his voice low as the minister droned on.

Cameron whipped his head around to look at Ben. "How did Denver take it?"

"Not real well as I remember. He stormed out of the café and told her he wouldn't eat in her joint again. Of course he was back the next day for breakfast acting as if nothing had happened."

Cameron looked at Mary, then over to where Denver stood alone at the edge of the crowd. "I wonder why Mary didn't mention that to me?"

"Probably for the same reason I'm just now telling you. She just didn't think about it as any big deal," Ben replied and then drifted away from Cameron's side.

Cameron looked back at Denver Walton. For the past six months or so he was rarely seen without Madison Billings at his side. Maddy was a beautiful blonde from a well-to-do family who also had a snarky side that made her far less beautiful once you got to know her.

She and Denver had been an item until about a month ago when the two had broken up for reasons unknown. Funny, Denver was a native of Grady Gulch and about Cameron's age, but Cameron didn't know much about the man. They hadn't run in the same crowd when growing up, and Cameron had no idea how Denver made a living other than spending Maddy's money.

Definitely Denver Walton deserved a closer look. As did Maddy, he thought, reminding himself that there was nothing to positively indicate the killer was male.

Denver was a flirt and it didn't matter if the waitress serving him was twenty or sixty, he used his considerable charm on all of them. Was it possible that Maddy had somehow taken offense to Denver's behavior with the waitresses at the café?

On the surface it seemed utterly ridiculous, but at this point Cameron was willing to look at everything and everyone in an attempt to make sense. Besides, he'd seen Maddy go off like firecracker lit by jealousy. It hadn't been a pretty sight.

The minister finally finished and the crowd began to slowly disperse. Cameron walked over to Sarah Blake and gave her his final condolences.

"I've placed all the details of whatever estate there is in the hands of Barney Kaufman," she said as he walked her to her rental car. Barney was a local lawyer. "So I won't be visiting your town again, but I thank you for your kindness to me while I've been here." She said the words in a tone that lacked any real depth of emotion.

"I wish you a safe trip home," Cameron replied.

"And I wish you a successful investigation," she returned. For just a moment a faint edge of sadness darkened her eyes. "Dorothy and I had little in common, but she deserves her killer being brought to justice."

"I intend to do just that," Cameron replied.

By the time he watched her rental car leave the cemetery that set on the north side of town, everyone else had gone except for his deputies on duty.

"Larry, I want you to go back to the office and find out everything you can about Denver Walton and Maddy Billings," Cameron said. "Ben, I want you to dig around in Thomas Manning's past. Find out where he came from before he arrived here, anything you can discover about his personal life. The rest of you hit the streets, keep your nose to the ground and find something that will move us forward. I'll be at the café should anything come up."

As Cameron headed to his car he fought the weight of the murders that threatened to slump his shoulders in defeat, break his back in ultimate surrender. But this was the job he'd chosen, this was what he loved doing, and he wouldn't be broken by some killer frightening his town.

Sooner or later a mistake would be made. Sooner or later he and his men would stumble on something that would take down the killer. He just hoped like hell it was sooner than later. The last thing he wanted was another dead body on his watch. There had been enough death here already to last a lifetime.

By the time he arrived at the café the place was hopping. Both Rusty and Junior were manning the kitchen and Mary and three waitresses were working the floor.

He knew he wouldn't have a chance to speak with Mary until the place quieted so he took a seat at a table for two in the corner and ordered a cup of coffee from Lynette Shiver when she arrived to attend to him.

Once she'd served him he settled back in his chair, knowing that he wouldn't be alone for long. Over the next two hours worried women stopped by his table for words of reassurance, men paused to give him support or to ask questions about the ongoing investigation. People simply stopped to mention something about Dorothy, an inconsequential fact that felt like a pathetic attempt to honor the woman who had been killed.

By the time Matt came through the door after school, most of the crowd had drifted away, heading back to their homes where they believed they were safe, that nothing like what had happened to Dorothy would ever happen to them.

Matt spied Cameron and beelined to his table, a wide smile on his boyish features. "Hey, Sheriff," he said as he slipped into the chair opposite Cameron.

"Hey, Matt," Cameron replied. "How was school?"

"Good." Matt shrugged off his coat and hung it on the back of his chair. "The most awesome part of the whole day was when Nathan Buckley went up to the teacher to tell her he didn't feel good and he threw up right on her shoes." Matt laughed and then slapped a hand over his mouth. "I know it's not nice to laugh, but it was totally gross and awesome at the same time."

Cameron grinned and remembered a time when he would have thought such a thing both gross and awesome. They smiled as Mary approached the table. "Hey there, my favorite son," she said as she ruffled Matt's blond hair.

"Hey there, my favorite mom," he replied with a grin.

"You want a snack?" she asked Matt, who nodded affirmatively, and then she looked at Cameron. "Can I bring you something? You've done nothing but fill up on coffee for the past couple of hours."

It was pathetic, that the fact that she'd even noticed what he'd been drinking or eating during the past couple of hours made his heart beat a tad bit faster. "Actually, give me whatever snack you're getting for Matt." He could tell his words pleased Matt.

"Two cowboy snackers coming right up," Mary said and left the table. Cameron turned his attention back to Matt. "So, what else is going on with you? You keeping your grades up? Staying out of trouble?"

"For sure," Matt replied. "I can't be a sheriff when I grow up if get into any trouble now. Besides, Mom would kill me. Right now I'm trying to figure out what I want to do for my birthday tomorrow."

"Birthday? I didn't realize tomorrow was a big day for you. Are you going to have a party? Invite all of your friends?"

Matt frowned. "That's kinda babyish. I know I want to go to Evanston and eat at the Dragon Wok restaurant. That's me and Mom's favorite place to eat besides here, but I want to do something else, too. I just don't know what."

"You have a pair of ice skates?" Cameron asked, knowing that lots of the kids owned skates for winter skating on local ponds. Matt nodded and Cameron continued, "This cold weather has made the pond out at my place perfect for skating. I can probably dig out my old skates from somewhere in the house. I used to be pretty good on the ice."

"That would be awesome!" Matt exclaimed, his blue eyes gleaming with excitement.

"What would be awesome?" Mary asked as she arrived back at their table with two plates containing slices of cheese and pepperoni, chunks of summer sausage and carrot and celery sticks with a small cup of ranch dipping sauce.

"Sheriff Evans says for my birthday tomorrow we can come out to his place and skate on his pond, then go into Evanston and eat at the Dragon Wok. That's exactly what I want to do for my birthday," Matt exclaimed with obvious happiness.

Mary's face didn't hold the same expression. "Oh, Matt, honey, Sheriff Evans is in the middle of a big investigation. I'm sure he doesn't have the time to…"

"To take off for an afternoon?" Cameron said, not letting her finish. "To be honest, it sounds like just what I need, a little downtime to help keep my sanity. I've been working crazy-long hours for the last couple of months and particularly in the last week. I'd love to spend some time with Matt and you for his birthday."

"Oh…I don't know…" Mary was obviously not feeling the same eagerness he was.

"Please, Mom. It will be so much fun," Matt pleaded, his hands clasped together before him as if asking an angel to answer his prayer.

Mary looked at her son's face and then shrugged and smiled. "All right, then I guess that's what we're doing for your birthday." She looked at Cameron. "We'll talk about the arrangements later."

As she returned to the kitchen Cameron and Matt ate their snacks, talking about ice skating and favorite Chinese food. When they were finished, Matt excused himself to find his mother. "Tell your mom when she gets a chance I still need to talk to her," he told Matt just before he scurried away.

Cameron wanted to find out about the exchange between Mary and Denver Walton. It was about fifteen minutes later that she returned to the table where he sat.

"Matt said you still needed to talk to me," she said as she sat in the chair her son had recently vacated. "Is this about tomorrow's plans?"

"No, although why don't you plan on being around my place at two. We'll skate for a couple of hours and then head into Evanston for dinner. I wanted to ask you about Denver Walton."

She frowned. "Denver? What about him?"

"Ben told me that a month or so ago Denver came in here asking about a job and got a bit huffy with you when you told him no."

Her eyes lit up with memory. "That's right, I'd forgotten all about it. But we all know Denver has more than a little bit of a temper. He cussed me out, told me he was never going to eat here again, then was back the next day for breakfast as if nothing had happened." Her brow crinkled with a frown. "Why? Is there some evidence that Denver had something to do with the murders?"

"No, nothing like that. But after Ben talked to me

I realized I don't know that much about Denver. What do you know about him?"

Mary shrugged and once again a tiny frown danced across her forehead, a frown Cameron would like to erase by running his fingers across it. He knew without a doubt that her skin would be soft and silky to the touch.

"To be honest, I'm not sure what Denver does for a living. I just assumed he did a little ranching and if he came up short for anything Maddy stepped in with her wallet."

"But Maddy isn't around anymore."

Mary smiled ruefully. "You know how those two have been, off again, on again. They just happen to be off right now, but I imagine it won't be long before they're back together again. Apparently he's invited Lynette on a date for this weekend. I was going to warn her before she went out with him not to get her heart involved with him."

Her smiled faded. "But I have to say since he and Maddy broke up, Denver doesn't seem to be hurting for money and he's always been a big flirt with the waitresses. He's driving a brand-new decked-out truck, so he must be working someplace and trying to move on from Maddy."

"I don't know about his social life but I intend to find out where he's working and a little more about his life in general."

"You know, you really don't have to indulge Matt for his birthday. I know how busy you are and everything that you have on your shoulders right now." She was giving him room to wiggle out of their plans, but he had no desire to back out.

"I think a few hours away from the investigation will be good for me. And I imagine you could use a break from this place, as well." He wished she didn't look slightly stressed by the idea of spending time with him. "Just a couple of hours, Mary…for Matt…for his birthday."

"Of course," she smiled at him but he could tell it was slightly forced. "Was there anything else you wanted right now? I really need to get back into the kitchen." She rose from the chair, poised to run.

"We're good for now. I'll see you tomorrow for the big birthday celebration."

"Okay… I'm looking forward to it." For just a moment there was a vulnerable wistfulness in her eyes, an emotion that gave him the hope that there might be a chance for something to develop between them. And then she was gone, leaving behind only the faint whisper of her perfume as she raced away from the table.

Mary, Mary, quite contrary, he thought as he leaned back in his chair, his thoughts momentarily filled with her. Sometimes it felt as if she were playing games with him, pushing against him and then subtly pulling him closer.

He knew she wasn't conscious of it, but she did seem aware of the intense chemistry that radiated between them. She seemed to fight against it rather than allow it to blossom and grow.

Although he was looking forward to spending some

downtime with her and Matt, he certainly hadn't forgotten he had a killer to catch.

Adam Benson entered his two-story home on Main just down the street from the Cowboy Café and the scent of baked chocolate instantly teased his nose.

"Somebody has been cooking something good," he said as he pulled off his hat and coat and hung them in the entry closet.

There was a faint squeak of a wheelchair and then Melanie Brooks, the woman he loved more than life itself, appeared in the doorway of the kitchen. Slender and with classically beautiful features, she always caused a catch in his breath whenever he thought of the fact that she was his, that she loved him.

"Pumpkin and chocolate brownies and fresh-brewed coffee. Nick and Courtney should be here anytime."

Adam looked at her in surprise and checked his watch. "At this time of night? After eight? I'm surprised they'd get Garrett out so late."

"They have a babysitter for him and I knew if I wanted us all to get together for a quick visit it had better be around this time of night because you've been working such late hours." She smiled up at him as he leaned down to give her a kiss.

Adam knew he'd never grow tired of kissing her, this wheelchair-bound dynamo who had agreed to marry him. She was his heart, his very soul and a woman he admired more than any other on the face of the earth. Despite the fact that she would live the rest of her life in a wheelchair, he never saw her as handicapped.

"Come in, my main man, and I'll show you the picture of the wedding dress I've been working on for half the day." He followed her into the large room that had once been a dining area but now served as their bedroom and her office.

She wheeled to the computer and with a touch of her fingers pulled up a frothy white concoction that looked like it belonged in fairy-tale land. "What do you think?" she asked.

"Isn't it bad luck for me to see this before the wedding?" he asked.

"Only if it's on my body," she replied.

"I think it's gorgeous. Is this your final design?"

She frowned and stared at the screen thoughtfully. "I'm not sure. Maybe, maybe not."

He'd already seen a dozen designs since the day they'd agreed on a Christmas wedding. He had a feeling he'd see a dozen more before she made her final decision.

At that moment the doorbell rang announcing Adam's brother, Nick, and his wife, Courtney. Within minutes they were all gathered around the kitchen table with coffee and brownies served.

They talked a bit about the family ranch where Nick and Courtney lived with their son and then Melanie said how pleased she was that her business of designing and making dance costumes was really beginning to take off. Of course it didn't take long for the small talk to turn to murder.

"It gives me the creeps to think that we've got another nut in this town," Courtney said.

"I know exactly what you mean," Melanie replied. "First Abigail Swisher tried to kill you and take your baby and then Jim Collins tried to kill me. Maybe it's something in our water system," she said half-jokingly.

"I'm hoping it's somebody who has moved to town recently," Adam said. "And I know Cameron is hoping the same thing." He pointed to his brother's empty coffee cup. "Ready for a refill?"

"No, relax, big brother, I'm good for now," Nick replied.

Almost three months ago when Nick had come home to the family ranch after being gone for two years, he'd arrived to find the ranch in disrepair and Adam drinking like a fish to drown out thoughts of their oldest brother, Sam, who was in jail pending his trial for attempted murder.

Nick had used a combination of a kick in the ass along with strong brotherly support to pull Adam out of his depression. The whole experience had made the two brothers' relationship stronger than it had ever been.

"I feel so sorry for Mary," Courtney said. "I can't imagine what she's going through with all this and, other than Matt, she really doesn't have anyone to talk to."

"She has Cameron," Melanie replied. "I mean, they seem to be good friends."

"True, but I was talking more about a girlfriend." Courtney took a bite of her brownie, washed it down with a quick sip of coffee and then continued. "I mean, isn't it kind of strange that she's been in town for eight years but doesn't have any close friends? She doesn't do lunch or go shopping with any girlfriends."

"What are you saying? That Mary should be on our list of suspects?" Adam asked.

"No, nothing like that. We all know that Mary wouldn't hurt a fly. I just think it's weird not to have a close girlfriend and in all the time I worked for her I've never heard her mention anything about her husband or her time before she came to Grady Gulch."

"I heard her husband died in a car wreck. Maybe his death is just too hard for her to talk about," Nick said. He frowned and reached to take Courtney's hand.

Adam knew he had to be thinking about how he'd reacted when their sister had been killed in a car accident. The day after Cherry's funeral Nick had left town to escape his grief. Adam had tried to escape his in the bottom of a bottle.

"And now, on a happier note," Melanie said as she looked at Courtney. "There's a rumor going around that Garrett is going to have a little brother or sister."

Courtney's cheeks grew pink. "I guess sometimes the rumor mill gets it right, although I'm not even eight weeks yet." She and Nick exchanged a glance that was filled with the love they had for each other.

Adam looked at Melanie and reached for her hand. "The minute we're officially husband and wife we're going to work hard to give Garrett and his new sibling a couple of cousins."

"I think that sounds like a great idea," Nick replied.

"So do I." Adam high-fived his brother as Courtney and Melanie rolled their eyes.

"I'm glad you two have our family planning all under control, but what I really want is for the creep who's killing women in this town behind bars," Melanie said.

Suddenly the pleasure of the evening was sucked out of Adam as he thought of the investigation that so far lead nowhere. Who was the person killing women and doing it so successfully? What kind of a monster were they chasing and would they manage to get him or her behind bars before another waitress wound up dead?

Chapter 5

The weather remained cold with temperatures below freezing the next day. Saturday afternoon Mary dressed in a pair of jeans and a pink sweater, wondering why she'd ever indulged Matt in his birthday wish to spend the day with Cameron. She should have put her foot down and just said no.

The sound of Matt cheerfully whistling "Happy Birthday" came from his bedroom as he eagerly readied himself for the day. And that was why she'd agreed to the plan for the day. Matt had barely been able to contain his excitement at getting to spend some quality time with Cameron for his big day.

She hadn't realized just how deep Matt's adulation for Cameron had run until now. But Cameron had been a constant male presence in Matt's life for the past eight years, the only constant male presence.

She should be grateful to have such a good, strong man as a role model for her son, but at the moment all she could think about were the nerves jumping around in the pit of her stomach and how often she'd fantasized about spending time away from the café with Cameron, a fantasy that she knew was dangerous.

It was just one afternoon, she reminded herself and Matt would be the center of attention, the birthday boy. There was no reason to think anything that happened today would change her relatively safe relationship with Cameron.

There was no question about the simmering tension between them each time they were together. She recognized that simmer for what it was…sexual longing. But she'd be a fool to follow through on it and so it continued to smolder but she never would allow it to boil over.

"Mom, it's time to go," Matt called from the living room, his excitement evident in the higher pitch of his voice.

"I'll be ready in just a minute," she called back. She and Cameron had agreed that she and Matt would meet him at his place to begin their day with ice skating on his pond and when they finished Cameron would drive the three of them to the nearby town of Evanston to eat dinner at the Dragon Wok.

With a final glance in the mirror and a flutter of nerves, she left the bathroom and joined Matt. "Skates, gloves, extra socks, neck scarf?"

"I've got it all," Matt replied as he patted the backpack he held in his hand. His blue eyes sparkled with eagerness. "We need to go. We don't want to keep Sheriff Evans waiting."

Mary glanced at her wristwatch. "We're fine, Matt. We told Cameron we'd be at his house at two and we will be. All I have to do is check in with Rusty before I leave."

Together the two walked from the back of the café to the kitchen where Rusty manned the grill and Junior was cutting up onions. "All set to head out?" Rusty asked.

"All set," Matt replied as he raced through the kitchen and headed for the café front door.

"Somebody's excited, but you look like you're facing a firing squad," Rusty observed.

"I'm just leaving my comfort zone."

"You should do that more often. You're here twenty-four hours a day, seven days a week. You need a life, Mary."

She smiled. "This is my life. You know to call me if there are any problems here," she said.

"Number two on my cell phone is Mary," Junior quipped and gave her his beatific smile.

"That's right," Mary replied. "I'll be back sometime after the dinner rush."

"We'll be just fine. You go and have a good time," Rusty replied.

Within minutes Mary and Matt were in her car and headed for Cameron's place on the south edge of town. As she drove, Matt kept up a steady chatter about what fun it would be to skate with Cameron. Mary had already told both of the males that she had no intention of skating. She would simply be their cheerleader on the sidelines.

Thankfully it was a perfect day. Although the air was frigid, the sun was bright overhead and there was not a single wisp of wind. It didn't take long for them to reach the attractive ranch house Cameron called home.

It was a nice place, with a long driveway lined with cedar trees. The house was white with grass-green shutters and trim. Neat and tidy, it appeared to be owned by somebody proud of where he lived.

As they pulled closer to the place, the pond appeared to the right, its icy surface glistening in the sun. "Awesome," Matt exclaimed, eying the pond. "It's bigger than I thought it would be."

The minute Mary pulled to a halt and shut off her engine, Cameron stepped out on his porch, as if he'd been watching for their arrival from the window.

Once again Mary's nerves tap-danced through her veins. Clad in a pair of worn, well-fitting jeans and a red-and-black flannel shirt, with the sun sparking off his deep brown hair and a smile curving his lips, he looked as handsome as she'd ever seen him.

Matt exploded from the passenger seat like a rocket and headed toward Cameron. "Ah, the birthday boy and his mother," Cameron said as Mary got out of her car. He clapped a hand on Matt's back. "Twinkie and I have been waiting for you."

"Twinkie?" Matt looked at him in surprise. "You have Twinkie here?"

By that time Mary had joined them on the porch.

The smile Cameron gave her warmed her like a pot-bellied stove on a cold wintry night.

"I have Twinkie for now," he answered Matt. "I'm looking for a good home for her." He opened the front door and gestured them inside. "How about we start the day with a cup of hot chocolate?"

"Sounds good to me," Matt said as he walked through the door and immediately encountered Twinkie dressed in a furry pink sweater. "Twinkie!" Matt dropped his bag on the floor and fell to his knees as the little dog leaped into his arms and slathered kisses on his cheek. Matt's giggles filled the room.

"It looks like Twinkie and I have the same fashion sense for a winter play day," Mary said as she took off her coat to display her own pink sweater.

Cameron smiled, his gaze sweeping over her. "Pink is Twinkie's best color, and it looks like it's yours, too."

Mary's cheeks warmed at his compliment, and she was grateful as he turned his back to her to hang her coat in the entry closet.

"Come on into the kitchen, I've got the hot chocolate ready to go." Matt finally relinquished Twinkie and as Mary followed the two through the living room she couldn't help but notice it was neat and clean, with furniture meant to comfort and embrace.

The kitchen gave the same impression, a bright, airy room decorated in yellow and white and with a large wooden table that was more fitting for a family rather than a single man.

"Please, sit," Cameron said. He smiled at Mary once again, that charming, warm smile that made him oh so dangerous. "Even though Matt is the official birthday boy, today is also one where somebody is going to wait on you rather than the other way around."

"Hmm, I like the sound of that," she replied and sank down into one of the chairs at the table.

Matt sat in the chair on her left, Twinkie futilely attempting to jump into his lap. He looked at Cameron, who shook his head. "Twinkies aren't allowed at the table," Cameron said.

Matt giggled. "She really is so sweet."

"I have a feeling Twinkie doesn't know she's a dog," Cameron said drily. Twinkie barked as if in agreement, the sound as tiny as her little paws.

"How come you're looking for a home for her?" Matt asked as Cameron moved to the stove where a saucepan emitted the heavenly scent of rich dark cocoa and warm milk. "I mean, I know about Dorothy, but why don't you just keep Twinkie here with you?"

"Twinkie needs somebody who is at home more often than I am," Cameron explained. "She needs somebody to take her out and play and give her lots of loving, and I'm not here enough to take care of her properly." He removed the saucepan from the stove and poured the contents into three large mugs. "Now, enough about Twinkie, who wants marshmallows?"

For the next thirty minutes they drank the creamy, rich cocoa and talked about birthdays and school and finally the two men began to challenge each other to skating contests.

"I hear a lot of big macho talk, but I don't see any action happening," Mary said teasingly. That's all it took for the party to move outside to the pond.

As she followed behind the two men toward the gleaming icy water, she realized at some point in the last half an hour, she'd relaxed. Cameron was so good with Matt, teasing him and yet maintaining the boundaries of adult and child.

He'd make an amazing father. He should be a father already. He should be married with children to fill the house that felt as if it were holding its breath, just waiting for a family to appear.

Cameron had obviously planned ahead. Three lawn chairs were situated around a fire pit where wood was already laid for a fire. "We have to keep the cheerleader warm," he said. He put a lighter to the wood and instantly got flames.

"Thanks." She sat in the chair closest to the fire and tried not to imagine what it would be like to be with Cameron every day and every night, to be the family that filled his house, the woman who shared his bed.

Impossible dreams for a practical woman. She knew that any relationship with any man was impossible for her. She could never be open and vulnerable enough with another human being to feel the intimacy that made a happy marriage. She would always be guarded, mindful of sharing pieces of herself and her past.

As Cameron and Matt finished lacing up their skates, she leaned back in the chair, warmed by the fire and simply enjoyed the show of the boy she loved and the man she might have loved gliding and spinning across the ice.

Cameron was surprisingly graceful on the ice, glid-ing in a way that showed he had spent many hours skat-ing in his past. She could easily imagine him and his brother, Bobby, spending wintry days here challeng-ing each other in spins and figure eights. Matt began a bit wobbly, but soon found his rhythm and the two glided side by side as if they belonged together, as if they were father and son.

The vision ached in Mary's heart for a moment and then she shoved it away, determined that the day be filled with laughter and happiness rather than regrets.

It was just after five when the three of them walked into the Dragon Wok in Evanston. The scent of exotic spices and soy sauce made Mary's stomach gurgle with hunger. She'd been too nervous about the day to eat ei-ther breakfast or lunch.

Her nerves had vanished, cast out by the laughter that had accompanied the afternoon and now she felt ravenous enough to eat the massive colorful papier-mâché dragon that hung across the length of the ceil-ing of the restaurant.

They were led to a booth in the back of the busy es-tablishment. Matt slid in next to Cameron and Mary sat alone on the opposite side, with their coats in a pile next to her.

"I'm starving," Matt announced and grabbed one of the three menus the hostess had left when she'd seated them. "Sometimes I wish Mom and Rusty would make Chinese food."

"Then we wouldn't have an opportunity to have special outings here," Mary replied.

"True," Matt agreed. "But I also want to order a bunch of things when we come here to eat."

"Just make sure you save room for the birthday cake I've got back at my place," Cameron said.

"You baked me a cake?" Matt asked in surprise.

Cameron laughed. "No, I didn't bake you a cake, but I *got* you one from the store. It's half chocolate and half white because I wasn't sure what you liked."

"White," Matt replied.

"Chocolate," Mary said at the same time and once again they all laughed.

That set the tone for the meal. As they enjoyed the soup starter, Cameron told them how he and his brother used to tell people that their grandparents were the founders of Evanston.

"Grandpa Emmett and Grandma Ida Evans made us small-town celebrities with the other kids in Grady Gulch, who actually believed our stories," he said. "Unfortunately it all ended when one of our friends found out that Evanston was named after Charlie Evanston who set up a cattle business in the early 1900s that became the town."

"Bummer," Matt said. "But that's what you get for telling a lie."

Cameron grinned. "That's right and you'd better remember that as you grow up, that nothing good ever comes out of lying."

Mary's guilty heart cringed when she thought of all the lies she'd told, all the lies she continued to tell, to live with each day that passed. She shoved these troubling thoughts aside, refusing to allow anything to ruin the rest of what had been a wonderful day.

It was over the main entrées that Matt asked Cameron about his brother. "I'll bet you miss him, huh? What was his name?"

"Bobby, and I miss him every day," Cameron replied. "He was the best of all of us, fun to be around and he loved working on my mom and dad's ranch. He loved animals and had a very gentle heart."

"How did he die?" Matt asked. Mary was ready to jump in and stop her son from asking questions that might be too personal, too painful, but Cameron gave her a look that indicated it was okay.

She remembered how difficult it had been for Cameron when Bobby had died. Cameron had shut down, turned off and she liked to think it had been those long nights after closing at the café that had finally brought him back to life, made him realize he wasn't honoring Bobby by grieving so deeply he kept everyone else out.

"He fell from the hay loft and broke his neck," Cameron replied. "We think he tried to pick up too big a bale of hay by himself and lost his balance."

"That's so sad," Matt said. "I always wished I had a brother or a sister, but it looks like that isn't going to happen anytime soon." He cast Mary a calculating glance. "But if I'm never going to have a brother or sister, it would be nice to at least have a little dog."

A burst of laughter escaped Mary as she gazed at her son and shook her head. "Whoa, I didn't see that one coming at all."

Matt leaned over his plate of General Tso's chicken to gaze at his mother with wistful eyes. "Mom, I've been thinking about it all afternoon. Twinkie needs me. I could spend all my spare time with her. I'd take her outside and play with her and she could keep me company when you're busy in the café."

Wisely, Cameron didn't say a word.

Mary took a bite of her sweet-and-sour chicken before replying to her son. "How about we finish dinner and discuss Twinkie as a new family member later," she finally replied.

"Okay," Matt replied although it was obvious he would have liked to continue to campaign for the pooch. "I need to go to the bathroom," he said instead. "I'll be right back." He scooted from the booth and disappeared down the hallway to the restrooms.

Mary watched him go and then leaned back in her chair with a sigh. "He's never asked for a dog before. He's never even asked for a lizard or a hamster."

Cameron smiled at her. "Ah, the charms of Ms. Twinkie." His smile faded and he looked at her seriously. "Just let me know how you want me to play it. I can discourage the whole dog thing if you want me to."

"Thanks." She flashed him a grateful smile in return. "To tell the truth, I'm not sure if I'm altogether against the idea. I never considered that Matt might get lonely when he's in the back of the café playing video games and watching television alone while I'm busy in the front. I suddenly feel like I've missed something, a loneliness, that he's been feeling and I haven't realized."

"Mary," Cameron reached across the table and covered her hand with his. Electric shocks zinged through her at his touch. So warm, so comforting, his big hand smothered hers with gentle care. "Mary, you're a great mom, and Matt is a great kid and you shouldn't beat yourself up about anything where he's concerned." He pulled his hand from hers and she was stunned by how much she wanted him to touch her again.

At that moment Matt came bounding back to the table and the conversation turned to what kind of ice cream went with which kind of cake.

"Chunky cherry ice cream and chocolate cake," Mary said.

"My favorite is rocky road ice cream over vanilla cake," Cameron replied.

Matt shrugged and grinned. "I just like cake and ice cream."

After the meal was finished they returned to Cameron's kitchen where he presented Matt with a cake big enough to feed a small army.

"Wow," Matt exclaimed, his attention torn between the cake holding his name in fancy red icing script and Twinkie who pawed at his leg in an effort to wind up in his arms. "Not now, Twinkie, we have to let Mom decide if you're going to come home with us." He slid a pleading look to Mary.

"I'm still thinking," Mary replied, her brow furrowed as if in deep thought.

"And I've heard that women always think better with chocolate," Cameron said as he slid a piece of chocolate cake before her.

"Maybe you better have two big pieces," Matt said to his mother, making both Mary and Cameron laugh.

When they finished with the cake and ice cream, Matt and Twinkie went into the living room to play and Cameron and Mary lingered over coffee.

"Are you sure you're really ready to part with Twinkie?" she asked.

He smiled. "She's definitely a charmer and I've grown attached to her, but that dog needs a boy, not somebody like me who is almost never home. Are you sure you're ready to take on a Twinkie?"

She laughed. "No, I'm not at all sure." She looked into the living room where Matt lay on his back on the floor, Twinkie on his chest like a wrestling victor. "But Matt seems crazy about her."

"I'll tell you what, Twinkie comes with a return policy. If things don't work out with Matt and Twinkie you can return the dog here and I'll try to make other arrangements."

"That's very nice."

He leaned forward slightly, just enough that she could smell his woodsy cologne. "I've been trying to tell you for the past eight years that I'm a very nice man, Mary."

His eyes were soft and more green than brown. The kitchen suddenly felt very small with too little oxygen to sustain breath. She jumped up from the table and carried her cake dish to the sink. "We need to get home. It's getting late. How long will it take you to get together all Twinkie's things?"

"About three minutes." He got up from the table. "I'll be right back."

True to his words, about three minutes later there were several bags next to the door along with a four-poster bed. "Don't let the bed fool you," he said to an ecstatic Matt who had, minutes before, told Mary she was the best mom in the entire universe. "She won't sleep in it. She likes to sleep in a people bed, curled up against their feet."

"Awesome, my feet always get cold during the night," Matt replied.

Mary grinned at her son. "You've never complained of cold feet before. Why don't you get this stuff loaded into the car and we'll head home. It's getting late."

Matt quickly pulled on his jacket and headed out the front door, a bag filled with dog food and dishes in one hand, the four-poster bed in the other.

"You've made this a birthday for him to remember," Mary said as she turned to face Cameron.

"You're the one who agreed to Twinkie," he replied. "But I will say this, I can't remember when I've enjoyed a day as much as this one."

"It has been nice," Mary replied, afraid of where this conversation might lead. Would he ask her out again? Part of her wanted to believe that she could at least spend some alone, quality time with Cameron without putting herself at risk, but the other, bigger part of her was so afraid. She'd been so afraid for so long.

Before he could say anything more, Matt returned. As he picked up Twinkie, Mary grabbed what appeared to be a bagful of Twinkie's clothing. With thanks and goodbyes, within minutes she and Matt were in the car and headed back to the café.

"This has been the most awesome birthday ever," he said, cuddling Twinkie close in his arms.

"You'll only take her outside through the back door, never through the café. You're responsible for seeing that she goes outside at least four times a day."

"I know, I know, Mom. She's my responsibility and don't you worry about a thing, I'll take care of her. You won't have to do anything except maybe love her just a little bit." Twinkie barked, her big brown eyes focused on her.

Mary smiled. "Don't worry, I'm sure I'll fall in love with the mutt. I won't be able to help myself."

The entire drive back Matt talked about three things, how awesome Cameron and his mother were, how great the day had been and how much he already loved his new dog.

It was almost closing time when they finally pulled into the café lot and parked. Few cars remained at this time of night and Mary realized she was exhausted as she got out of the car.

Spending time with Cameron had been heavenly, but she'd been tense, on guard off and on during the whole time. Now she was just ready to close up the café, get Matt settled in with his new little friend and go to bed.

Rusty stood behind the counter as they walked in. One of his bushy eyebrows raised when he saw the dog that Matt carried. "Must have been some birthday celebration," he said. "I was wondering what happened to Twinkie with Dorothy gone and all."

"Now you know," Mary said. She looked at her son. "Take Twinkie to the back and get him all settled in."

Matt didn't need to be asked twice. He disappeared into their living quarters with the dog tucked safely in one arm and the bag with food and dishes slung over the other.

"How'd things go here?" Mary asked as she set the little dog bed on the floor and placed the bag with clothing on top of the counter.

"Busy afternoon and evening, but everything ran smoothly," Rusty replied. He nodded toward two couples seated at a four-topper. "Once they're finished, I'll shut down the place. You go on back and relax. I've got things under control here."

"Thanks, Rusty." She smiled at him gratefully. He was the one person she'd depended on throughout the last five years and he'd never let her down.

He'd shown up at the café one spring day driving a rusted-out pickup and looking for a job as a cook. He definitely appeared to be a man down on his luck and Mary had decided to give him a chance. It was one of the best decisions she'd ever made when it came to the café. Rusty might look like a boxer, but he cooked like a well-trained chef.

"Before you go, this came in the mail today." He reached beneath the counter and held up a box. "It's addressed to Matt. I figured it's a birthday present for him."

"Thanks, I'll take it back to him and I'll just say good-night." She grabbed everything and carried it back to her living room. She set the brown box on their small kitchen table and then took the little doggie four-poster and the clothes to Matt's room where he was playing with Twinkie in the middle of his bed.

"You have a package on the table," she said as she placed the little doggie bed next to his. "Probably one of your friends sent you a present."

"Awesome." Matt bounded off the bed, Twinkie at his heels and went to the table where the package awaited. Wrapped in plain brown paper, the postmark was Grady Gulch and the return address was the café. Maybe one of the waitresses had sent it, Mary thought.

Matt tore the paper off the box and then ripped the tape and opened the lid and frowned.

"What is it?" Mary asked, moving closer.

His frown deepened into a touch of confusion. "It's a stuffed animal." He reached inside and pulled out a stuffed green frog wearing a small gold crown.

Mary's heart plummeted to the floor as she stared at the frog…the exact frog that her husband had brought to her in the hospital on the day that Matt had been born.

Gonna take more than a stuffed frog to turn that kid into a prince, he said, his eyes gleaming with a proprietarily light that had nothing to do with pride and made her slightly sick to her stomach.

But he was dead. She'd seen to that. So, who else had known about the frog? A shiver raised the tiny hairs on her arms and waltzed up her spine with agonizing ice.

"There's no card or anything," Matt said, pulling her back from the terror that threatened to consume her. "It's nice that somebody thought of my birthday, but it's a little bit babyish."

"You're right, you're a little old for stuffed animals," Mary said, grateful her voice betrayed none of her inner turmoil. "Why don't we put it on the top shelf in your closet and maybe at school on Monday some friend will tell you it came from him."

"Sounds good," Matt replied and then stifled a yawn. "I think I'll take Twinkie out for a fast walk and then maybe we'll go to bed."

"How about we both take Twinkie outside," Mary suggested, suddenly afraid to let Matt out of her sight. They hooked a small leash onto Twinkie's jeweled collar and left by the back door that led to the four cabins behind the café.

As she watched her son and the tiny dog walking the area, her head whirled with possibilities and suppositions. They all led back to the same time and place of terror.

The anniversary card…the prince frog…the dead waitresses…somehow they were all tied together. She knew with a horrifying certainty that they were all linked to her.

She could pack their things, take the money from the cash register, the stash she kept in her closet and they could disappear. She'd done it before, she could do it again…go far away and start all over.

A new town…a new name…an aura of safety.

She watched Matt through a veil of sudden tears, his laughter at Twinkie's antics like a dagger through her heart. The last time she'd run away, she'd easily uprooted a two-year-old.

This time she'd be tearing an eleven-year-old from

his school, his friends and the only home he'd ever known for the uncertainty of a life on the run. She couldn't do it again. She loved Matt too much to pick up and run. Her sins had finally caught up with her and she realized she was tired of running, and besides, Matt deserved more than that kind of a life.

She quickly swiped the tears from her eyes as Matt and Twinkie came bounding back to her. "All done," Matt said proudly, like a new parent. He picked up Twinkie in his arms. "And now I think we're ready for bed."

It took a half an hour for Matt to take a shower and change into his pajamas. While he was doing that Mary sat on the edge of his bed and played with the little Chihuahua mix who had already stolen her son's heart.

A little over an hour later Mary stood in Matt's doorway, watching him sleep with Twinkie curled up at his feet. Grief ripped through her, crushing her heart and twisting her insides like a well-wrung washrag.

Maybe the frog really had come from a school friend of Matt's. Or maybe one of the waitresses had left it for him, finding the frog silly and cute and thinking of him as Mary's little prince.

She tried to cling to that tiny ray of hope but it could find no purchase in her cold, frightened heart.

She knew the truth. Somebody had found her. Somehow her past had finally caught up with her.

Tomorrow was Sunday and Matt had a playdate at Jimmy's house. Even though Sundays were busy in the café, at the moment business was the last thing on her mind.

Tomorrow she'd call Cameron and tell him the truth about herself, about her past. It would be one of the most difficult things she'd ever done, but she knew now that it had to be done.

Tomorrow life as she knew it would end, and she stifled a sob with the back of her hand as she worried that, once she spoke with Cameron, once she spilled her secrets, she'd never see her son again.

Chapter 6

To say that Cameron was having a bad morning was a vast understatement. He'd awakened just before dawn, his thoughts not only filled with moments of the day he'd spent with Matt and Mary, but also with worries about the unsolved murders.

It hadn't been the warmth of thoughts of Mary and Matt that had driven him out of bed, but rather the haunting of the dead and his frustration with the lack of leads in the case. He could only hope that somebody on his team had come up with something yesterday while he'd been off duty, although he knew that if any real leads had been discovered somebody would have called him.

It was just after six when he got to the office. He holed himself up in the small room with a fresh cup of coffee, a stale donut left in a box from the night crew and the files of the three murders he desperately wanted to solve.

Candy Bailey had died in one of the cabins behind Mary's café. For a long time Cameron had believed her boyfriend, Kevin Naperson, was guilty despite the fact that his father had alibied him for the night and time in question. Even when Shirley Cook had wound up dead, Cameron had wondered if Kevin was responsible, attempting to take the heat off himself for Candy's murder by killing another woman he had no ties to.

But Dorothy's death had put a whole new spin on things. There was no way he believed Kevin Naperson had the calculation and cunning that this killer had displayed. There was no way Cameron believed he was chasing a young adult who wasn't that smart to begin with. Kevin was simply an unfortunate young man dating a woman at the wrong time.

Cameron also didn't believe that this was the first time his killer had killed. He was simply too good at it and showed no signs of deteriorating or losing control.

He ate the cinnamon-covered donut, hoping for a sugar rush that would get him through another long day, then leaned back in his chair and took a sip of the strong brew, wishing it could magically infuse his brain with some answers.

They were still running background checks on some of the newer people in town, but that didn't mean the killer wasn't a native of Grady Gulch. Besides, no matter how many tools you had at your fingertips, thorough background checks took both time and manpower and ultimately the sanction of a friendly judge.

A knock on his door surprised him as he looked at his watch. Only six-thirty. The door opened and Ben Temple poked his head inside.

Cameron motioned him in. "A little early, isn't it, Deputy Temple?"

"For you, too," Ben replied. He eased down in the chair opposite Cameron and swiped a hand through his short, curly dark hair. "I've been having bad dreams. Sleep isn't so pleasant right now."

"I hear you," Cameron agreed, thinking of the images that haunted his dreams when he closed his eyes at night. He reared back in his chair and shoved the files he'd been staring at to the side. "So, what did I miss yesterday?"

"We all worked on doing as many background checks as possible and reinterviewed some of the people that we initially talked to with the original two crimes. Nothing much came from those interviews, but I did find out something very interesting about one of our newer members in town."

"Who?" Cameron leaned forward.

"Thomas Manning. Apparently seven years ago he lived in Oklahoma City and was married to a woman named Nancy." Ben's blue eyes gleamed with the first spark Cameron had seen there for a long time. "Guess what Mrs. Manning did for a living?"

"She was a waitress," Cameron replied, his heart beating just a little bit faster.

Ben nodded. "She worked as a waitress at a truck

stop on the north side of the city. Thomas was an English professor at one of the community colleges. Anyway, apparently serving up burgers wasn't all Nancy was doing while she was at work in the evenings. One night she left a note for Thomas and told him she had fallen in love with a truck driver and was taking off over the road with him. Thomas and Nancy divorced soon after she left town."

Cameron raised his elbows to the desk and steepled his fingers thoughtfully. "This definitely makes Thomas a person of interest." He dropped his hands to the files he'd pushed aside moments before. "How do you feel about a road trip?"

Ben shrugged. "Footloose and fancy-free, you know that's me. Just tell me where to go and what to do."

"Why don't you plan to spend the next couple of days in Oklahoma City? See if you can find any of Manning's coworkers at the college, maybe talk to people who knew both him and Nancy. Also talk to local law enforcement and see if there were ever any domestic calls to their residence, find out if any women working as waitresses anywhere there have met untimely deaths. Also, see if you can find out what happened to Nancy after she left with her truck-driver lover."

Ben nodded. "You mean find out if she's still among the living."

"Exactly," Cameron replied.

"But this could be the break we've been looking for, right?"

Cameron hesitated a moment and stared at the wall just over Ben's shoulder. "It could be. But it could also mean nothing, just one of those odd coincidences that sometimes haunt a case. I mean, why here? Why now? If his wife left him five or six years ago, then why would he move to a small town and start killing waitresses now?" He looked back at Ben. "Maybe you can find those answers in Oklahoma City."

Ben rose, as if eager to get going. "I'll find out everything I can and will check in with you by phone as soon as I get any answers."

"You should be able to get it all done by Wednesday. That gives you two days to dig, so I'll expect you to check back in here sometime Wednesday late afternoon."

As Ben left the office, Cameron reached for his coffee once again, his thoughts whirling. Was this the break they'd been waiting for? He didn't want to get his hopes up. Right now all they had was a man whose ex-wife worked as a waitress and nothing at all to tie Thomas to the murders.

He couldn't put all his eggs in one basket. He still wanted to check out Denver Walton for no other reason than he spent a lot of time at the café, had acted out with Mary when she hadn't given him a job and had some sort of new financial support that didn't include Maddy Billings.

Despite Mary's protests of Rusty's innocence in all this, Cameron also planned on checking out the cook's background. Five years ago when Mary had bought the café from the previous elderly owner Rusty had appeared out of nowhere, a loner…a drifter who had decided to stay in town after Mary had given him the job as head cook.

Few people knew anything about him, but the one thing everyone did know was that Rusty had a temper…a legendary bad temper. He had the opportunity to know the waitresses better than anyone else. He would know about their hours, their social lives and who was vulnerable and who wasn't.

It was possible the waitresses who had been killed hadn't played nice with the tough, demanding cook. With some action or another they might have pushed Rusty into a fit of rage that had ultimately ended in their deaths.

At eight o'clock Cameron met with the rest of his men to plan the duties for the day, which basically consisted of them completing the interviews and background checks he'd already set into motion.

Discouragement hung heavily in the conference room where they all met. It had been almost a full week since Dorothy had been found dead and each of them knew that the more time that passed, the less the odds of finding any clues to the killer.

It was just after nine when Cameron dismissed the group after giving them a pep talk he didn't even believe himself. When the conference room was empty, Cameron remained, his shoulders tight with tension and a headache attempting to grab hold of his forehead.

Had Ben stumbled upon a real clue? Had Thomas Manning moved to town for a new beginning and harbored a killer rage directed toward any waitress? Had his wife's betrayal burned in his gut until it had finally exploded?

The next logical step was to bring Manning in for questioning, but Cameron was reluctant to do so until he heard back from Ben. Information was power, and the more information Ben could gather about the man, the more power Cameron would have to interrogate Manning and hopefully break him if he was guilty. The idea of a neat-and-tidy confession was the only thing that eased Cameron's headache.

He finally left the building, needing to walk and think. The streets were fairly deserted, most people either at church or opting to stay home and out of the blustery wind and frigid temperature. Thanksgiving was still a little over two weeks away, but it felt as if it were January.

They could not only use a break in the case, but a snap in this cold streak would be nice, as well. He pulled his collar up closer around his neck as he began a trek down the sidewalk. As he passed each storefront he paused to wave at whoever was inside, knowing that his presence on the streets just made people feel safer.

It was a false sense of security, not just for the people he served, but also for himself. He was conscious of the possibility that one of the people he waved to during the day might be the same person who was skulking around in the dead of night seeking a vulnerable woman to kill.

Just because Thomas Manning's wife had been a waitress who'd left him didn't mean he was the killer. Once again he reminded himself to check with his men to make sure they were checking into all the waitresses' husbands and significant others to make sure that nobody had an issue with their spouse working at the Cowboy Café.

There were cases where motive wasn't necessarily a big issue, but in these particular murders Cameron couldn't help but think if he could just figure out the motive he'd be much closer to identifying the guilty.

His cell phone jangled from his coat pocket and he pulled it out to see Mary's number displayed. He frowned. Although he'd like to think she was just calling to hear his voice, maybe to thank him again for spending yesterday with them, he knew she had to be calling for something less personal. In fact, he couldn't remember the last time she'd called him...if ever.

"Mary?" he answered.

"Hi, Cameron. I was wondering if you could come by the café right now."

Her voice sounded higher pitched than usual, strained as he'd never heard it before. "Sure. Is something wrong?"

There was a long hesitation and for a moment he thought the call had been dropped or she'd hung up. Just when he was about to hang up and call her back, she spoke, her voice a mere whisper.

"I need to talk to you. I think I might have some information that can help you in the investigation."

Adrenaline pumped through him. "What kind of information?"

"I'll talk to you when you get here." She clicked off.

Cameron pocketed his phone and headed back to the

office where his car was parked. Information? What kind of information could she possibly have now that she hadn't had yesterday?

And why had she sounded so stressed? As if she were afraid not just of some unknown entity, but of him, as well?

Nervous tension paced Mary back and forth in her small living room, eating at her insides as she contemplated what she was about to do.

She was on the verge of destroying everything she'd worked so hard for over the past eight years. She would lose the café, the respect of everyone here in town, but worse than all of that, she was about to put herself in a position to lose her son forever.

She choked on a sob and swallowed it, knowing she had to be strong. She would not only have to be strong for herself, but also for Matt, who wouldn't understand, who wouldn't remember who and what they'd escaped so very long ago.

Although telling Cameron all of her secrets was the very last thing she wanted to do, she knew it was the right thing to do, the best thing she could do for her son and for the town they'd grown to love.

At least she could assure Matt a good future with somebody who cared about him. And, hopefully, someday Matt would be mature enough, understanding enough, to find forgiveness for her and her past actions someplace in his heart.

She finally sank down on the sofa, grateful that Matt was at Jimmy's and Rusty was in charge of the café.

Maybe after Cameron heard her story, he would lead her out of here through the back door, handcuffed with her head hanging in shame.

She straightened her slender shoulders and drew in a deep breath. No, not shame. She would never be ashamed of what she'd done even though it had been one of the worst things a human could do to another. Rather she would hold her head up high, not in pride, but rather in acceptance. She'd done what she'd had to do to protect herself, but more important, to protect her beloved son.

The nerves that had jangled inside her since she'd made the decision to call Cameron slowly calmed as she drew in another deep breath and embraced a final resignation.

Somehow she'd always known this day would come. She'd hoped it wouldn't, but a small part inside her had known that she would have to answer for the split-second decision she'd made years before.

And now that day had come. There was no way to ignore the anniversary card or the frog with the crooked gold crown that had been delivered to Matt for his birthday. Somebody from her past had found her. She feared they were already meting out a form of justice to her, causing the deaths of the people who worked for her, the women who had been her friends.

She couldn't live with the knowledge that she might be responsible for any more deaths. A knock on her door jangled the nerves that had so recently calmed.

"Mary, it's me…Cameron."

Tears filled her eyes at the sound of his deep, familiar voice. She got up from the sofa and quickly swiped the tears away. She wanted to be strong. She needed to be strong to get through what happened next.

She opened the door and gestured Cameron inside, unable to meet his gaze with hers. "Why don't we sit at the table," she suggested, as she worried a strand of her hair between two fingers.

"Okay." He shrugged off his coat and tossed it on the sofa, then sat in a chair, dwarfing the table with his size. She sat in the chair across from him and finally forced herself to meet his gaze.

"Thanks for coming." Her voice cracked and she cleared her throat. She folded her hands on top of the table, hoping to keep their trembling under control.

"Mary, what's going on?" His gentle voice pulled a mist of tears to her eyes. "What kind of information do you think you have that might help me solve these murders?"

For a long moment she wasn't sure where to begin to tell the story that had ultimately brought her to this place and time. She finally decided the beginning was always the best place to start.

She leaned back in her chair, pulled her hands from the top of the table and kept them tightly clasped in her lap. Hopefully he wouldn't notice how violently they trembled. "When I was twenty-one I was working as a waitress in an upscale restaurant in San Francisco. My parents were dead and I was trying to make it on my own with a paltry salary and whatever tips I got. It was a tough life, but I was getting by okay."

He looked at her curiously and she knew he was

wondering where she was going with this. But he sat back as if patient enough to allow her to get there in her own way.

"I'd only been working there about two months when I met Jason McKnight. He was very handsome and quite charming and seemed to be taken with me. Over the next couple of months he came into the restaurant regularly and always sat in my section.

He flirted with me and kept asking me out and finally I agreed to go out with him. For the next six months he wined and dined me and I discovered he was a very wealthy, influential man, but what was important to me was that he treated me with a respect and tenderness I'd never known before. I felt like Cinderella who had finally met her prince."

For a moment she was cast back into time, back to when she had believed dreams could come true and there really was a Prince Charming for everyone and she'd found hers.

She released a shuddering sigh. "When he asked me to marry him, I readily accepted. I thought I was so in love. The wedding was a whirlwind and I scarcely caught my breath before I suddenly I found myself Mrs. Jason McKnight, attending lavish dinner parties and charity balls. We rubbed shoulders with judges and politicians, with movie stars and the upper crust. Jason expected me to be the perfect wife, the perfect hostess and I tried so very hard to please him." Her hands began to tremble again in her lap and she squeezed them more tightly together.

"But you didn't always please him," Cameron said,

his tone as flat as the slightly dangerous darkness that had swept into his eyes.

"We'd been married about six months the first time he kicked me in the thigh so hard I thought he had crippled me. He told me I'd been flirting with somebody at the party we'd attended, which of course wasn't true."

"So, what happened?"

She shrugged. "He kicked me and screamed at me and then went downstairs to his study for yet another drink. I crawled into bed and finally fell asleep. The next morning I woke up in a bed full of roses and Jason effusively apologizing and chalking the whole thing up to the fact that he'd been drunk, too drunk to really know what he was doing. I made the same mistake so many women make.... I believed him and so I forgave him."

"And then something happened again," Cameron said softly.

"Of course," she replied and released a weary sigh. "Cameron, I was a textbook case of an abused woman. Each time he hurt me he made excuses for himself and it didn't take long before I began to blame myself for his behavior. Maybe the flower arrangement in the center of the table hadn't been as fresh as it should have been, perhaps I should have paid more attention to the items on the menu for an important dinner party. There was so little I knew about the kind of lifestyle we were living. I was raised by an alcoholic mother who didn't teach me anything but how to clean her up after a bad night."

She raised a hand to twirl the strands of her hair.

"And if I wasn't blaming myself, then I was the one making excuses for Jason. He was a wealthy, powerful man with lots of stress and who sometimes drank too much. Besides, I felt powerless. I didn't have any friends, I had no money of my own. I was isolated and alone in my misery. I didn't know how to get out…and then I got pregnant."

"And you hoped, you prayed that somehow that would change things," Cameron said, as if he'd heard the story a hundred times before.

"Exactly." God, she'd been such a fool, believing Jason's excuses and promises, afraid to leave yet equally afraid to stay. "The pregnancy went without incident and for the first time since he first hurt me, I had real hope. He'd cut down on his drinking and we seemed to be in a honeymoon stage."

She knew the term was appropriate since the good times occurred between abusive incidents in a domestic violence situation. It was flowers and jewelry, intimate dinners and romance…and then the tension began to build to an explosion once again.

"The honeymoon period lasted through my entire pregnancy and with each day that passed I began to believe that Jason was truly a transformed man.

"But something happened that changed all that." Cameron's features were taut with tension, his eyes holding little spark of life as he stared at her. He seemed to go to a dark place inside himself in order to prepare for the rest of her bleak tale.

"It started up again when Mike…Matt…was three months old. Jason didn't like Mike crying. He didn't like the time that I spent with him. He didn't bond with Mike at all, in fact I think he hated his own son. Jason started to drink more and I could feel his rage escalating. Each day I waited for the explosion that I was sure would come."

She paused, her body and mind remembering the simmering terror of those days and nights. As perverse as it seemed, she'd almost wished for a beating that would relieve the stress of the anxiety of waiting for it to happen.

She splayed her hands on the top of the table, palms down to assure that the trembling would halt. "The explosion came when Mike was almost two years old." Her mind filled with the memory of Jason's face, his dark eyes flat and cold as a snake and his mouth compressed together in a tight line that always portended imminent danger.

"We were all in the den supposedly enjoying quality family time. Jason had been knocking back drinks while I chased Mike around to keep him entertained. The backhand across my face came out of nowhere and the force of it threw me to the floor. I instantly curled up into a fetal ball as Jason began to kick me over and over again. And with each kick a rage began to form inside me. I knew before morning came, I'd take Mike and leave…if I lived through the beating."

Cameron's hands on the top of the table had curled into fists, as if he wished Jason were here in the room with them and he could mete out a bit of macho justice of his own.

"He finally stopped kicking me, but he wasn't finished yet. He walked over to where Mike stood crying and viciously shoved him down. He pulled back his arm with his hand fisted and I knew he intended to punch Mike. That's when I got the fire poker."

Her heart raced inside her chest, threatening to erupt from her skin just as it had on that fateful night. She was grateful that Cameron said nothing to stop the story from spilling out of her.

She had to finish it. She would be destroyed, but she might save lives. She had to do the right thing and that meant telling Cameron what she'd done so many years ago.

She unclasped her hands and sat up straighter in her chair, holding Cameron's gaze intently, expecting that with her next words the softness in his eyes would transform into something much different. She got up from the table, unable to sit as she finished her tale.

She took several steps away from the table and then turned back to look at Cameron. "He was just about to hit Mike when I slammed him over the head with the poker. It was one thing for him to abuse me, but there was no way I was going to allow him to hurt my child. That first blow sent Jason to the ground on his belly and then something snapped inside me and I hit him again…and again. I couldn't stop hitting him. I killed him, Cameron. Nine years ago I killed my husband and then I took Mike and we went on the run."

Chapter 7

She trembled from head to toe as he tried to process what he'd just heard. He wasn't sure at what point he felt as if he'd been kicked in the gut, but he was half-breathless with shock, trying to process what she'd just told him.

In essence she'd just confessed to a murder. What he didn't understand was why she thought this information might help him with this particular investigation. If her husband was dead, then he couldn't be here now killing women. This revelation didn't do much to move his current case forward, but she'd put herself… and him…in a bad situation.

"Are you going to arrest me?" She held her hands out as if expecting him to slap on handcuffs immediately.

"Right now what I'd like for you to do is sit back down. I have some questions for you."

She nodded and slid back into her chair. "Before you start asking me questions, I have one for you." Her blue eyes suddenly swam with tears. "I know it's a lot to ask and I have no right even to consider it, but if I'm charged with Jason's murder and I end up going to jail would you take care of Matt? He cares about you so much and you're the only male constant that has been in his life. I know how good you'd be to him and at least I wouldn't have to worry about his well-being."

Cameron held up a hand to halt her, the request squeezing tight in his chest. "Mary, you're getting ahead of yourself here." He leaned back in his chair and swiped a hand through his hair, still trying to digest what he'd just learned.

"Why do you think what happened nine years ago has anything to do with what's happening to the waitresses here and now in Grady Gulch?"

As she told him about the anniversary card she'd received and the stuffed frog that had come for Matt, Cameron's stomach clenched tighter and tighter.

"Don't you see? It has to be somebody from my past…a friend of Jason's who knows what I did, somebody who hates me and has decided to hunt me down to punish me, to make me pay."

"Now? After all these years?" A headache began to pound at Cameron's temples. "Let's back up," he said, needing to know what happened between the moment she'd killed her husband and now. "You beat your husband with the fire poker and then what?"

She frowned, obviously not wanting to go back to that place and time, but knowing she needed to answer his questions. "I finally dropped the poker and realized what I'd done."

Swallowing visibly, she stared at the wall just over his shoulder. "I was in a panic. I knew that if I called the police and tried to explain what had happened, if I told anyone about the years of abuse nobody would believe me. There were no hospital records to back up my claims. No police had ever been called to our house. I also knew that Jason had important friends who would see to it that I got the death penalty. So, I packed up a suitcase with a few things for myself and Mike. Thankfully Jason kept fairly large amounts of cash in his wallet, so I took that and left. I picked Mike up in my arms and took the suitcase and we walked for what felt like miles before I felt safe enough to get on a bus."

"To where?" he asked.

"To anywhere. Just away from there, from the death and the thoughts of what I'd done. We wound up in Arizona and stayed there almost a month in a ratty motel room. Every minute of every day I waited for a knock on the door that would be the police to arrest me. I decided it was time to move on and from there got on another bus that took us to Texas. It was in Dallas that I met some street people who got us fake identifications and that's when I became Mary Mathis and Mike became Matt Mathis."

"And who were you before you were Mary?"

Her blue eyes went hazy with a hint of pain, as if she didn't want to remember who she had been before she'd become Mary Mathis…owner of the Cowboy Café. "Samantha Roberts and then I was Samantha McKnight and then for a long time I was nobody. Finally I found my identity, my true self, as Mary Mathis, owner of the Cowboy Café and productive member of the community of Grady Gulch."

She placed her hands back on the top of the table and he couldn't help but notice that they still trembled. "So, what happens now?" she asked. "Are you going to take me to jail?"

"Do you have intentions of running again?"

"I'm finished running." She said it with a certainty that he believed. "I'm tired of looking over my shoulders, waiting for karma or the law to catch up with me. It's time I face the consequences of my actions."

"You can relax, Mary. I'm not arresting you today." He wanted to do a little research into all this. He needed to find out if a warrant had been issued for her at the time of the incident and what the original investigation had yielded.

The truth of the matter was, despite his professionalism, he wasn't in a hurry to put a woman he cared about behind bars. Eventually it might come to that, but not until he had more information. For the moment she had a reprieve.

He got up from the table, still reeling a bit from what she'd told him. "Go on about your business as usual. I'll be in touch later and we'll see if we can sort all this out." He pulled on his jacket and moved toward the door to exit, but she stopped him by grabbing him by the arm.

"You didn't answer my question," she said, her eyes burning with fervent need.

He frowned, unsure what she was talking about.

"Matt. Promise me, Cameron. Please, promise me that if something happens to me, when I have to go away, you'll take care of him and raise him to be a good man like you." Tears splashed on her cheeks and even though he'd just learned that he might have to arrest her, he couldn't help himself, he pulled her into his arms.

She melted against him as she had so many times in his dreams, but he'd never dreamed he'd be holding her, smelling the sweet raspberry scent of her hair under these particularly strange circumstances.

In his dreams she'd always come to him with want, not need. But it was desperate need that emanated from her now, the need to know that whatever the future held for her, her son would be safe and loved.

"I promise," he whispered against her ear. "I promise that Matt will be just fine." He couldn't promise her anything more than that. He couldn't tell her that everything would be okay and that her life would continue as it had been.

Things were different now. There were obviously serious issues that needed to be addressed and at this moment he had no idea what her future might hold.

He held her tight until she finally lifted her face to look at him once again. Even with her cheeks tearstained and her blue eyes rimmed with red, she took his breath away with her fragile beauty.

He had no intention of kissing her, but as he stared down at her and saw the tremble of her full lower lip, without thought he leaned down and covered her mouth with his.

She hesitated a moment and then returned the kiss, opening her mouth to his. Her arms wound tightly around his neck. It might have been wonderful if he hadn't tasted such desperation in her kiss. It lasted only a moment and then he reluctantly stepped back from her. He wished he could hold her forever, that somehow he could unhear what she'd just told him about herself, about her past.

But he couldn't ignore what she'd said and he couldn't completely dismiss the idea that somebody from her past was now making her pay for her husband's death by killing people she cared about. He needed to get to the bottom of the murder she'd confessed to and find out if she was a wanted fugitive.

With a murmured goodbye, he stepped out of her private quarters and into the bustling café, his head whirling with so many thoughts he felt half-nauseated.

He spoke to nobody as he grabbed his hat, plopped it on his head and left the restaurant. It was difficult to think of the woman he'd known for the past eight years as a victim of spousal abuse or as a murderer.

Even if she really had killed her husband, at the time she probably would have been able to make a case for self-defense, but so many years had now gone by and her actions immediately following the crime would make it extremely difficult for her to have any kind of a defense.

Nine years. She'd carried this with her for over nine long years. If it were all true and if one of Jason Mc-

Knight's friends were responsible for the death of the waitresses, then what had taken him so long?

When she'd left her home that fateful night, had she covered her tracks that well? What mistake might she have made in the past couple of years or months that had given somebody the information to find her location?

As far as he knew, in all the advertising he'd seen for the Cowboy Café, there had never been a picture of either Mary or Matt. No strangers had been in town in the years since she'd moved here asking subtle questions about her or her son.

Or was this all some sort of a coincidence that had nothing to do with the murdered waitresses?

He hated this.

He hated the whole thing.

For the first time since he'd taken his oath as the sheriff of Grady Gulch, he hated his job. He'd wanted to be the man to make a family with Mary and Matt. He definitely hadn't wanted to be the man to arrest Mary.

"I don't want to be disturbed unless somebody is bleeding or has the name of the killer," he told his secretary, Bev, as he headed for his office.

Once inside he closed the door, sat at his desk and powered up his computer. It was probably going to take him hours, but somehow, someway, he had to go back in time and find out the truth. He had to find out what had happened to Jason McKnight and whether Mary Mathis was the warm, loving woman he'd always thought she was or a cold-blooded, cunning killer named Samantha McKnight.

* * *

Mary didn't immediately return to the front of the café after Cameron left although she knew the lunch rush would be in full swing. She was too fragile from her confession and all the memories that had flooded through her. She was too much on edge to go out and make nice with all of her diners.

Instead she sank back down on her sofa and tried to keep her thoughts from drifting back in time again. Unfortunately, it was impossible.

Memories of her marriage that she'd shoved away for so many years now haunted her, pouring into her brain. She was not only sickened by the violence she'd suffered at Jason's hands, but also by how easily she'd fallen into the domestic abuse trap.

She'd been a perfect victim waiting to happen, without family and with only a few fellow waitress acquaintances. She'd been blinded by Jason's overt charm, and yes, the more-than-comfortable lifestyle he offered to her had been equally appealing at the time. She'd been so alone in the world, working long hours and living in an area that hadn't been safe.

He'd won her over not only with roses and jewelry, but also in the way he'd looked at her as if she were the most important person in his universe.

She'd loved him on the day they'd married and hadn't realized how insidiously he'd slowly taken away all control she had, how slickly he'd made her feel as if she was nothing without him.

It wasn't until Mike's birth that the violent incidents happened more often. Jason obviously didn't like to share and he definitely didn't like vying for his wife's attention with his new little son.

Eventually her love for Jason had turned to something deeper than terror, something harder than hatred. He was her captor, her tormentor, and the beautiful mansion where he'd brought her to live had become a prison.

By the time of their final showdown she'd felt powerless, trapped and unable to escape. She'd almost given up on getting away, finding a better life. She'd almost lost all her hope.

But the minute she'd realized he intended to inflict pain on her precious baby boy, she'd snapped. Even now when she thought of the violence that had erupted out of her it made her sick to her stomach.

She'd never felt those kinds of feelings before and knew she would never feel them again in her lifetime... unless somebody threatened Matt. Only for him did a killing instinct rise up primal and strong inside of her.

She'd already proven she'd do whatever necessary to keep her son from harm and she would go there again if she thought Matt were in danger.

And now Cameron knew what she was capable of, what kind of a woman she had been. He knew that she'd not only killed a man, but had run away rather than stick around to face the proverbial music.

But even in those frantic moments of half thoughts when she'd stared down at the man who had been her husband, the man she had killed with a fire poker, she'd known that there was no possibility that she'd ever get a fair trial. She'd known that she'd be tried and convicted and they'd throw away the key forever.

As she'd grabbed up her sobbing almost two-year-old son and held him close to her chest, she'd truly believed that running had been her only option. She couldn't fight Jason's friends, she couldn't stand up to his power or influence.

And now it didn't matter. The decisions she'd made then had now been placed with Cameron. He held her fate in his hands and she expected no succor from him. He would do what he had to do as a lawman despite any personal feelings he might have for her.

She felt the ticking of a clock…the ticking away of time to the arrest she knew would have to come. Before that happened she had to have a talk with Matt. She had to explain to him what had happened, that the story she'd told him about a father who had died in a car accident wasn't true.

It would be the most painful conversation she'd ever had with anyone in her entire life, but Matt needed to hear the truth from her before Cameron acted, before Matt heard some form of the story from a classmate or an unthinking adult. It was an ugly, awful story that should come from her.

She checked her watch. Matt wouldn't be home from Jimmy's until later in the day and if she sat here and thought for too long about everything that had been and everything that was about to come, she'd go completely out of her mind.

She needed to get back to work and keep her mind

busy with pleasing customers while she waited for her fate to catch up with her.

By the time Matt came home she had changed her mind and decided to wait to talk to her son until she heard from Cameron. She had no idea what the future held, but decided she didn't want to burden her eleven-year-old son with the baggage of her former life until absolutely necessary.

At least she had Cameron's promise that Matt would be okay. Mary might not be around to watch him grow up, but she knew without a doubt that Cameron would see to it that he grew to be the kind of man who would make Mary proud.

Myriad thoughts—of not seeing Matt grow to a man, of missing him learning to drive, his first girlfriend or his prom, of not seeing him married, not enjoying grandchildren—nearly cast her to her knees with a keening grief.

"Are you okay?" Lynette asked her at closing time.

"I'm fine. Why?" Mary looked at the pretty waitress who had been practically dancing through her duties all evening.

"You just seem kind of withdrawn...quiet," Lynette replied.

"And you seem unusually happy," Mary countered, not wanting to think or talk about her own somber mood and the reasons for it.

Lynette smiled. "Denver was in earlier to eat. We went out last night and had such a good time together that he's taking me into Evanston for dinner tomorrow night." Her smile faltered slightly. "And Maddy came in after he left and spent her whole time eating and shooting me looks to kill."

"So, she doesn't want Denver, but she also doesn't want anyone else to have him, either," Mary said.

"Apparently," Lynette replied drily. "But Denver told me he was the one who broke up with her, that he was finally done with her for good and he doesn't need her money or anything else from her anymore. He's ready to move on and find somebody who can really be his soul mate."

"Just take it slow. Denver has a history of dating somebody new but also going back to Maddy," Mary replied. "I don't want to see you get hurt."

Lynette flashed her a bright smile, her eyes gleaming with a touch of cynicism and intelligence. "Don't you worry about me, Mary. I'm not about to let some sweet-talking, sexy cowboy break my heart. It's more likely that Maddy will come in here and stab me with a fork."

Lynette laughed and shook her head. "At the very least I wouldn't be surprised if she keyed my car or tried to poison my cat."

"She is a nasty piece of work," Mary agreed, thinking of the pretty blonde who had been given too much by overindulgent parents and now considered whatever she wanted her due.

Minutes later, with the café empty and Mary all alone, she hesitated before turning the Open sign to Closed and missed the fact that she knew Cameron wouldn't appear at the door for a last cup of coffee of the night.

But why would he come back here tonight or any

night for a bit of alone time with her? He probably felt nothing but disgust for her now.

She was a criminal, somebody who had run from the law. She was a killer, for God's sake, and he was sworn to uphold the law.

The spark of chemistry she'd always felt whispering between them would now be gone. He would never look at her the same way again.

But maybe, just maybe, by coming clean to Cameron he might find a lead that would stop the killing of the innocent women who worked for her. Maybe the ultimate sacrifice she felt she'd made in telling Cameron her secret would count for something and the killer would be caught.

She double-checked to make sure all the doors were locked before heading to her own quarters. If what she believed was true, then somebody from her past was in town killing waitresses in a misguided, sick effort to punish her.

And sooner or later that same person would probably tire of killing surrogates and would eventually come after her. She checked on Matt, who was peacefully sleeping with Twinkie curled up at his feet and then she went into her own room to get out of her clothes and into the oversize T-shirt that she slept in.

Maybe she was jumping to conclusions. Maybe the card and the frog had simply been weird coincidences. Maybe there was nobody from her past seeking retribution after all these years.

If it wasn't coincidence, then she hoped Cameron

could use the information to find the killer that had followed her from her former life before he killed again.

However, she also realized that if the murders were happening for another reason then she had completely destroyed her life by confiding in Cameron.

He stood in the shadowed darkness by one of the cabins behind the café, his eyes narrowed as he saw the last light go off in Mary's living quarters.

He knew that the sheriff had been there for part of the morning and wondered what, if anything, Mary had told him about her marriage. By now she had to have known that she hadn't outrun her past. The anniversary card and the stuffed frog should let her know that she hadn't run far enough to escape retribution.

Action—reaction. There were always consequences for your actions and he was here in Grady Gulch to remind her of that fact.

It had felt good to kill Candy Bailey and Shirley Cook. He'd taken great pleasure when he'd sliced Dorothy Blake's throat, knowing that he was taking away from Mary, destroying the people who worked for her, the people she loved.

But the thrill of the kills were beginning to wear thin, like an endless preshow before the main event. Impatience tapped through his veins. He'd like to sneak into her room right now and end this…end her.

But he'd been so careful so far, and he knew impatience and impulse made mistakes. That's how others had been caught before and he had no intention of ever being caught.

With Mary Mathis's death, the reign of terror in Grady Gulch would come to an end, but it would take years before people stopped talking about the time when good women, when hardworking waitresses from the Cowboy Café were murdered in their beds. It would take years before they stopped talking about him.

Chapter 8

It was just after midnight when Cameron reared back in his chair and rubbed his tired, gritty eyes. He'd been on the internet for so long the words now swam before his strained eyes, but he'd wanted to be thorough.

And what he'd discovered didn't jibe in any way with the story Mary had told him earlier in the day. Something wasn't right and he was determined to get to the bottom of it. But it was too late tonight to contact Mary.

He powered down his computer, a deep weariness stabbing his back between his shoulder blades. He stood and stretched, working out the kinks that were a result of sitting too long in front of the monitor.

Once fully stretched out, he walked over to the printer and grabbed the pile of items he'd printed off throughout the evening in his research. He'd not only spent the afternoon and evening on the computer but had also made dozens of phone calls to California in an attempt to confirm Mary's story.

He hadn't told any of his other deputies what Mary had confided in him. He'd wanted to have all his ducks in a row before executing an old arrest warrant or instructing his men to investigate further, but his research had only made things muddier.

Crazy. Either she was crazy or there had been a cover-up of massive proportions. In any case, none of it made any sense.

With it being too late to confront Mary on everything he'd learned, he headed home. As he drove he found himself replaying the kiss he and Mary had shared. There was no question that it had stirred up a wild desire inside him, but he wasn't sure whether she had kissed him with her own desire or with a form of unconscious manipulation in mind.

She'd been desperate not to be arrested, half-hysterical with the need for him to agree to take care of Matt should things go bad and she be sent away. It was possible all of that had combined to allow her to not only eagerly accept but also reciprocate his kiss.

When he reached home, still too wound up to go to bed, he made himself a ham-and-cheese sandwich and sat at the large kitchen table, remembering when the kitchen had been filled with Mary's and Matt's laughter. He almost wished Twinkie were here to break the empty silence of the house that surrounded him.

While he'd always had more than a little bit of a crush on Mary, he'd never really followed through with it by asking her out or attempting to create a real relationship with her. And he knew that for a long time part of the reason had been Bobby.

Bobby's untimely death had nearly broken Cameron. He'd loved his brother like he'd never loved another human being. He'd always known he'd been a disappointment to his parents, but Bobby had made him feel like he was the greatest, like Cameron could do or be anything he wanted.

They had been best friends as children and had remained so until Bobby's death. That death had made Cameron leery of relationships, fearful of loving and losing.

As much as he'd fantasized about having Mary and Matt here permanently, about having them in his life forever, the idea scared him just a little bit. Forever hadn't lasted with Bobby. Forever hadn't lasted for Candy, Shirley or Dorothy. Bad things happened and people disappeared.

Yet he couldn't deny that Mary pulled him in, made him wish for things that both excited and frightened him. It had been her strength that had become his own after Bobby's death when he'd plunged into a depression that had nearly overwhelmed him. She'd helped him through it and he'd come out whole on the other side, even more drawn to Mary than he'd been before.

He finished his sandwich, took a fast shower and then headed to bed, knowing that sleep would be a long time coming.

Surprisingly sleep must have come immediately for the next time he opened his eyes, it was to the early-morning light just beginning to streak bright pinks and oranges across the eastern horizon.

He didn't linger in bed, but instead dressed quickly and headed out to his parents' place. It was too early to do much of anything else but he knew his mother and father would be up. Despite their advanced age, they were ranchers, up before dawn and in bed just after dusk.

It was time for him to stop by for a quick visit even though the visits were rarely happy ones. Cameron always had the feeling that his parents believed the wrong son had died, that if given the opportunity they would easily sacrifice Cameron to have their precious Bobby back.

As he pulled up he was surprised to see Kevin Naperson, the young man who had initially been a suspect in the murders, coming out of the barn with a shovel in his hand.

He froze at the sight of Cameron's official car, his breath visible in frosty puffs in the frigid morning air. He didn't move as Cameron parked and got out of the car.

"I'm not doing anything wrong. Your dad hired me as a handyman around the place," Kevin said before Cameron could say a word. Kevin raised his chin slightly, as if anticipating trouble.

Cameron had been all over Kevin's ass when his girlfriend, Candy, had been found murdered, but with each subsequent murder and now with the information he'd gained from Mary he had little reason to believe Kevin had anything to do with any of the crimes.

"I'm sure Dad could use some extra help around here," Cameron replied and then headed toward the front door, aware of Kevin staring after him.

As he stepped inside the house he was greeted by the scent of freshly baked biscuits and fried sausage mingling with lemon polish and lavender. It was a familiar scent, but he didn't feel at ease. He walked through the living room that had once smelled like home, but that had been before Bobby's death.

He entered the kitchen to find his father at the round oak table, a plate of biscuits and gravy before him. His mother hovered nearby, her face wreathing into a gentle smile as she saw Cameron.

She wiped her hands on the checkered apron she'd worn for breakfast-making for as long as Cameron could remember. "I knew there was a reason I made extra sausage gravy this morning. Sit." She gestured him to an empty chair at the table. "You know how much you love my sausage gravy."

Cameron sat at the table and smiled even though it had been Bobby who'd always loved their mother's gravy. "Thanks," he said as his mother put a cup of coffee at his elbow.

"Saw Kevin Naperson outside," he said to his father, who hadn't looked up from his plate since Cameron came into the kitchen.

"Things were getting away from me. Without Bobby around it was way past time that I hired on somebody to help with the chores and livestock around here." Jim Evans finally looked up at his son, his weathered features expressionless.

"I can't depend on you being around here to help out at all considering what's going on in town. It sounds to me like you got your hands full with your own problems." He focused back on his plate.

"Those poor women," Edna exclaimed as she placed a plate of biscuits covered in steaming gravy in front of Cameron. "Do you have any clues?"

"Not many," Cameron admitted.

"Sounds to me like you're no better at sheriffing than you were at ranching," Jim replied.

The arrow of pain that shot through Cameron wasn't quite unexpected. He was finally becoming accustomed to his father's hurtful quips…almost but not quite.

"I'm doing the best I can and that's all I can do," Cameron replied. The rest of the breakfast was filled with conversation between Cameron and his mother, who told him about everything that had happened with the neighbors, her best friend's newest grandchild and how the forecast called for snow in the next week.

Halfway through the conversation Jim finished his breakfast and left the room without a parting word. A few minutes later Cameron heard the slam of the front door and knew that his father had left the house.

Edna sank down next to Cameron and covered his hand with hers. "Try not to let him bother you too much," she said softly. "He's a bitter old man and he talks mean to almost everyone these days. Bobby's death broke something inside him and I don't think he's ever going to get fixed."

"I know. It's all right," Cameron replied, but his mother's words didn't take away the fact that Bobby's loss had forever transformed Cameron's tenuous relationship with his father into something much worse.

After finishing his breakfast Cameron left his parents' house and headed toward the Cowboy Café. It was late enough now that Mary would be open and he had important issues to discuss with her.

The café offered up warmth and savory scents, and as usual George Wilton sat at the counter, a cup of coffee between his wrinkled hands and a frown on his grizzly features.

"I'm telling you, Mary, the coffee is too weak. You need to use another scoop or something. Hell, I might just as well stay home and make my own damn nasty coffee if yours isn't going to get any better than this."

Mary nodded to Cameron and smiled at George. "I'll try to remember to add an extra scoop when I make the next pot," she replied. She left the old man and gestured for Ginger, one of the other waitresses working, to take her place.

As she approached Cameron, her gaze shot to the manila folder he carried and the smile that had curved her lips slowly faded.

"Can we talk privately?" he asked.

He saw her inhale a deep inward breath as if for courage and then she nodded and motioned him toward her back quarters. Thankfully Cameron knew Matt would have already left for school and they would be alone for this discussion.

Everything he had learned from the internet and by talking to the authorities in California the day before had created numerous questions that needed answers.

Somehow he had to sort out the confusing mess she'd handed to him when she'd confessed to her husband's murder.

When they reached her living room she turned to look at him, her blue eyes widened with obvious fear. "Mary, don't look at me that way," he said softly. "I'm not here to arrest you. I'm here to tell you that you didn't kill your husband, that according to everything I've learned, Jason McKnight is still very much alive and well."

Mary gasped in astonishment, her heart pounding a thousand beats a minute as she stared at Cameron in disbelief. She shook her head and back away from him. "I was there, Cameron. I saw him lying on the floor, I know how hard I hit him. Again and again I hit him with that fire poker."

"But did you check his pulse before you ran? Did you see if he was still breathing? Or did you just assume he was dead and take off?" Cameron motioned her to the small kitchen table in the corner of the room.

She stared at him for a long moment and then moved to the table and sank down into a chair. After shrugging out of his jacket and hanging it on the back of the chair, he sat next to her. She was acutely aware of his familiar woody-scented cologne and the body heat that radiated from him.

It was a single sensory sensation to cling to while the entire world whirled and shifted beneath her feet. Jason alive? Was it possible?

Had he still been alive when she'd packed the clothes for herself and her son? Had he still been breathing when she'd grabbed his wallet from his pants pocket and taken what money was there? Had he been conscious when she'd slammed out of the front door, running for her life and for her son's life?

"I spent all day yesterday and most of last night on the internet and on the phone, trying to learn all that I could about the murder of Jason McKnight," Cameron said as he placed the manila folder of papers in the center of the table. "And what I discovered is that there was no body, there was no investigation and there was no murder."

She stared at his lips, as if afraid if she didn't see them forming the words she wouldn't understand what he was saying. "I…I don't understand."

Cameron opened the folder and pulled out what was obviously a printout from a news page from the *San Francisco Examiner* newspaper.

He shoved it toward her and she picked it up to see that it was dated on the day after she'd fled their home believing that she'd beaten Jason to death. Financial Wizard and Philanthropist Attacked in Park, the headline read.

The story indicated that Jason McKnight had been beaten and robbed in a neighborhood park near their home by an unidentified masked man. He'd sustained substantial injuries but was listed by the hospital in serious but stable condition.

Mary looked up from the article to Cameron. "But it's a lie. He didn't get those injuries from a robbery. I gave them to him. Why would he lie about the attack?" A million thoughts raced through her mind but the one that kept surfacing to the forefront was the utter joy in the realization that she hadn't killed him, that she wasn't a murderer after all.

She wasn't going to go to jail. She wasn't going to lose Matt. She'd be here with him to see him grow into the amazing man she knew he would be. She would be here for each and every special moment in his life.

"Maybe he lied because he didn't want you arrested," Cameron said, his gaze sober. "Maybe he wanted to make you pay in a way different than a jail sentence for assault."

Mary stared at him, her joy short-lived as she realized the implications of his words. "Did you find any information about where he is now?"

Cameron shook his head. "All I know for sure is that he still owns the house in San Francisco where the two of you lived, but it's now run by paid staff and he's supposedly been living out of the country for years. A year after the attack he divorced you on abandonment issues."

"Abandonment?" The entire world had gone mad and swallowed her whole. He'd divorced her on abandonment issues? At least she was no longer legally bound to the monster. "What about his business?"

"McKnight Enterprises moved to Switzerland six years ago and I had no luck finding anyone who could or would tell me Jason's whereabouts during the last six months or so. Supposedly he's there, but I have no proof that's the case."

"Then he's here," she said, her heart once again beating frantically.

"Would you recognize him after all this time?"

"Surely I would," she said, her hesitation obvious in her voice. "His features are burned into my brain, at least the way he looked the last time I saw him. I'm certain I haven't seen anyone here in Grady Gulch who even remotely resembles him. But he's got to be behind this. He told me a hundred times when we were married that if I ever left him he'd hunt me down and kill me, that he'd make me suffer in ways I couldn't begin to imagine." Her voice cracked when she thought of the women who had died because of her…because of what she'd done to Jason. She'd had the temerity to stand up to him, to beat him down and leave him and she knew there would never be forgiveness or forgetfulness in his heart. And so three women were dead because she'd cared about them, because they'd worked in her café.

Cameron's hand covered hers, as if he knew the direction of her thoughts. "Mary, this isn't your fault," he said softly. "Somebody killed those women, but it wasn't you. You loved those women and I don't want to see any self-blame in your eyes."

He squeezed her hand tightly and then released it and leaned back in his chair. "If you haven't seen Jason here in town, then he's either sneaking around after dark and not being seen by anyone or he's paid somebody else to do his dirty work for him."

"Either is possible," she admitted. "Jason was filthy rich when we got married and over the years I'm sure that hasn't changed. He could name a price that might push somebody into doing something like this. I just can't imagine who."

"We're going to figure that out," Cameron said with a steely determination. "If Jason is anywhere in this state, we'll find him and if he has some henchman working for him we'll find him, too. If what we believe is true, then we now have a motive for these killings and we know what we're looking for. I just don't want to get total tunnel vision and think this is the answer to everything. Nine years is a long time to hold a grudge."

"But this is a theory that finally makes some sort of horrible sense," she said, still reeling with the information she'd just learned. Although it frightened her to think about Jason being somewhere in the area, she couldn't help but feel as if a thousand-pound weight had been taken off her shoulders. It was a weight she'd carried for too long.

"I just wanted to come by first thing this morning to let you know that you don't have to worry about being arrested. You aren't wanted for any crime." Cameron rose from the table and started to grab his coat, but before he could Mary got up as well and impulsively wrapped her arms around his neck.

Instantly he embraced her and pulled her close. "Thank you," she said fervently as she gazed up at his handsome face. "I feel like you've given me back my life, given me back my son."

And with all the raw emotions suddenly rushing through her, she felt more alive than she could ever remember feeling. "For the first time in my life I'm not afraid of you learning about my past, I don't have any more secrets that could destroy me."

As she gazed up at Cameron, she knew he was going

to kiss her and she wanted it…she wanted him. She'd wanted him so badly, for so long, but had been too afraid to get close, too afraid he'd discover that she was a murderer. Now there was no secret keeping her from him and as his lips touched hers, she welcomed his kiss and melted closer into him.

It was crazy, it was the beginning of the breakfast rush in the café, but Mary had no desire to leave this room, this man who now held her with such command, yet who kissed her so tenderly.

He pulled her closer and she leaned into him, close enough that she could tell he was aroused and she wanted him in her bedroom, beneath her sheets where she'd dreamed about him so many times in the past eight years.

The kiss seemed to last forever, an explosion of want that had been building for what seemed like an eternity. Cameron kissed far better in real life than in her fantasies, his lips a sweet combination of tenderness and demand.

It was he who broke the kiss, dropping his hands from around her waist and stepping back from her. His eyes were a deep golden hue with green flecks that sparked like emeralds.

"Mary…I…"

"I want you, Cameron," she said hurriedly, before the spell between them was broken, before his eyes lost the aching want that filled their deepest depths. "I've wanted you since the first time you entered the café and hung your hat on the wall, the first time I took your breakfast order, but I've been afraid to follow through because of what you might find out about me."

His gaze flared even hotter at her words. "But maybe this isn't the best time for you to be acting on those feelings." Although he said the right words, as far as she was concerned there was no better time than this moment.

"Matt's in school, the café can run just fine without me and there's no better time than now." With an energized desire rushing through her she reached out and took his hand in hers and pulled him toward her bedroom door.

The last time she'd had sex with a man it had been a night that Jason had taken her roughly, with only his need to dominate and control in mind, with only his own desires in charge.

She knew with Cameron it would be different and no matter what the future held, she wanted the tall, solid lawman to hold her in his arms, to make love to her and show her what making love could be.

He didn't stop her from pulling him forward and when they entered her bedroom he once again took her in his arms and kissed her with enough emotion that it nearly stole her breath away.

His hands tangled in her hair and she once again wound her arms around his neck, pressing herself into the solid strength of him. "I won't lie to you, Mary. I've thought about this—about being with you—for years," he whispered into her ear. His warm breath coupled with his words shot a wave of warmth through her.

This time when she stepped away from him it was to

pull her T-shirt over her head. There were no thoughts of the café or murders, no worries about arrest or anything else. All her thoughts were of Cameron and making true the fantasies she'd had about being in his arms.

As she pulled off her T-shirt and tossed it to a chair next to the bed, Cameron stared at her for a long moment. "You're just as beautiful as I ever imagined," he said, his voice husky, and then his big fingers fumbled frantically at his shirt buttons.

They undressed like two teenagers, frenzied with the fear of discovery, of interruption. The morning sunshine streaked through her window. Cameron clothed was amazing, but Cameron undressed was like a statue of a Greek god. His broad shoulders emphasized his slender waist and hips. His skin glistened with a faint bronze hue that made her want to touch him all over.

While he took off his socks, she slid beneath the blankets on the bed, her heart rapping a rhythm she scarcely remembered. He joined her in the bed and, as he gathered her in his arms, she felt his heartbeat matching the racing speed of her own.

She would never forget the horror of her marriage to Jason, but she had a feeling that no matter what the future held, making love to Cameron would brand him in her heart from this day forward.

Chapter 9

Cameron felt as if he'd entered a dream world. All rational thought had escaped his brain the moment he'd kissed Mary. Now with her naked body pressed against his he was lost in her warmth, in her sweet scent.

As their lips clung together he filled his palms with her full breasts, loving the way her nipples instantly rose in response and she gasped in pleasure against his mouth.

On some level he knew what they were doing was wrong, that the timing was off and they'd never even been on a date. There had been no courtship and yet he couldn't imagine how something that felt so right could be wrong in any way.

There were no thoughts of crimes or criminals, no disturbing visions of the dead as he moved his mouth along the curve of her jaw and down the slender column of her neck. She grabbed hold of his hair, and his tongue slid across one of her turgid nipples, teasing the tip with gentle flicks.

"Cameron," she whispered his name as he captured the nipple in his mouth, loving the taste of her. There was no question in the single word that escaped her lips, just a sense of wonder that made him want to please her like no man had ever pleased her before and never would again.

With this thought in mind he set about to drive her insane with desire, to make her body sing beneath his slow caresses and soulful kisses.

They moved together as if they'd made love a thousand times before, and Cameron had done so in his dreams for years. He knew her taste, the feel of her silky skin against his hands, the whispered sighs of delight that escaped her with each touch.

What surprised him was that she gave as she received, eagerly stroking his skin, pressing her lips against his throat, his chest. He couldn't get close enough to her and she seemed just as insistent.

The desire he felt that was already at fever pitch only rose higher when she encircled his hardness in her hand. He gasped and held his breath, afraid that by her intimate touch it would all end before it had truly begun.

He strained against the need for his own release, wanting nothing more than to part her legs, enter her and finish whether she was with him or not. But he wasn't going to do that. He wanted her with him all the way.

Instead of focusing on the sensations she wrought in him, he slid his hand down the flat of her stomach, along her inner thigh and found her moist center with his fingertips.

Instantly her fingers around him slackened as she arched up her hips to meet his feathering touch. A low moan escaped her lips, and he moved his fingers faster, wanting her to reach her release, needing her to completely shatter before he took her.

She grasped the sheets on either side of her, her eyes fluttering as she shuddered with her climax. It was the sexiest, most amazing thing Cameron had ever seen and immediately he moved between her thighs, needing to bury himself in her heat.

She welcomed him, grabbing his buttocks to pull him in closer, and as he sank deep within her he felt as if he'd finally come home. For several long moments he didn't move, but remained perfectly still, with the warmth of her breath on the underside of his jaw.

He wanted to stay frozen in this moment, buried deep inside her and her gaze holding his with a sense of sweet wonder. But he couldn't help the primal needs of his body, his own need for release. He pulled his hips back and stroked back into her in a slow rhythm that had her gasping his name with surrender.

Faster and faster he moved against her, her fingernails raking erotically across his back as his own release built closer and closer.

His climax overwhelmed him, and he stiffened against her, crying out her name. They remained unmoving, still engaged with him holding the bulk of his weight on his elbows.

"I should bring you good news more often," he finally said.

She laughed, the joyful sound wrapping around his heart. "Oh, Cameron, that was amazing and you've given me back my life," she said.

Just that quickly all the elements of the case thundered back into his mind. He kissed her on the forehead and then rolled away from her. "I'll be right back." He grabbed his clothes from the floor and padded naked across her living room and into the bathroom.

It was only as he got dressed that the full ramifications of his news to her struck him. Her abusive ex-husband was alive and possibly killing people she cared about, women in his town.

As he exited the bathroom she disappeared into it and Cameron sat back down at the kitchen table to wait for her.

Making love with her had been more amazing than any fantasy or dream he'd ever entertained. He could still smell the faint raspberry scent of her lingering on his skin, a fragrance that made a new desire for her roar through him.

But he couldn't think about that now. This had simply been a beautiful respite in the hell that was going on all around them. He had more important things to think about, more important things to discuss with her than what this had meant to each of them or when would be the next time they could get together intimately.

She came out of the bathroom once again dressed for

her day at work, but with a smile and a twinkle in her bright blue eyes that hadn't been there before.

"I can't tell you how much I wanted that to happen," she said as she sat in the chair next to him. Her cheeks were flushed and her lips slightly swollen and he'd never seen her looking so achingly beautiful.

"Mary, I've cared about you and your son for a very long time, and as happy as you are to discover that you aren't a murderer, you have to realize that in all probability Jason is either here in town or has hired somebody to do his dirty work…and that dirty work probably includes your eventual murder."

The shining light in her eyes dimmed slightly and her smile fell as she held his gaze. "I know that," she replied soberly. "And I'm hoping that you'll find him before that happens. At least now you know what you're looking for. If he paid somebody, then that person would suddenly be flush with cash, and if he's here in town, somewhere sooner or later somebody will see him."

Cameron nodded, his mind already working the details of what needed to be done. "I've downloaded a picture of Jason taken ten years ago, the latest picture of him I could find, and I'm going to distribute it all over town. Granted, he could have changed some in those years, but hopefully somebody will recognize him. I'm also going to check around to see who maybe has bought a flashy new car or is tossing around cash that he or she shouldn't have. But in the meantime I'm worried about you."

"I'm a little worried about me, too," she admitted with a self-conscious laugh.

"Why don't you and Matt move in with me for a while?" Although he made the offer with her safety in mind, there was no question that he liked the idea of her and Matt beneath his roof.

"Cameron, you have a killer to catch. The last thing you need is to babysit us." She swept a strand of her blond hair behind one ear and looked around the room. "We're as safe here as we would be anywhere. The café is full of people from dawn until late night." She raised her chin a notch higher. "Besides, I'm not going to let him chase me away from my home, from my livelihood. He took enough away from me when we were married."

She leaned forward, her eyes burning with a fervent light. "Just find him, Cameron. Find whoever it is before they kill somebody else…before he does get to me."

What he wanted to do was wrap her up in body armor to keep her safe. What he'd like to do was whisk her and her son far away from Grady Gulch until these crimes were solved and somebody was in jail. But he could tell by the determined glint in her eyes that neither of those were options.

"Then I'd better get moving," he said reluctantly as he got up from the table. "I've got a killer to catch."

She stood, as well. "And I have a café to run."

For a moment they simply looked at each other and then she moved to him, raised up on her tiptoes and kissed him on the cheek. "Thank you, Cameron."

"For what?" he asked.

"For not arresting me the minute I confessed to murder, for taking the time to check things out and discovering the truth. Thank you for making me feel like a beautiful, desirable woman for the first time in years and reminding me that lovemaking isn't all about pain and degradation."

Her words created a lump in the back of his throat and as he kissed her on the forehead he swore that he'd do everything in his power to make sure that she and Matt survived to live a full and happy life in his town… hopefully with him.

Once back at the office, it didn't take him long to get things rolling. He sent Ben to the printer with the photo of Jason McKnight and with the instructions to make enough flyers not only to be posted in Grady Gulch but in Evanston, as well.

It was possible that Jason McKnight could be staying in the neighboring town and only coming into Grady Gulch in the dark of night for his reign of terror.

He also assigned a couple deputies to check more closely into both Denver Walton's and Thomas Manning's financial records.

The fact that Denver was driving around in a brand-new truck with no means of visible support was troubling, as was Thomas Manning's history with his waitress wife. Both needed closer scrutiny.

They could possibly be on Jason McKnight's payroll. Denver might have joined the dark side in a desperate escape from Maddy and her money and Thomas for personal reasons of misguided revenge.

Once again he logged on to his computer to look up up Jason and Samantha McKnight. He wound up finding a grainy newspaper photo of their wedding. She was clad in a simple long white dress with beading across the bodice. She looked young and innocent and with the expectancy of love shining from her eyes. The photo broke his heart as he knew all her expectations had been shattered by a violent, abusive man.

Jason was suave and slender in a black tuxedo. His black hair was perfectly styled and he had the features of an aristocrat, but it was the flat, cold proprietary gaze at Samantha that turned Cameron's stomach.

He had to find Jason McKnight, and if Jason wasn't around but was rather pulling strings from afar, then Cameron had to find his puppet.

As he thought of Mary and the danger she was in, his heart crunched painfully in his chest. He had to protect her at all costs. He wasn't about to lose something just as it had been found.

Concentration was next to impossible for Mary as the afternoon wore on. She screwed up two orders and, during every spare minute, found herself drifting off into thoughts of Cameron and what they'd shared.

The fact that she hadn't murdered Jason was both a curse and a blessing. She would never again have to look over her shoulder waiting for a tap from a lawman with a warrant, and yet now she had to keep vigilant to make sure Jason didn't get a chance to finish what she'd always thought he'd do during their marriage—kill her.

At some point during her marriage she'd begun to believe that she would die at Jason's hand and her greatest fear had been that Matt would be left to live the horrendous life she'd lived with her husband. Even now the thought of Jason putting his hands on Matt shot sheer terror through her heart.

She wasn't sure how she felt about what had happened between her and Cameron earlier that morning. Making love with him had been a gift, an amazing affirmation she'd desperately needed.

Was she in love with him? She wasn't sure. She'd always admired not just his physical stature, but his intelligence, his morality and his solid dependability. She'd loved their late-night talks about movies and the weather and whatever else entered their minds.

Still, she'd spent so much time telling herself any kind of a relationship with him was impossible. It didn't quite feel real and that made her realize she was in no way ready to jump into a relationship with any man. She felt as if she'd just been given back her life and now she had to make sure she stayed alive.

There was no way she could think about a relationship with anyone until the danger to her staff and herself had passed. As long as Jason was out there, whoever she got close to would be at risk, as well.

Her wayward thoughts were interrupted by a commotion in the kitchen. As she headed in, Junior Lempke raced out, obviously escaping Rusty's temper.

"What's up?" she asked the big man who was scrapping down the grill and cursing up a storm.

"Regina is making me crazy," Rusty said. "She doesn't take the orders right and then they come back to me with complaints. I'm sick of it. I'm sick of her."

It was the first time Mary had ever heard him bitch about a waitress. "I'll talk to her," she replied in an attempt to halt one of Rusty's temper tantrums before it became one of his legendary ones.

"You do that," he said curtly. "Shirley used to be the same way, God rest her soul. She was a good woman, but she screwed up her orders a lot, too. It just makes it so much easier if everyone does their jobs right the first time."

As Mary went to talk to Regina, Mary's heart thundered with an unexpected rumble of uneasiness. It was odd that Rusty had not only complained about Regina but had also mentioned Shirley Cook, as well.

Rusty's cabin behind the café was completely isolated. It would be easy for somebody to come and go from there without anyone being the wiser.

Just a coincidence, she told herself. There was no way she could believe that Rusty was behind the murders. Besides, how would Rusty meet Jason? The cook was busy at the café most of the time and Rusty certainly didn't appear to have come into a windfall of money recently.

Don't get overly paranoid, she thought as she pulled Regina aside and told her she needed to take more care with her orders. She had to trust the people she surrounded herself with on a daily basis, otherwise she would go completely mad.

At dinnertime Maddy Billings showed up alone, a sour look on her pretty face as she glanced around the café, obviously looking for Denver and Lynette, who Mary knew were together on a date in Evanston.

Maddy flopped down in a booth near the door, her expression as sour as a lemon as she slammed her zebra-print purse on the booth seat next to her. Mary decided to wait on her and approached her with a friendly smile. "Hey, Maddy, nice to see you this evening."

Maddy sniffed disdainfully, as if sitting in the booth she'd often sat in with Denver was far below her standards. "I see that Lynette Shivers isn't working tonight, so I suppose the rumors are true and she's with Denver tonight."

"I'm sorry, I don't keep track of my waitresses when they're off duty," Mary replied smoothly. "Now, what can I get for you?"

"If she thinks she's going to have a relationship with Denver then she's sadly mistaken. Denver has belonged to me since we were teenagers. Oh, we have our little spats and he comes in here and flirts with all the waitresses, but he always comes back to me where he belongs." She raised her pointy little chin as if for punctuation.

"Maddy, I'm just here to feed you," Mary replied evenly.

Maddy sighed with impatience as if what she really wanted was to discuss at length her dysfunctional romantic life. "Just give me one of those dinner salads and a diet cola." She dismissed Mary with a wave of her hand.

Although Mary wasn't one to get involved with town romances, she almost wished Denver would find a nice woman and settle down, a young woman who wasn't Maddy Billings, a woman who didn't think she could buy people and love.

Denver did like to flirt with the waitresses, and if

Shirley and Dorothy had been young and carefree like Candy and Lynette, then Maddy would have been on the top of the suspect list, at least before Mary had learned that Jason was still alive.

What if it wasn't Jason who was responsible? After all, it had been years. For all she knew Jason could have moved out of the country, divorced her and then forgotten all about her and Matt and built a new life with a new young woman he could dominate and control. And yet that didn't explain either the anniversary card or the stuffed frog.

By the time the dinner rush began she had the mother of all headaches, torn between every theory of the case that flittered through her mind. What if Cameron focused only on the Jason angle and missed the real killer who could be a Grady Gulch native with motives they had yet to discern?

There was no guarantee that Jason was behind everything that had happened here in Grady Gulch. The anniversary card hadn't been signed and might have had something to do with the café, not with her. The stuffed frog could have been from any one of Matt's many friends. Maybe she'd overreacted to both because of her own guilty conscience.

Jason could simply be a red herring that would deflect law enforcement's attention from the real killer and the real motives for the murders.

The only thing that soothed her aching head was thoughts of the moments she'd spent in Cameron's arms that morning. He had been passionate and yet with an innate tenderness that had soothed many of the ragged edges of her soul, tattered remains she hadn't even known had been left behind by her marriage.

Cameron had given her hope again, a hope she believed she'd never feel again. He'd made her believe in all kinds of possibilities. She could find happiness again, she could find the kind of love she deserved with a special man, a man who could be a loving stepfather to Matt.

That night after the café closed, as always Mary checked on her son and found him still awake. "Can't sleep?" she asked as she sat down next to him on his bed.

"I'm trying, but I'm really not very sleepy."

She reached out and stroked a strand of his blond hair off his forehead and realized it was time he knew the truth about her past…about his father.

"I need to talk to you about something that's not going to be very pleasant," she said.

Matt sat up and rubbed his eyes, his gaze curious in the light shining in from the living room. "Talk about what?"

Mary stared at his sweet little face and her heart felt heavier than she could remember in a long time. She'd somehow always expected this moment to come, but she'd never realized how difficult it would be.

She not only had to tell her son that she'd lied about the car accident that had supposedly taken his father's life, but she also had to tell him that his father was a monster.

"I've lied to you."

Her words made Matt's eyes widen in shock. "You lied to me? About what?"

Slowly, haltingly, she told him everything, about the abuse, about the night she'd taken him and fled and that it was possible his father might be doing bad things now to punish her.

Matt took it all surprisingly well, with few questions and the comment that if the man who was his father had beaten Mary, then he was glad that man wasn't in their lives. "If he's a killer then I hope Sheriff Evans catches him and puts him in jail forever."

They hugged, and Matt settled in to sleep, but Mary had a feeling there would be more questions from him as he processed the information she'd told him.

She took a quick shower and then changed into her nightshirt. With a cup of freshly brewed plum tea in hand she walked to the windows that faced the small cabins in the distance.

It had been in one of those cabins that the whole madness had begun, with Candy Bailey's murder. Of the four cabins only one was occupied now by Rusty. A faint light spilled from the front window of his tiny cabin.

The other three cabins were illuminated faintly by the light of the big, fat moon overhead. The cabins had always been a safe place for people, particularly women in need. When she'd first come to Grady Gulch broke and with a two-year-old, the owner had allowed her and Matt to live in one of those cabins.

Over the years since Mary had taken over, she'd often had a down-and-out waitress living there, wanting to pay forward the kindness she'd received when she'd first come to town.

Now those cabins only signified isolation and death. She would never forget Candy's lifeless body and she didn't think she'd ever allow a vulnerable woman alone to stay in one of them again.

A small gasp escaped her as she thought she saw a figure move between two of the cabins. She froze, her heart crashing against her ribs as a frantic terror rose up the back of her throat.

Was it him? The killer? Was it Jason coming to finally make her pay for what she'd done to him? But he didn't appear to be moving toward the café.

In the blink of an eye the figure was gone, making her wonder if she'd seen somebody or not. Tall trees surrounded the small structures and a light breeze stirred among the nearly bare branches. Had she only seen a dancing shadow of a tree branch in the moonlight?

Should she call Cameron or was she merely jumping at shadows? She took a step backward, aware that she was silhouetted by the light in the room. With a trembling hand she placed her cup on the coffee table and turned off the light, plunging her room into darkness and then moved back to the window. An icy shiver slid up her back, one that had nothing to do with the coolness of the room.

Once again she peered outside, this time her vision better without the light on in the room. Nothing. Nothing but a faint night breeze shifting the tree branches in a ghostly landscape.

She didn't know how long she stood at the window, a frightened sentry guarding her home and her son before she finally convinced herself she was being silly. She was jumping at tree movement, seeing shadows of killers who weren't there.

With a tremulous sigh she finally moved away from the window and headed into her bedroom. She still felt spooked, but was certain she was overreaching due to a heightened sense of imagination.

All the talk of Jason had brought back hurtful and horrific memories that had haunted her throughout the day. Still, she found some comfort as she burrowed beneath the covers on her bed, within the sheets that still smelled vaguely of Cameron.

She could love him, if she let go and allowed herself, but at the moment she was afraid that in loving him she'd put him at risk. She was afraid that she'd put him in the sights of a killer who wanted to destroy everything she cared about and, finally, she was scared that somehow, someway, if it were Jason behind all this, she wouldn't survive him again.

Chapter 10

It was only ten o'clock and Cameron had already thought about calling Mary twice just to assure himself she was okay. But he knew she would be busy with the morning rush and that business would probably slow down midday because the forecast was for a band of snow to move in later in the afternoon.

He turned around in his chair and gazed out the window, where he was met with a sky the color of dark steel, the clouds low and appearing laden with something they were determined to cast down.

Just what he didn't need, a couple of inches of snow to complicate things. Snow always brought with it a slew of traffic accidents, slips and falls and dozens of other issues he didn't have the time to deal with, not with a killer plotting his next move.

What he needed to do was find Jason McKnight. Posters of the man had been hung all over Grady Gulch and Evanston. Hopefully, if he was in the area, somebody would see him and call the TIP line they'd set up.

Deputy Larry Brooks was in charge of managing that dedicated phone line, which so far had yielded the typical opportunity for every nut in the county to call in. Sam Canfield had been the first call, telling Larry that he'd seen a cigar-shaped mother ship drop Jason off in his field and from there Jason had disappeared into the woods on the property.

Clarissa Defoe had called in to let them know that Jason had been her lover for the past five years. Clarissa was ninety-two years old, on an oxygen tank full-time and lived with her only son and his wife.

At the moment, Cameron was waiting for Denver Walton to arrive for an unofficial chat. Denver had, indeed, come into a big windfall. According to his bank records, a month ago fifty thousand dollars had been deposited into his account from an unknown source.

It had been about that time that Denver and Maddy had broken up and Denver had bought a new pickup truck. Cameron intended to confront the man about his new financial situation and see if he had any ties at all to Mary's ex-husband.

He looked up as Ben Temple entered his office and flopped down on the chair next to Cameron's desk. "I spent all day yesterday talking to people who knew Thomas Manning and his wife. According to everyone I spoke to, Thomas is a timid, book type who didn't appear overly upset at the time that his wife left him."

"Trouble in the marriage?" Cameron asked. Neighbors usually knew more about the couple next door than people realized.

"Nothing overt," Ben replied. "No domestic abuse issues, friends and coworkers said that Thomas was a rather passionless kind of guy, hard to get to know, but nobody ever saw him lose his temper and he never spoke ill of Nancy after she left him."

"Still waters run deep?" Cameron mused.

"Maybe, but if he's been paid off as a hit man then he's hidden the money well. He lives a simple life that hasn't changed in the last couple of months. There's been no unusual activity in his bank account."

"But we both know money is easy to hide. Offshore accounts are fairly easy to set up. Hell, for all we know he has a stash underneath his mattress."

"I heard you have Denver coming in for an interview."

"I figured he was a good a place to start as any. He seems to have come into a bit of money lately. He lives alone on an isolated little piece of land and can pretty much come and go as he pleases. He doesn't seem to have a legitimate job that I know about, so I figured maybe it's time we need to have a talk."

Ben nodded. "Denver's an odd duck, lives alone on that little place his parents left him when they moved to Florida. The only real connection he's ever had with anyone here in town has been Maddy Billings. They've been a couple off and on since they were teenagers."

"Apparently he's dating Lynette Shivers now," Cameron replied.

One of Ben's dark eyebrows rosse. "Hope it sticks, that Maddy Billings is bad news. Her and her high-falutin' attitude. She's been so nasty to so many people here in town she's gonna have a problem finding anyone who might want to date her."

Cameron gazed at the young handsome single deputy before him. "Maybe you should take her out, see if you can straighten out her attitude a little."

Ben snorted. "Obviously you suffer a secret hatred of me even to consider such a thing. I'd rather stab myself in the eye with a fork than take Maddy Billings anywhere."

Cameron laughed and at that moment Larry Brooks poked his head in the door to let him know that Denver had arrived and was waiting in the small interrogation room down the hall.

"Time to get to work," Cameron said as he rose from his desk. "Hopefully by the end of this interview I'll know if we can take Denver off our suspect list or move him straight up to the top."

He and Ben parted ways in the hallway, Ben heading toward the front door of the office and Cameron to the interview room. The room was small, with a one-way window and held only a table and a couple of chairs. It was a typical interrogation room that was rarely used.

Denver sprawled in a chair like he was at home in front of his television, his big black winter jacket thrown over the chair next to him. "Hey, Sheriff," he said easily as Cameron entered the room.

"'Morning Denver." Cameron eased down in the chair opposite the handsome, dark-haired man.

"You want to tell me what I'm doing here? I didn't even have time for breakfast this morning. Was I seen jaywalking or maybe spitting on the sidewalk?"

Cameron ignored Denver's attempt at levity. "Would you like a cup of coffee or something else to drink?" Cameron asked.

Denver shook his head and leaned forward in his chair, his easygoing smile falling from his lips. "I'd just like to get out of here. So, whatever you need to do, let's get it done."

"I want to talk to you about Jason McKnight."

"Who?" Denver looked at him in apparent confusion.

"Jason McKnight, the man who paid you handsomely to terrorize Mary Mathis by killing off the women who work for her." Cameron watched Denver's features closely. "The man who's pulling the strings behind all these murders."

Denver slammed his back against the chair, his eyes widened in surprise. "What in the hell are you talking about? I don't know any Jason whoever and I sure as hell have nothing to do with the murders. I loved those women who worked at the café. They were friends of mine."

"Are you working, Denver? Nobody I've talked to around town seems to know exactly how you make a living."

Denver's eyes darkened slightly. "I raise a few cattle and have some crops. I get by okay."

"Rumor has it you get by with the help of Maddy Billings's wallet."

Denver's cheeks flushed slightly. "I won't lie, Maddy

has helped me out now and then financially, but I'm done with her and I'm done with her money. I've finally discovered my pride." He tilted his chin upward.

"Then talk to me about your new truck, about the fifty-thousand-dollar deposit in your bank account," Cameron said.

Once again Denver appeared shocked. "You've checked my bank account?"

"I'd check your underwear if I thought it would lead me to the killer," Cameron replied drily. "Now, talk to me about that money."

"It was an inheritance from my grandfather. I've got all the papers at my place. You can check it out. It's all legit," Denver exclaimed, rising half out of his chair. He eased back down and looked Cameron straight in the eyes. "It's what gave me the courage, the freedom, to finally break away from Maddy, the freedom to find out who I am as a man, but one thing I know for sure is that I had nothing to do with those women's deaths. I cared about those women."

There was a truth that rang in his words and shone from his eyes, a truth that Cameron reluctantly found himself believing. "Bring me the paperwork all about your inheritance," he said, disappointed that he was fairly certain Denver Walton had just slid off the top of his suspect list, leaving him few people left to investigate and a murderer to catch before he killed again.

For the first time in years Mary got up, got dressed and then laid back on the sofa to rest her feet before beginning the day. Matt awakened her when he came in to tell her he was leaving for school and asked if she were sick.

She jumped up from the sofa, stunned by the relative lateness of the hour and assured her son she wasn't sick, but just a sleepyhead who had fallen back asleep after getting up and dressed.

It was almost eight-thirty by the time she hurried from her back rooms and into the café kitchen, where things were already in full swing.

Rusty manned the grill like an old pro while waitresses turned in orders at a pace that let her know the café was unusually busy.

"Sorry I'm late," she said as Rusty raised an eyebrow in her direction. "I got up and then fell back asleep on the sofa. Thankfully Matt woke me before he left for school."

"Sleeping in…that's a first."

"I guess I stayed up too late last night." After thinking she saw somebody around the cabins, she'd had trouble going to sleep and knew it had been after two before she finally drifted off into a dreamless sleep. "How's it going?"

"It's going," Rusty replied. "Junior didn't show up for work, I figure he got his schedule screwed up again."

Mary nodded. It wasn't unusual for Junior to occasionally not show up for a shift because he'd gotten confused about what shift he was supposed to work. "He'll probably show up around two for the evening shift. You need help with prepping or anything? I can take over Junior's jobs if you need me."

"Nah, hope you don't mind but when it became obvious that Junior wasn't going to show up I called in James to bus tables through the lunch hour." James Waldron was a high school graduate who worked for Mary whenever possible.

"Sounds like you have everything under control."

Rusty flashed her a quick smile. "That's why you pay me the big bucks."

Mary laughed as she left the kitchen and moved into the café dining area where the breakfast rush was winding down. George Wilton was at the cash register, paying for "the worst breakfast he'd ever had in his life," Marianne and Bob Unger lingered over coffee. The middle-aged married couple came in every Monday for breakfast and after all their years of marriage it was still obvious that they only had eyes for each other.

John and Jeff Taylor, the twins who had recently moved to the area from someplace back east, were chatting to the couple seated at the table next to them. Brandon Williams sat alone at a table for two, a chair pulled aside to accommodate his motorized wheelchair.

She felt sorry for the vet, who had lost the use of his legs in a bomb explosion that had also left his face scarred. Once when visiting with him for a moment she'd noticed what appeared to be makeup on his forehead and realized he'd apparently made some sort of an attempt to hide the worst of his facial scarring.

Still, it was hard to feel too sorry for him as he was a gregarious man who didn't appear to suffer any self-pity because of his situation. He was a favorite among the waitresses, not only because he tipped well, but also because he had a terrific sense of humor.

Everyone looked happy and cared for, and Mary was pleased to see the three waitresses bustling between tables to make sure all the guests stayed that way.

She poured herself a cup of coffee and sank down at the stool behind the long wooden counter, where at the moment nobody sat to eat.

She wished Cameron was here, seated on the other side of the counter, gazing at her with his beautiful hazel eyes. But it was a foolish thought. The less she had to do with Cameron, the less danger she felt she placed him in.

If their theory was right and Jason or one of his paid minions was killing people close to Mary, then the last thing she wanted was for anyone to know the true depth of her feelings for Cameron.

For some reason she wasn't afraid for Matt. Even as evil as she believed Jason to be, she didn't think he'd want to kill Matt. He would simply want to own him. He'd want Mary to die knowing that Matt would be with him for the rest of Matt's youth.

She shoved these troubling thoughts out of her head. She didn't want to think about Jason or the killings, although she was acutely aware that it had been one week ago today that Dorothy's body had been found in her bed.

As always when she thought of the three victims her heart crunched with the pain of loss. She didn't want any more victims, not in this town that she loved, not from the café that was her life.

Rather than focus on the trauma of the last week, she walked around the café, greeting her diners and visiting with each for just a minute. It was what everyone called the "Mary" touch, the personal attention she tried to give everyone who entered her establishment.

"Good morning, Brandon," she greeted the scarred, bald war veteran. "Hope you're finding your breakfast to your liking."

Brandon patted his bulging stomach. "I'm afraid I find all your food to my liking. If I keep eating here I'll need two scooters to get myself around town." He winked one of his blue eyes. "Unfortunately I'm a man who hates to cook and this place makes it far too easy to eat well despite my inadequacies."

"We're always glad to see you here," she replied and then moved on to visit with the twins for a few minutes.

Even as she put on her pleasant face and went about her usual business, she couldn't help but think about Jason. Surely he'd stick out in this rough-and-tumble town with his elegant features and slick dark hair. Even in a pair of jeans and a flannel shirt, he'd poke out like a sore thumb. But if he'd hired somebody to do his dirty work, then he'd never have to make a personal appearance here in Grady Gulch.

It was between the lunch and dinner rush, when the café was fairly empty that Mary thought about that moment the night before when she thought she'd seen somebody skulking around the cottages.

She hadn't been inside any of them since Candy's death. Maybe it was time to check them out and make sure no vandals had done any damage and no squatters had taken up residency without her knowledge.

"Rusty, have you ever seen anyone around the other

cottages out back?" she asked as the burly cook sat on a stool drinking a cup of coffee and eating a thick ham sandwich.

He shook his head. "Never. It's definitely deserted out there. It's just me and the raccoons and deer. Why?"

"I was just thinking that I haven't been out there to check on the other cottages for a while and maybe it's time I did." She grabbed her coat from a hook on the back door.

"You going now?" Rusty asked, around a mouthful of ham and cheese.

"Now is as good a time as any," she replied. "I can get out there and check things before the snow moves in."

"Want me to come along?"

Mary looked out the back door in the direction of the cabins. It was the middle of the day and Rusty had just told her he never saw anyone around. She felt perfectly safe just peeking in the windows to make sure that inside the cabins were in the same condition they'd been when she'd last seen them.

"No thanks, I'll be fine. But if I'm not back in fifteen or twenty minutes, call the Sheriff," she said jokingly.

As she stepped out into the frigid air she could smell the snow and thought she felt a couple of flakes on her face. The forecasters all indicated an early, harsh winter, which was bad for business. When the snow fell and travel was difficult, people stayed home to eat rather than venturing out.

She'd weathered many tough winters before and, God willing, she'd live to survive another. Hopefully

Cameron and his team would keep everyone in town safe through the long, hard season. At least they'd had a busy breakfast and lunch so far that day because if the weathermen got it right, and the snow moved in for real, their dinner crowd wouldn't amount to anything.

The cabins weren't far from the back of the café and she had no creepy-crawling feeling that she was being watched or shadowed.

The cabins were set up like studio apartments, with a small kitchenette and a bathroom and one medium-sized room that served as both living room and bedroom.

Although each had its own key, Mary had never kept the empty cabins locked. There was nothing in there to steal, and while she didn't mind somebody in need squatting there for a night or two, she needed to know if that was the case.

As she approached the first one the only thing she felt was sadness, for the first cabin was where Candy had been killed.

She peered through the window and saw the remnants of the crime-scene investigation that had taken place. Fingerprint dust still lingered on the few pieces of furniture that had been moved out of place as the deputies had sought clues. The bed was missing the top mattress and the whole cabin interior spoke of loss.

Candy's family had come and picked up her personal items, so nothing of the young girl remained, only the scene of the crime.

Mary tried to tell herself that she wasn't responsible for Candy's death, that even if it was Jason behind the murders they could have happened to anybody in any town where Jason might have found her. But that didn't stop Mary's heart from filling with sadness.

In order to keep Jason from torturing her by hurting those she loved, she would have had to stay on the road, moving from place to place for the rest of her life, and that wouldn't have been possible with Matt in tow.

Matt had needed a town, a place to call home. He'd needed stability and normalcy and he'd had that for the past eight years. She hoped he continued to have that and she prayed that nobody else would have to die, that Cameron and his deputies would find the guilty party and put him away for the rest of his life.

As she walked the short distance to the second cabin, the sky gave up more of its moisture and snowflakes began to fall in earnest, fat flakes from the steel sky.

She figured she'd take a quick peek into the windows of the other two empty cabins and then get back into the warmth and comfort of the café. With the snow band already moving in, the dinner rush would definitely be small.

When she got back inside she'd call Lynette and Ginger and tell them they could have the night off. There was no point running at full staff capacity if the crowd was going to be unusually small and by the look of the sky overhead things were only going to quickly deteriorate.

According to the weathermen they were expecting three to six inches of the white stuff between this afternoon and morning. If the forecast came true then tomorrow would be a slow day, as well. Hopefully with it being such an early snowfall it wouldn't stick around too long and there would still be some nice days left in the month.

She reached the second cabin and frowned as she realized black curtains were drawn tightly closed across the windows. The cabins didn't come with curtains... so who would have hung them here and drawn them completely shut?

Leaning close to the front door she placed her ear against the wood, but heard no movement inside, nothing to indicate that anyone was there. She remained that way for several minutes, but discerned no sound...nothing beyond the door.

Heart suddenly pounding, she placed her hand on the doorknob. It turned easily beneath her hand. So, whoever had hung the curtains hadn't locked the door. But why the curtains, other than to keep prying eyes out?

What was it that might be inside that somebody wouldn't want anyone else to see?

Once again she pressed her ear against the door, but heard nothing at all. She drew in a deep breath and opened the door. The room was in darkness and she immediately flipped on the switch that turned on the overhead light...and then let out a gasp.

An old gray sleeping bag was open on the threadbare sofa and a colorful throw rug decorated the beige linoleum floor. A table lamp sat at an odd angle on an upended orange crate, the shade broken. Cans of food were lined up on the counter next to a small microwave, but none of this was what made her heart nearly stop.

It was what was on the wall that made her gasp in

horror. Tacked to the beige paint on one of the room's wall were news clippings about the murders and pictures of all the victims.

Had she found Jason's secret lair?

Was this where he'd been hiding out? In her very own backyard?

Her heart crashed the beat of horror as she backed up and hit the broad chest of somebody standing just behind her.

She whirled around and horror turned to shock. "Junior," she exclaimed as she stared at the man she'd trusted as much as she'd trusted her own son.

Junior's features screwed up as if he were about to cry. "Ah, Mary, now you've ruined everything," he said in dismay.

Chapter 11

After Denver's interview, Cameron had every intention of bringing in Thomas Manning for a chat, but he'd discovered that Manning was out of town, back in Oklahoma City to attend a conference at the college where he'd once been a professor. He'd sent Ben Temple to follow the good professor and keep an eye on him while he was out of town.

Cameron had grabbed a quick lunch from a fast-food place at his desk, brought in by Larry Brooks, and then had decided to check in on Mary, afraid that if the snow came as predicted he wouldn't be able to stop by to see her at closing time that night.

It was just after three when he left his office and headed for the café. As he drove, fat snowflakes splatted across his windshield, forcing him to turn on his wipers to see the road clearly.

He met little traffic on the way to the café. Hopefully most of the folks knew to stay at home when the weather turned bad, but he knew from experience that there were always some yahoos who decided snow and ice were the perfect time to test their driving skills.

When he reached the café, the parking lot was nearly empty and despite the fact that he was wishing Mary's business ill, he hoped the lot stayed empty until the snowstorm passed and some of what had been forecasted had melted away. At least by morning the streets would be plowed by both city vehicles and ranchers with the appropriate tractors.

He parked in front and got out of his car, hurrying toward the door through the snowflakes. As he entered, he automatically hung his hat on a hook and looked toward the counter.

His favorite blonde wasn't there. In fact, he didn't see her anywhere in the café. Nobody was seated at any of the tables and he could hear Rusty's voice as well as several female ones coming from the kitchen area.

He followed the voices to find Rusty and two waitresses chatting. "Hey, Sheriff," Rusty greeted him.

Cameron nodded in return. "Where's Mary?" he asked, not seeing her anywhere in the kitchen.

"She just went out back to the cottages to take a quick look around and make sure no vandals or squatters have moved in," Rusty said. He gazed down at his wristwatch. "She's only been gone a few minutes."

"She went by herself?" Cameron asked, a tiny alarm sounding in the back of his head. He didn't want her going off anywhere all alone.

He didn't wait for a reply but instead stepped out the back door and sucked in his breath at the frigid snowy air that slapped him in the face. The snow was falling in earnest now, quickly covering the ground and obscuring visibility.

As he drew closer he immediately saw that the door to the second cabin was open and it was there he headed, his heart beating an unexpected rhythm of anxiety.

He should have thought about the cabins. Damn it, he should have thought that one of them might be a potential den for a madman. But with Rusty staying out here, he'd just assumed the others were vacant. Now he cursed that assumption.

When he got nearer he saw that dark curtains hung at the window and his heart beat a little quicker. He pulled his gun, an automatic habit when approaching an unknown situation.

He moved to make a sideways approach, not wanting to alert whoever was inside that he was there. He leaned against the building just outside the door, drew a deep breath and then whirled inside to see Mary standing in the middle of the room and Junior Lempke standing before her as if to block her exit.

Junior turned around, his eyes wide as his hands shot straight up in the air. "Don't shoot me, Sheriff Cam, I ain't done nothing wrong."

Cameron met Mary's gaze. She shrugged as if she didn't have a clue what was going on. A quick sweep of the room chilled Cameron's blood like the falling snow outside couldn't possibly do.

The news clippings about the murders tacked to the wall stunned him. Junior? Junior Lempke? He hadn't even been on the list of suspects.

"Does somebody want to tell me what the hell is going on here?" he demanded, not removing the barrel of his gun from the center of Junior's body. Adrenaline fired through him with a heat that could melt the snow on the ground outside.

"I was out here checking on the cabins and noticed the curtains in this one. I'd just stepped inside when Junior showed up and now you're here," Mary said, her voice reflecting both relief and the same kind of stunned disbelief that Cameron felt.

Cameron turned his attention to Junior. "What's going on, Junior. What have you done?" The young man standing before him would have been the last person Cameron would have thought capable of the crimes, but this place, the clippings, spoke of an obsession with the women who had been killed.

Too many serial killers liked to keep souvenirs of their crimes and the clippings and pictures on the wall could definitely be considered souvenirs.

Tears began to stream from Junior's eyes. "My mom, she told me that I'd never be able to have a place of my own, that I'd always have to live with her. But this was my place, all by myself."

Awkwardly he ambled over to the lamp and touched the broken shade. "I bought this with my own money at the thrift store, and I...I got the microwave at the same store. I can live here and turn on my lamp when it gets dark and cook in the microwave for myself and maybe have friends come over. My mom is wrong and I want to prove her wrong. I'm responsible and this is my place all to myself." He jutted his chin forward, his eyes still gleaming with tears.

Cameron holstered his gun, his gut instinct telling him that Junior had no weapons on him, that he was harmless and harboring some misguided mission. He pointed to the wall with the clippings. "What's that?" he asked.

Junior's eyes once again filled with tears that spilled onto his cheeks. "That's my sad wall. They were all my friends and now they are all gone. But I'm making a happy wall over there." Junior pointed to the opposite wall and pulled a photo out of his coat pocket. "This is my first picture for my happy wall." He handed the photo to Cameron.

It was a picture of Junior and Mary standing side by side at the picnic Mary had sponsored last summer for her staff. Junior stood tall and proud, and Mary's face was wreathed with a smile that softened her features.

He handed the photo to Mary, who looked at it and released a deep sigh. It was obvious to him that Mary didn't believe Junior had anything to do with the murders, either.

This was like when Cameron was twelve and Bobby was eleven and they'd gotten angry with their parents and had built an elaborate fort up in hay loft. They'd stocked it with cookies and fruit and decided they could live there alone for the rest of their lives.

Of course the rest of their lives had ended when darkness came, when the old barn had creaked and groaned and made frightening noises. That's when they'd decided maybe sleeping in the house in their own beds wasn't such a bad idea.

Junior had wanted his own fort, a place where he could pretend he was in charge and away from his over-protective mother. He'd wanted to feel normal…like a man.

Junior Lempke wasn't the killer they sought. Cameron knew it in his gut. He completely believed Junior's story. "Are you going to arrest me, Sheriff Cam?" Junior asked, his voice trembling like that of a young child's. "My mom is really going to be mad at me if I end up in jail."

"No, I'm not going to arrest you, Junior," Cameron said and slid a glance to Mary, who nodded her head in agreement.

"But you have to get your things out of the cabin," she said. "I can't let you use this place, Junior." She gazed toward the open door where the snow was fall-ing in sheets of white. "You wait until this snow moves out and then you get your things from here and never come around the cabins again."

Junior's lower lip quivered. "Am I fired, Mary?"

Mary moved over to stand next to him and placed a hand on his shoulder. "Of course you aren't fired. What would I do without you, Junior? You help me keep the café running smoothly."

Junior's chest puffed out with pride and Cameron admired Mary's compassion, her gentleness with Ju-nior. "You need to get on home now," Cameron said to the man. "I doubt if Mary is going to need you in the kitchen. The snow is going to keep everyone inside for the night."

"Call me tomorrow, Junior, and I'll see if I need you to come in to work," Mary added.

Junior pulled his cell phone from his pocket. "Two is for Mary."

"That's right," Mary replied.

"Okay, I'll call you tomorrow," and with that Junior turned and ran out of the cabin.

Mary appeared to deflate, slumping down on the sofa atop Junior's navy sleeping bag. "I stepped in here and knew I'd found Jason's lair...right in my own backyard. My heart beat so hard it hurt and then I turned around to see Junior standing in the doorway. He told me I'd ruined everything and for one insane minute I thought he was the killer, and then you showed up."

She reached over and attempted to straighten the lamp shade on the crooked lamp. "Poor Junior. He just wanted to feel normal, to have his own place without his mommy around."

"Junior isn't our killer," Cameron said and sank down next to her on the sofa, instantly engulfed by the familiar raspberry scent of her. "But you got lucky because this could have been where the killer was staying. You could have walked inside this cabin and never left it again." His heart filled his throat at the very thought. "You should have never come out here alone."

"I know. I was foolish." She looked at him and offered him a half smile. "Although I did tell Rusty that if I wasn't back inside the café in twenty minutes to call you."

"A lot of bad things could have happened to you in twenty minutes." He took the strand of hair she twirled between two fingers and instead twirled it between his finger and thumb. Despite the circumstances she looked lovely with her cheeks pinked by the cold and her black winter coat making her hair appear almost as pale as the snow falling outside the cabin.

He so wanted to kiss her. When he'd walked into the cabin and had seen Junior standing in front of her and the wall filled with the news clippings, he'd thought about how easily he could lose her.

Dropping the piece of her hair, he leaned forward, wanting a kiss to assure himself she was really safe, but was surprised when she jumped up off the sofa and headed for the door. "We'd better get back to the café before we can't find our way back."

She had her back to him and he knew in his gut that she'd intentionally avoided his kiss. Maybe she regretted those moments they'd shared in her bed. He'd hoped the time they'd shared had been a beginning, but maybe he was wrong. Maybe it had simply been an awakening for her and there was no place in her future for him except as the local lawman. Maybe the truth of the matter was that he was simply a transitional man to her and nothing more.

He rose from the sofa. "Yeah, we should get back to the café. I forgot to leave breadcrumbs behind me and the snow is really coming down."

Together they left the cabin and raced toward the café's back door. By the time they reached the kitchen, they both looked like snowmen.

As they shook off the snow that covered them, Mary sent all her waitresses home but one for the night shift and then turned to Cameron.

"Thank you and now you'd better get out of here because I'm sure you're going to have a busy night with the weather and everything else that's going on," she said as she walked with him out of the kitchen and into the main eating area.

He grabbed his hat from the hook on the wall, wanting to say something…needing to say something but unsure what it was. "Don't be foolish again," he finally said gruffly and then he walked out into the near-blizzard conditions.

Chapter 12

Just as Mary expected, the café was dead for the evening rush. The snow continued to fall until dusk and then finally stopped, leaving behind about three inches of the fluffy stuff.

She popped popcorn for her and Matt and they sat at one of the tables eating from the big bowl and drinking hot chocolate. As she talked to her son about snow days and making snow angels and how excited she'd been the first time she'd seen snow, in the back of her mind her thoughts were of Cameron.

While they'd sat in the cabin she'd seen the kiss in his eyes before he'd leand forward and fear had shuttered through her, fear for him.

What if Jason stood just outside the window, watching them?

What if Jason somehow figured out how deep in her heart Cameron had crawled? Then Cameron would have a target placed firmly in the center of his back.

Mary couldn't let that happen. Cameron had owned part of her heart long before they'd fallen into bed together. She knew he wanted her again, but that wasn't going to happen, either.

Her biggest fear was that Jason would never be done with her, that he would just keep killing waitresses and friends and neighbors until there was nobody left in town but the two of them and Matt. He wouldn't stop until she was as alone, as isolated as she had been when they'd been married. Maybe she'd be insane by then, her mind fractured from all the losses she'd endured.

"Mom? Are you okay?"

Matt's voice pulled her from her horrible thoughts. "I'm fine," she assured him with a forced smile and patted his hand on the table. "I was just wondering if this snow is going to melt by morning."

"I hope not! I'm ready for a snow day from school. Jimmy and I already have plans to build a snowman in front of the café and put a cowboy hat on his head."

"Hmm, sounds just like the kind of advertising I could use," she replied with a smile. "But I wouldn't count on a snow day so early in the school year. I have a feeling the plows will be out all night cleaning off the roads."

Rusty left the kitchen carrying an old checkerboard set and challenged Matt to a game. As they played, Mary walked over to the window and stared outside where night had quickly stolen over the land despite the fact that it was just a little before seven.

Mary had never been afraid of the dark before, but since learning that Jason was still alive and the murders had occurred in the middle of the night, darkness brought with it a simmering anxiety that gnawed at her soul.

However, she didn't expect Jason to come at her in the night. She had a feeling he'd want to see her face in the starkness of sunshine, in the brightness of light when he came for her. He'd want her to see his glee when he killed her and wrapped their son in his arms.

The evening seemed endlessly long. At eight she sent home Regina, the only waitress working, and that left only Rusty in the place.

She allowed the checker games to last until nine and then she sent Matt to bed just in case the school buses ran in the morning.

"You might as well head home," she told Rusty. "If anyone comes in I can handle the grill, although I'm not expecting anyone this late on such a night."

"I heard the latest forecast on the radio earlier and this is all supposed to melt off in the next couple of days," Rusty said as he pulled on his coat. "And they'll have the roads cleared by morning now that it's stopped snowing. I imagine it will be business as usual tomorrow."

"I hope so," she replied. "It's far too early in the year for this place to have a quiet night like this."

"Definitely." Rusty pulled his collar up and withdrew a pair of gloves from his pocket. "I'll lock up the back door as I go and see you in the morning."

"'Night, Rusty," she said.

Minutes later Mary sat at one of the tables nursing a cup of hot tea. She'd already locked the front door and turned the sign in the window to closed. She didn't expect Cameron to stop by at closing time nor did she expect anyone else to come in for a quick meal.

She should just go on to bed and take advantage of an early night, but she wasn't a bit sleepy. Far too many thoughts weighed heavy on her mind.

When would the killer strike again? Would the next victim be another waitress or Mary herself? She hadn't had a chance to ask Cameron who he'd taken off the suspect list and who might have been added onto it.

Was Denver's new truck bought and paid for by Jason? She'd heard through the grapevine that the twins, Jeff and John Taylor, were planning on a new barn in the spring…possibly financed by her crazed ex-husband?

Or had Thomas Manning been easy pickings as Jason's dupe? Thomas had a waitress wife who'd betrayed him. Had he maintained a simmering rage after that, a rage that had eventually been tapped into by the manipulative Jason?

Or was the murderer just a local rancher down on his luck, with a stomach to kill and a willingness to take whatever money Jason might offer him?

She didn't want to think about her feelings for Cameron, not with the headache that had begun to pound with a nauseating intensity across her forehead. She cared about him, but their passion had exploded under odd circumstances.

She didn't know if what she felt for him was love or gratitude. She wasn't sure if she thought she loved him because he was the only man she'd allowed remotely in her life.

She finished her tea, rinsed the cup and then turned off the overhead lights, leaving on only the faint glow of the security lights above the counter.

Maybe an early night would ease some of the anxiety that had become a constant thrum inside her for the past couple of days. It certainly wouldn't hurt her headache either to get an extra hour or two of sleep.

Within thirty minutes she was in her bed, wishing she didn't feel so alone, wishing that Cameron was beside her. If the world was a different place and she'd met Cameron at a different time would he be the right man for her?

She'd once thought Jason was perfect and obviously that had turned out badly. She wasn't sure she trusted her own instincts when it came to men. There was no way she believed that Cameron was anything like Jason, but she also didn't know if she was drawn to him simply because he was the keeper of her secret and the first man she'd interacted with intimately since Jason.

It was easy to imagine love for lust and a sense of security. Easy to imagine loving a man who was solid and moral and adored by her own son. But did that mean she was *in* love with Cameron?

She fell asleep before an answer could form in her

head and awakened disoriented as she heard a crackling noise and smelled the scent of something burning.

At first she thought it was some kind of a dream, but as complete consciousness claimed her, she realized it wasn't a dream, it was very real.

Had she left the grill on in the kitchen? Had Rusty left on an appliance that had shorted out? She rolled over and turned on her bedside lamp, shock jerking her upright as she realized the room was filled with dark smoke.

It took a moment for the last of her sleep to completely fall away and reality to grab her by the throat with sheer panic. The café was on fire.

Matt! His name screamed through her head. She had to get to her son.

She jumped out of the bed and raced to her bedroom doorway, stunned to see that the sofa had been turned on its side and was not only engulfed in flames but also blocked any entry or exit from Matt's bedroom.

Despite the roar of the fire and the fact that Matt's bedroom door was closed, she screamed his name at the top of her voice, and then half collapsed with a coughing spasm. Her eyes burned and began to tear from the black smoke that roiled in the air.

Horror stuttered through her as she realized she couldn't get to Matt's room…to Matt himself, unless she could somehow move the blazing sofa from where it sat.

The red-and-yellow flames lighting the room made it look like a rendition of hell. But true hell was knowing that her son was on the other side of the burning barrier.

She was about to attempt to push the sofa to one side when over the din of the fire she heard a shatter of glass from her bedroom and somebody yelling her name.

She raced back to the bedroom to see Cameron at the window. "Come on," he yelled, urging her out the window.

"I can't," she cried. "I can't get to Matt." She began to cough again, nearly falling to her knees.

"I've got him. Matt's out here with me. He's safe, Mary." Cameron reached a hand through the broken glass. "Come on. You need to get out of there now."

Trusting that what he'd told her about Matt was true, she grabbed his hand and he helped her out of the window. At the same time she heard the distant sound of sirens. Hopefully they were from an approaching fire truck.

Matt stood shivering in the snow, tears streaming from his eyes. "Mom, Twinkie is still in there," he said with a sob. "I couldn't find her in the smoke when the man told me to get out of my window." His tears falling on his cheeks glistened as if on the verge of turning into ice. "She's gonna die in there."

Cameron's features looked hard and determined in the faint light of the moon and the whisper of smoke that had drifted outside. He handed Mary his car keys. "Go on, the two of you get in my car and turn on the heater before you both get frostbite or worse."

Matt turned and ran toward Cameron's car. Mary hesitated. "What are you going to do?" she asked as they hurried around the building.

"I'm going in to get Twinkie."

Despite Mary's protests, there was no way Cameron was going to force Matt to live with the fact that cute little Twinkie had fried in his bedroom. The kid would be traumatized for the rest of his life.

Although Mary tried to stop him, clinging to his arm and begging him not to attempt a rescue, Cameron was determined. He raced back to Matt's room and climbed in through the broken window and hit the floor.

The room was dark except for the faint glow of the greedy fire beneath the closed door. The fire made a hissing noise, as if it were a dark and ominous snake attempting to sneak beneath the door.

The smoke stung his eyes and pressed tight against his lungs. He stayed low to the ground, where the air was still just barely breathable. "Twinkie," he called.

The heat in the room grew more and more intense and he expected the flames from the burning sofa to jump to the bedroom door at any moment. If that happened he'd have no other choice than to abandon the room and leave the dog behind.

"Twinkie," he yelled again, grateful to hear men's voices coming from the other side of the bedroom door. Apparently help had arrived.

At the same time Cameron felt a furry little body run into his head. "Twinkie, thank God." He grabbed the trembling dog to his chest and then backed up to the open window.

With the dog safely in his arms he exited the building, grateful to see the volunteer fire truck nearby with hoses already in use.

He ran across the snowy landscape to his car. Matt

opened the back door, his arms opened to receive his precious dog. "Thank you," Mary said, her eyes filled with tears.

He nodded. "Just keep the doors locked and the car running so you stay warm. Don't open the doors for anyone but me and if somebody tries to get in, then drive away and I'll find you later."

Mary nodded solemnly, as if she realized what Cameron had already assessed, that this fire could have simply been a diversionary tactic to get Mary and Matt out of the café and into the snow alone and vulnerable.

Thank God Cameron had been doing hourly drive-bys and checking out the perimeters of the café and had seen the fire blazing when he had. By the time Cameron arrived, Matt had already climbed out his window and was crying for his mother and Twinkie.

When Cameron realized Mary was still inside, his heart had frozen with fear. Now, with all three of the occupants safe in his car, he raced back to see that the firemen were pulling their hoses back through the broken main door of the café.

The chief of the fire department, aptly named Smokey Johnson met him in the kitchen. "Fire is out, only mortality is a sofa and some smoke damage mostly contained to the main room in the back. No question that it was arson, probably gasoline poured over the sofa material. There's a broken window in the room, probable point of entry for whoever lit the fire."

Smokey pulled off his helmet, his ragged features indicating exhaustion. "We don't get called out at three in the morning very often."

"Thank God you got here before any real damage was done or somebody lost their life," Cameron replied. He slapped Smokey on the back. "I'll be in touch for your official report sometime tomorrow. In the meantime if you all could board up the broken windows before you leave I'd appreciate it. I've got Mary and Matt in my car and I want to get them someplace safe and warm for what's left of the night."

"We'll take care of everything," Smokey replied. "And when we're finished we'll let your men move in for whatever they need to do." Cameron knew he could depend on the fire chief, who had served efficiently in his capacity for the past ten years.

After speaking with Deputies Larry Brooks and Brent Walkins about their own crime-scene investigation in the café, Cameron hurried back to the car, his goal now to get Mary and Matt settled in at his place.

The interior of his patrol car was nice and toasty and Matt had already fallen back asleep with Twinkie curled up on his chest.

However, Mary still had the shell-shocked look of a woman somebody had just tried to kill. Her hair was wild around her face and one cheek sported a smear of smoky residue.

"I'm taking you to my place," Cameron said as he put the car into gear and headed out of the Cowboy Café parking lot. He was grateful she didn't object. He wasn't exactly in the mood for objections from anyone.

"How bad is the damage?" Her voice sounded faint, as if she were trapped in a dream and couldn't wake up.

"You're going to need a new sofa and there's a lot of

smoke damage, but that can be fixed with a little elbow grease and some new paint."

He felt her gaze on his as he carefully maneuvered the dangerous curve he had to drive in order to get to his ranch. "You know it was probably Jason. He was probably hoping the whole place would come down."

"Maybe, but I was doing cursory checks around your building throughout the night. It was on this last check that I saw Matt standing outside his bedroom window in the snow, crying for you and his dog."

Mary straightened in the seat. "You weren't the man who broke his window? You didn't tell him to get out of his room?"

Cameron shot her a quick glance, his jaw tense. "No, he was already out when I arrived."

Mary worried her fingers together in her lap and shot a quick look over the seat to her sleeping son. "Matt told me somebody tapped on his window, then broke it out and told him to get out of the building because it was on fire. It had to have been Jason."

She stared out the passenger window and then turned back to Cameron. "He must have run away when you arrived. Jason's intention was to kill me and take Matt. Thank God you came when you did." She shivered, as if any other scenario filled her with ice.

With the thick layer of snow, Cameron hoped his deputies would be able to find footsteps to follow that might lead them to tire tracks and from those they could at least figure out what kind of vehicle the person was driving or something physical about the person who had left behind footprints.

Mary fell silent and Cameron desperately tried to keep his attention on the snowy road and not on the length of her legs that was bared by the shortness of her oversize black T-shirt.

As he tried to ignore Mary's bareness and maneuver the slick roads, his mind also worked over the elements of the entire case. Three dead bodies, an abusive ex-husband who couldn't be located and Mary. There was no question in his mind now that Jason McKnight was behind it all. But was he working alone or was he working with somebody here in town?

And where in the hell was he holed up?

His men had been working over the past week to check out every abandoned barn, shed and building. Any stranger walking the streets would be noted by somebody and brought to his or one of his deputies' attention, but so far that hadn't happened.

"Maybe you should just take us to the motel," Mary said, breaking the silence that had grown between them.

"I'd feel better if you were at my place." He'd wondered how long it would take for her to protest his plans.

"And I'd feel better if we weren't."

He shot her a glance of surprise. She stared out the front window, as if not wanting to meet his gaze. Was her reticence because of what had happened between them before?

"Mary, if you're worried that I'll somehow take advantage of you or you're regretting what happened between us, then let me assure you that I will be a complete gentleman."

"That's not it." She turned to look at him, her eyes

shimmering in the illumination from the dashboard. "Don't you understand? Jason is hurting all the people I care about. I don't want him to think that I care about you in any way and put you in danger."

Her words warmed him, but also made him more determined than ever that she and Matt would stay with him until this was all over.

There was no question in his mind that the end was near, that Jason had honed in on Mary rather than any of her waitress friends. The fire tonight proved that he was finished playing games with her. He wanted her dead and Cameron was determined to do everything in his power to make sure that didn't happen.

He just hoped it was enough.

Chapter 13

There had been little conversation once they reached Cameron's house. Cameron led Matt and Twinkie to a small guest room with a double bed covered with what appeared to be a multicolored handmade quilt and a chest of drawers.

Mary was taken to the guest room next door, one that obviously got more used than the room where Matt and Twinkie slept. It held a double bed and dresser with a mirror and the room was decorated in sky-blue.

Mary took a quick shower, pulled on a pajama top that Cameron had provided and then tumbled into bed. The top smelled vaguely of Cameron's cologne and thankfully she immediately fell asleep.

She awakened at dawn, for a moment disoriented as she gazed at the room around her. The sun was just beginning to awaken behind the opened blue curtains at the window. She stared at them in confusion. She didn't have blue curtains in her bedroom.

She sat up and memories of the night before tumbled through her head. The fire. The panic. Her utter, gut-wrenching fear for her son. Cameron returning to the burning rooms to rescue Twinkie.

She was surprised to see the closet door open and some of her clothing hanging there. Apparently at some point during the night somebody had brought clothes for Mary and Matt from the café to Cameron's place.

She got out of bed and quickly grabbed a pair of jeans and one of her Cowboy Café T-shirts, then raced across the hall to the bathroom to wash her face and brush her hair.

When she felt prepared to face whatever the day might bring, she left the bathroom and instantly checked on Matt, who remained sprawled asleep on the bed with Twinkie curled up against one ankle.

She followed the scent of fresh-brewed coffee down the hallway and into the kitchen, where she found Cameron seated at the table, files and papers strewn before him. He looked up in surprise at her appearance. "Good morning, I didn't expect to see you so early." He shoved some of the papers aside and pointed to the empty spot. "Help yourself to the coffee and come join me." He closed a couple of the files.

"I don't suppose you managed to get Jason behind bars while I was asleep," she said as she poured herself a cup and then joined him at the table.

"No such luck," he replied. "I've got my deputies

checking the whereabouts of Denver and a couple of other men at the time of the fire. Thomas Manning apparently got home from Oklahoma City late last night and so he's not off my hit list of suspects." Cameron released a deep sigh and motioned to the files before him. "I was just going over everything again for the hundredth time, trying to see if there was something, anything we missed, but so far nothing is popping."

"Last night was the most up close and personal he's gotten with me," she said as she lifted the cup to her lips. As she thought of the fire, of that moment when she feared she wouldn't be able to get Matt out alive, she needed the hot brew to heat the icy chill that swept through her.

She took a sip and then looked out the window. "Looks like the snow has moved on."

"Left behind about three inches, but is now heading for Kansas. The roads have been plowed and we're in good shape. We're just supposed to stay cold for another day or two and then a warm front is moving in."

"That will be nice." It seemed so odd to be sitting at his table talking about the weather with her business, her home, her very life, in utter shambles. She glanced at the clock on the oven.

"I need to get Matt up for school in just a few minutes. Could you drive him there and then drop me off at the café?" she asked.

"Are you sure you wouldn't like to take a little time off and keep the café closed for today?" he asked, his concern deepening his voice.

She shook her head vehemently. "He might have

burned my sofa, but thankfully, from what you told me last night, the café itself is still ready for business. He doesn't get to win, Cameron, at least not in me closing down the café. In all the years I've owned it we've never shut down for a whole day for anything and I'm not about to do that now."

He held her gaze for a long moment, as if assessing her inner strength. She raised her chin, knowing the kind of strength she had inside her, a survivor strength that had seen her not only through the past nine years but also the years she'd spent as Jason's abused wife.

"I'll tell you what, I'll take Matt to school each day and you to the café, and I'll pick you both up there when you're finished for the day, but in return you agree to stay here with me until all danger has passed."

"But that could be months," she protested. "He could just keep killing waitresses, tormenting me for months…until we're all crazy."

"I don't think so," he countered soberly. "I think things are coming to a head. Last night he got close… too close. He's taking bigger chances and I think he's ready for the main event."

"I can't figure out why he just didn't slit my throat last night. He got into our quarters without me or Matt hearing him. Why not just finish me off then?" She took another drink of the coffee, needing it to battle the coldness that filled her each time she thought of Jason.

"I can't answer that," Cameron replied thoughtfully. "Maybe he just wanted one more opportunity to terrorize you completely, a final chance to show you how powerless you are and how powerful he is." Cameron's fingers whitened as he gripped his coffee cup handle tightly. "He could have killed you last night and yet he didn't. He wanted you to know that he holds the ultimate power of life and death where you're concerned and he decides when it's time for it to end."

"I get it," she replied drily.

"He may be winning the battles, Mary, but that doesn't mean he gets to win the war," Cameron said firmly. He set his cup down and instead reached across the table for her hand.

It felt right, his big hand covering her smaller one. She was a strong woman, but Cameron was a strong man and she knew they just might make a good match... if she lived long enough.

Cameron watched Mary's face as they entered what had been her living room. The sofa was a melted mass of wood and blackened material, the walls darkened from all the smoke that had unfurled against the paint. Matt's artwork that had decorated the walls were curled and blackened around the edges, but at least they were mostly still intact.

The smell of smoke lingered in the air despite the scent of frying potatoes and onions that Rusty had going in the kitchen.

"A new window and sofa, a fresh coat of paint and several loads of laundry and it will all be as good as new," he said, in an attempt to take away the stunned look from Mary's face. "It could have been so much worse."

She blinked a couple of times, as if warding off the

threat of tears. "I hated that sofa anyway," she finally managed to say, the words a mixture of laughter and a sob.

Cameron threw an arm around her shoulder and pulled her close against him. "You'll get through this, Mary. You're strong. You've been to hell and back and I'm not about to let anything else bad happen to you or your son."

She forced a smile up to him. "Then you better get going. You aren't going to find the bad guy sitting here having breakfast." She moved away from him and into the kitchen.

He followed behind but she ignored his presence as she talked to Rusty about breakfast service. Cameron left the café, knowing she was in good hands, but unsure where he stood with her. Right now he was her protector, but what would he be to her when this was all over?

Earlier, when he'd dropped Matt off at his school, he'd gone inside and spoken to Matt's teacher to let her know that Matt was to be released only to him or Mary and should remain inside the classroom until one of them arrived to pick him up. He was also forbidden to take recess outside without close supervision. The last thing he wanted was a snatch-and-grab of Mary's son. That would be the straw that broke her completely.

He headed to his office, eager to hear what his deputies had to share about their investigation into the fire scene the night before.

He met Ben Temple coming in. Ben had returned from Oklahoma City late last night when Thomas Manning had come back to town. Cameron motioned him into the office. "So, how did you find the big city?"

"Boring except for the drive home in the snow. That was a little bit of a challenge." He sat in the chair opposite Cameron's. "I'll tell you, I don't know if Thomas Manning can be bought off and paid for as a serial killer, but while he was in the city he took all of his meals at the truck stop where his wife used to work."

"Interesting. And what time did he make it back here to Grady Gulch last night?"

"Just a few minutes after midnight."

Cameron reared back in his chair and rubbed the center of his forehead. "So, he would have had enough time and could have set the fire at the café."

"It's definitely possible."

"I think it's past time to bring him in for some questioning."

"Agreed," Ben replied. "Want me to bring him in?"

"That would be great. As soon as I get Smokey's report and the investigative report from Mills and Walkins, I'll be going over those and there might be somebody else I need brought in."

That was the beginning of one of the most frustrating days of Cameron's life. Within an hour Ben had returned to announce that Manning wasn't at home, nor was he at the café or anywhere else that anyone had seen him that morning. They agreed that Ben would sit outside his house and bring him to the office as soon as he showed up.

Smokey's report yielded nothing more than what he'd told Cameron the night before. Somebody had broken through the window, crawled through and had shoved the sofa from the center of the room to block Mary from getting into Matt's room. That person had then poured gasoline all over the sofa and had lit it on fire.

What made it even worse was that after talking to Matt this morning Cameron knew that the person who had set the fire had broken Matt's bedroom window and made certain the young boy had awakened and gotten out to safety.

Matt couldn't describe the man, he hadn't seen him. He only knew that the breaking glass in his bedroom had awakened him and a deep voice had commanded him to get out, that his life was in danger from a fire. Matt could smell the smoke and so he'd done as he'd been told and had scrambled out the window.

By the time Matt got out, within seconds Cameron had arrived and there had been no sign of anyone else in the area.

Although fresh snow should have yielded footprints, the area around Matt's window was a muddled mix of prints…Matt's and Cameron's and Mary's. They were so mixed up and smeared it was almost impossible to discern what other prints might have been there.

The firefighters had also marred the pristine snow around the entrance of the café where the glass door had been broken for entry. He only hoped that when Mills arrived to give his report he and the other deputies might have found some prints somewhere in the general area that could help lead to the suspect.

It was just around noon that Larry showed up, not

only with his own report but with a handful of others from the deputies who had been on scene.

"Tell me something good," Cameron said as he gestured Brooks into the chair across from his.

Larry winced and placed the written reports on Cameron's desk. "Wish I had something good to say. The only real piece of evidence we discovered were boot prints leading away from the café."

"From where to where?" Cameron asked, hoping this was finally the break they'd been waiting for.

"From the back of the café to the street. Unfortunately the street had already been plowed and we lost the prints there."

"So, whoever was responsible headed toward Main Street. Do we know what size the boots were?"

"Ten and a half or eleven…and wide width with heavy tread. I'd guess our perp is between two hundred and two fifty pounds. Definitely not a woman's boot."

"And a fairly good-sized man." Cameron blew out a sigh. "What about tread pattern?"

"I checked with three of the local stores and most of the boots sold in each of them bear the same kind of tread. It's a common boot sold in the area."

"Of course it is," Cameron said with frustration. "We aren't any closer to finding this guy than we were when Candy Bailey was murdered and what scares me more than anything is that I think he's at his breaking point. The clock is ticking for our next victim." And he was scared to death that the next victim would be Mary.

At three forty-five that afternoon, with no more clues coming to light, Cameron walked into the school to pick up Matt. The boy's face wreathed in a big grin at the sight of Cameron and it was at that moment Cameron knew he could love this boy as his own.

"Hey, Sheriff Evans," Matt said as he grabbed his book bag from a hook near the door of the room. "I told Mrs. Perry that you'd be here right on time. I told her you were the dependable kind."

Cameron nodded to the teacher who smiled from her position at her desk. "I wasn't worried about it," she replied. "Even if you're a few minutes late I can always use the extra time to grade a few papers."

Matt sidled up next to Cameron. "I'm ready when you are. Thanks, Mrs. Perry," he said.

Cameron nodded to the teacher and then the two left the building and got into the car. "Everyone asked me about the fire today," Matt said, buckling himself in. "It was cool until lunchtime and then I got sad and I couldn't help it. I started to cry." He shot a quick glance at Cameron, as if to gauge his reaction to Matt's confession.

"Sometimes you just get so emotional you can't help but cry," Cameron said, keeping his gaze on the road. "Do you know why you were crying?"

Matt fidgeted in his seat. "It's just weird, you know, that my real dad is basically a monster who has killed women who I liked and now wants to kill my mom. I just got a little freaked out, you know scared that maybe I'll grow up and be like my dad. Anyway, Mrs. Perry sent me to the counselor's office and we talked."

"Did it help?" He shot a quick look at the boy.

Matt nodded. "Mr. Wheeler talked to me about nature and nurture stuff and that my dad was just a blip in my life and I'm more likely to be like my mom and the men in my life now...more like you." Matt turned his head and looked out the side window. "Most of the time I pretend you're my dad."

Cameron's heart squeezed tight and for a moment no words would form in his head. Sheer emotion nearly overwhelmed him. If he could ever conjure up a son in his imagination, it would be a kid like Matt. "You know I'm always here for you, Matt," he finally managed to say. "If you ever need to talk about something, I'm available."

Thankfully at that moment he pulled up in front of the café. "Are you coming in?" Matt asked him.

Cameron shut off the engine. "I believe I will. I haven't had lunch so I guess I'll grab an early dinner."

Before Cameron could get out of the car Matt laid a small hand on his arm. "Thank you for going back into the fire to get Twinkie. That was the bravest thing anyone has ever done for me in my whole life."

Cameron smiled. "Your mother has done some pretty brave things for you, too."

"I know, I'm lucky to have both of you in my life." With those words Matt exited the car. Cameron was slower getting out, his head racing with thoughts of Mary and Matt.

There was no question that Cameron wanted them in his life, not just temporarily, but forever. But there was also no question that he'd felt Mary distancing herself from him the moment after they'd made love.

She'd only been under his roof last night because

her place was uninhabitable. It certainly hadn't been a choice she'd made eagerly with her heart. Once her place was ready for her, she'd go back.

He also had a terrible fear that once Jason McKnight and anyone else involved with the crimes was no longer a threat, Mary Mathis would find some fine cowboy to hitch her star to, and Cameron would simply be the man who had awakened her to a future of possibilities.

Chapter 14

The first time Mary saw her living room she felt as if she'd been sucker-punched. The actual event of the fire felt like a bad dream that had occurred in the middle of the night. In the light of day, she saw how quickly, how easily the fire might have spread, how easily she might have been trapped and died in her attempt to get her son out of his room and to safety.

Evil. She felt it getting closer with each day that passed. It was an evil that she'd never felt before, not even in the years she had lived with Jason. This evil had deepened and matured over time. It was no longer an impulsive, alcohol-driven rage, but rather one that had patience and cunning.

She'd spent only a few seconds staring at the fire damage and then had gotten to work in the café. The breakfast rush was busy, with the main topic of conversation the fire that had taken place in the back rooms.

Everyone was sympathetic. Even George Wilton, who for the first time ever had no complaints about his coffee or his breakfast.

She realized by now that most of the people in town knew that the suspect was her ex-husband, but nobody mentioned it to her and for that she would be forever grateful.

The lunch rush was just as busy, with people coming and going, wanting the inside information of the fire and any other gossip that might be floating in the air.

The brightest spot in her day was when Matt came in, followed by Cameron. As Matt raced to the back room to see the damage, Cameron sat on one of the counter stools.

"Drinking or eating?" she asked.

"I'd like a burger and a scotch, neat."

She smiled. "I can help you with the burger but you'll have to go to the Cowboy Corral or someplace else for the scotch."

"I was afraid you'd say that. Guess I'll take a burger and fries and a vanilla milkshake."

She nodded. "I'm assuming last night yielded no new clues."

She could tell that he hated that she'd asked and that he hated even worse his reply. "Nothing except the possibility that our perp wears size ten or eleven in snow boots with a tread pattern on the bottom that is common to most snow boots sold in the state."

"At least with that information you can rule out small-footed men."

"What size shoe did Jason wear?"

"A ten and a half." She leaned slightly forward, allowing her to catch his familiar scent. "I feel it, Cameron. I feel *him* getting closer with every minute that passes. He's evil, pure and simple. When we were married he swore he'd make me pay if I ever left him, he promised that he'd kill me and now he's doing just that and he won't be happy until I'm finally dead."

She'd had a horrible sense of impending doom that she'd been unable to shake since awakening to the blazing flames in her living room the night before. She felt as if the end game could occur at any moment and her greatest fear was that after all these years Jason would ultimately win.

"Mary. I'm not going to let that happen. You have to trust me." There was a burning determination in Cameron's eyes that she desperately wanted to believe, but he was only one man and at the moment Jason seemed so omnipotent.

"I'm going to see you to work each morning and I'm going to take you and Matt to my house each night. When you aren't here surrounded by people, I'm going to be stuck on you like white on rice," he said.

She smiled at his silly cliché. "Let me go place your order." She left the counter and went into the kitchen where Rusty and Junior were working side by side on prepping for the dinner rush.

Minutes later she served Cameron his meal and then moved away from him, not wanting anyone to see her lingering around him. It was certainly probable that Jason or whoever was working for him knew she and Matt were staying at Cameron's place, but there was no reason to give them the idea that it was anything except professional safekeeping, especially after the fire.

Thankfully, for the past eight years of being in Grady Gulch Mary had never shown any overt romantic interest in any man, although she'd certainly had plenty of the single cowboys hit on her.

There had been some speculation about her and Cameron, the waitresses had even teased her about it. But nobody knew anything beyond the perception that the two of them shared a deep friendship. Nobody knew about that morning in her bed, when he'd made love to her so exquisitely, when he'd breathed life into a lifeless body and soul and made her believe in love and happiness once again.

However, at that moment she'd believed that it would just be a matter of hours, at the most a day or two, before Cameron would have Jason behind bars and she could continue her life without fear. She didn't believe that anymore.

Now her constant companion was a kind of fear she'd never known before. She suspected each and every man who entered her café doors, had learned to be suspicious of every crackle of a tree limb, each unusual noise that might reach her ears. She didn't like the woman she was becoming, afraid to love, afraid to care about the people who had been in her life for the past eight years.

Thankfully the dinner rush kept her busy and shoved all troubling thoughts from her mind. Matt spent his time working on his homework at a table in the corner and then playing a handheld video game until they could leave.

When closing time came gratitude sprang through her as Cameron walked through the door, ready to take her and Matt back to his place. He looked tired and stressed, but also like a safe barrier to ward off evil.

"Everything okay this evening?" Cameron asked once they were in his car.

"Fine. Of course, the fire was the hot topic—excuse the pun," she replied.

Matt laughed and Cameron cast her that slow, sexy grin that exploded a fireball of heat in the bottom of her belly. She didn't ask him what, if anything, he and his deputies had come up with during the afternoon and evening. She feared his answer would be the same as it had been when he'd come in to eat…basically nothing.

The conversation on the drive back to Cameron's consisted of Matt's school-day adventures, the fact that the plows had done a great job clearing the roads and how much Twinkie had probably missed them all during the long day.

As they walked into Cameron's front door, Matt was greeted by Twinkie, who danced and jumped on his new owner as if unable to get enough of him. After a quick visit outside, Matt and Twinkie headed for the guest bedroom he was temporarily calling home.

Cameron motioned Mary to the sofa. "I'm about to have that scotch I mentioned earlier today. Would you like something to drink?"

"You have any wine?"

"A bottle of red."

She nodded. "A glass of red wine sounds heavenly."

As he left to go into the kitchen she leaned her head back against the sofa and closed her eyes, fighting against a wave of discouragement.

For the first time in her life she wished she had a best friend, somebody who knew her entire history and lived in another town. She would have sent Matt to them, away from this place of danger and tension, away from the man determined to own him.

She wished she had a best friend who she could talk to about her conflicting emotions where Cameron was concerned. She wished she had somebody to confess about their bed time together and how those magical moments in his arms had only managed to confuse her more.

But throughout the time before she'd landed in Grady Gulch she'd traveled light and stealthily, not making friends, not allowing herself any close acquaintances.

She knew that much of the latest gossip was about the fact that the number one suspect in the fire and the murders was her ex-husband, although nobody had said anything to her face. Except George Wilton, who had finally had the temerity to say something to her about it.

"So, sounds like you married a real bastard," he'd said as he was finishing up his dinner.

"Something like that," Mary had agreed and then left the old man to his meal.

She now opened her eyes and straightened as Cameron entered the room, carrying a goblet of deep red wine and a smaller glass of amber liquid.

He eased down next to her and handed her the glass of wine. She tried to ignore the scent of him that smelled like home and security. "Ah, this is just what I needed," she said before taking a sip and then setting the glass carefully back on the coffee table. "Actually, what I probably need is to chug the whole bottle."

He grinned at her. "You can do that if you want. You'd be safe here…and drunk, but I wouldn't want to think about the headache you'd have tomorrow."

She picked up her glass again and took another sip of the wine. "I've never been much of a drinker." She stared at the deep red liquid. "Drinking is dangerous when you're keeping secrets. You have a little too much, talk a little too much and suddenly you've said more than you intended to say and perhaps put yourself and your son in danger."

"It must have been tough, believing you were running from the law, afraid to make friends with anyone or stay in one place for long," he said, his eyes the soft green-brown hue that threatened to pull her in and hold her there forever.

"It was tough." She broke eye contact with him to take another sip of the wine and then continued. "If it had just been me it wouldn't have been so difficult, but I had Matt to consider." Her mind swept her back to bad places, sleeping under bridges, hiding out in motel rooms that weren't fit for humans. Afraid. She was always afraid of what would happen when her money ran out or if she was stopped by the police for any reason and they discovered she was wanted for murder.

"It was horrible," she finally said. "By the time we

landed here in Grady Gulch I was both broke and exhausted. I stepped into the café carrying Matt. Violet Grady took one look at me and him and before I knew it I was staying in one of the cabins out back, working here in the café. Violet was babysitting Matt during my shifts."

She couldn't help but smile as she thought of the eighty-two-year-old owner of the café. Violet Grady had been a strong, opinionated woman whose husband had built the café that she'd kept running years after his death at the age of seventy-seven.

"She never asked me a single question about where I'd come from," Mary said. "She told me she didn't care much where people had been, that it was where they were going that mattered."

Cameron smiled. "That sounds just like Violet. She was definitely a character, but had a heart of gold."

Mary's smile faded and a new grief swept through her. "I had three wonderful years of working for Violet before she came to me and told me she was terminally ill and didn't have long to live. Since she had no children and no family left, she considered me and Matt her only family. She wanted to leave everything to me, but I refused. Violet was nothing if not persistent. We finally came to an agreement that I'd buy the café from her for five hundred dollars."

Mary looked at Cameron incredulously. "A paltry sum for a future for me and my son."

"Violet didn't need your money. Despite the fact that she lived in the back quarters of the café and dressed from clothes she got at the thrift store, she was an extremely wealthy woman. She loved you and Matt. She once told me that she thought the two of you were a gift from God, the daughter and grandson she'd never had. You should have taken what she had to give. She wound up leaving her fortune to a pet humane society."

"That's a great place for it to go. She changed my life by selling me this café for a pittance, gave me the hope of a future for me and my son and I've tried to honor her memory by the way I run the café."

He touched the back of her hand. "You've done a fine job honoring her and you'll continue to do so for as long as you want." She started to pull her hand away from his, but he tightened his grip, his eyes holding a wealth of emotions that both thrilled her and frightened her a little bit.

"Mary, there's something I need for you to know," he said. "I'm in love with you. I think I've been in love with you since the first time I walked into the café and saw you there. When this is all over I want you in my life, I want you and Matt as my family." The words tumbled from him in one long breath, as if he'd been holding them in for a very long time and couldn't halt their escape.

Mary pulled her hand away from his, her heart thudding the rhythm of uncertainty. She wished he hadn't spoken the words aloud, at least not now...not yet. She wished he hadn't basically thrown the ball of their future relationship into her court. She wasn't ready for this. She wasn't sure she was ready for him.

"Cameron, you know I care about you very deeply, but everything is such a jumbled mess in my head, in my life right now." She hated how her words dimmed the sparkling light in his eyes and tugged a tiny frown into the center of his forehead. "I just… I don't want to…"

"It's okay," he said, halting her awkward, stumbling words. He finished his drink in one large swallow and then stood. "It's getting late and I'm going to call it a night. Do you need anything else?"

She'd hurt him by not being able to tell him that she returned his love, that she wanted the same things he did for the future—a future together—but she couldn't tell him what he wanted to hear. "No thanks, I'm fine. I think I'll just sit here and finish the last of my wine."

He gave her a curt nod and carried his glass into the kitchen. As he walked back through the living room he murmured a good-night and she did the same, her heart heavy.

Alone.

She was alone the way she always had been, alone and afraid and now with a heart half-broken. There was nothing more she'd like than to give Cameron her future, but what he didn't understand was right now she didn't quite believe she had one.

Cameron stared up at his darkened ceiling, feeling not only like a fool, but also with a heartache he hadn't experienced since Bobby's death.

She didn't love him. He'd made a mistake, misjudged her. He'd put his heart out for her to take and she'd rejected it. Somewhere in the back of his mind he knew he shouldn't be surprised. Their lovemaking had been nothing more than an impulsive release on her part, an act that really had nothing to do with love.

His job was to protect her and Matt, and that was his only job, his only role in her life. It wasn't his place to love her or need her. Somehow, someway he had to move forward knowing that.

He awakened the next morning with his heart still heavy, but with the resolve to be the friend and protector that Mary needed no matter how painful it was to him.

It was early enough that he was the first one up. He showered and dressed in his uniform for the day and then went into the kitchen to make coffee.

While he waited for the brew to drip through, he stood at the window and stared outside where the sun was just peeking up over the horizon.

He shouldn't have confessed his feelings to her in the midst of the chaos, with the anxiety that a bomb could explode at any moment. Maybe if he had waited longer her reply would have been different.

He jerked away from the window, once again feeling like his thoughts were foolish. The truth of the matter was that he'd probably been right when he'd believed that he might be her transitional man. He'd clean up the danger around her, he'd shown her that lovemaking could be wonderful again and that was all that his role in her life would remain, what it was meant to be.

All his fantasies about her and Matt living in this house, filling it with life and laughter had been nothing more than the fantasies of a lonely man. Maybe it was time he looked around at some of the other women in town who had made it quite clear they would be up for a date with him. Still, the idea of dating anyone else held no appeal. Loving Mary had become a habit he had to learn to break and what he needed most was time.

It was almost eight when he dropped Matt off at school and then got back into the car to drive Mary to the café. She'd been quiet since getting up, distant and introspective.

As they drank coffee and Matt got ready for school, their conversation had been strained and superficial. He wished he hadn't told her how he felt. He wished he would have kept his feelings deep inside so they could continue to enjoy the light, easy friendship they'd had before last night.

"Nice to see the sunshine," she said as they headed toward the café.

"A day or two of this and the snow will be completely gone," Cameron replied. As he pulled into the café, he frowned at the amount of cars and trucks already parked. There was even a delivery truck pulled up from Riley's Furniture Store.

"What the heck?" Mary muttered from beside him. "Do you know anything about what's going on?"

"Don't have a clue," he replied honestly.

Together they got out of the car and he was surprised to see that the Open sign on the café was still turned to Closed. The café was always open by six-thirty in the morning. Why were all of these people here and why was the café still closed?

Obvious concern created a creased frown across Mary's forehead. She pushed open the door that was unlocked. Cameron was just behind her as a group of people with paint cans and rollers, paintbrushes and cleaning supplies all yelled surprise in unison.

Several waitresses were there, as well as Rusty. Junior stood next to George Wilton who wielded a paint roller like it was a foreign object that had magically appeared in his hand. There were other familiar faces and even Brandon Williams was there in his scooter, his lap filled with a variety of cleaning supplies and rags.

Courtney Chambers stepped forward, her pretty face wreathed in a smile. She wrapped Mary in a big hug and then stepped back from her. "You have done so much for all of us and now we think it's time we give a little back to you. We're here to clean up and paint the back rooms and we've all chipped in and bought you the navy-and-beige sofa that was in the window at Riley's Furniture Store. You told me once that you thought it was pretty. Hopefully by tomorrow you'll have your place back the way it should be."

As she was talking, Mary's eyes had welled up with tears. "We figured we'd all work through the morning and get as much done as we could," Courtney continued, "and then you can go ahead and open up for lunch and some of us will continue working in the back while the others man the café. Does that sound like a plan?"

The tears spilled onto Mary's cheeks and she nodded her head affirmatively and then turned and ran back out the front door.

"I think we must have overwhelmed her," Courtney said as Cameron went after her.

She ran straight to his car and got into the passenger seat. He climbed in behind the steering wheel and didn't say anything as she cried for several minutes, her face averted from him.

She finally pulled a tissue from her purse, swiped at her cheeks, and the unexpected weeping became tiny sniffles. "I never expected…" she began.

"That people around here care about you? That they would do what they could to help you if you needed it? You've obviously underestimated your own worth with the good people of Grady Gulch," he replied gently.

She dabbed at her eyes and turned to stare at him, the blue of her gaze hollow and empty. "I have to leave here," she said. "We need to go to the school and pick up Matt and then he and I need to leave." Despite the emptiness of her eyes, there was an urgent desperation in her voice.

"Don't you understand, all those people are potential victims. If Jason sees that they care about me at all, then he'll go after them. He'll kill them and it will be because of me." A new sob caught in her throat.

"And where are you and Matt going to go?" he asked.

She stared at him and that delicate frown he found both charming and troubling appeared across her forehead. "Somewhere…anywhere…just away from here."

"And wherever you go he'll find you again and then you'll have to run once more. Matt will never know a real home and friends again. He'll learn to be afraid of everyone, afraid to get close to anyone. Is that what you want for him? For yourself?"

She closed her eyes and leaned her head back, as if exhausted, broken by the very thought. "No, that's not what I want for either of us."

"I thought you were through running away, that you were ready to stop and take a stand. At least here you have people who love you surrounding you. At least here you have support and you aren't alone."

He wanted to touch her so badly, just a reassuring tap on her hand, a quick embrace to let her know she was where she belonged. But he was afraid to touch her now, especially after last night. He had no right.

"Stay, Mary. Stay here where you've built your life, where Matt is happy and feels like this is his home. Stay and let me and my men end this for you here and now."

"But what if it doesn't end here? What if it never ends?" Her voice trembled with the frailty of her emotions.

"It ends here, Mary," he said firmly, believing what he told her. "One way or another it ends here. You have to trust somebody. Trust me. Trust in this town and us. Trust in these people who care about you, people who have embraced you and your son."

He held her gaze and watched her eyes soften and lose some of the abject fear that had radiated there only moments before. She finally cast her gaze back toward the café. Her shoulders straightened as she sat forward. "This is *my* home. This is *my* town and he has no place here." She looked back at Cameron and nodded. "I should have made a stand against him years ago, before things got to where they did. I should have been strong enough to walk away from him the very first time he hit me. You're right. I'll make my stand here."

She opened the car door and stepped outside. As he followed her back to the café he only hoped…he prayed that this wouldn't be a stand that ended in her death.

Chapter 15

Mary spent most of the morning with her heart in her throat as her friends worked hard in her living quarters to turn things right again for her and her son.

The burnt sofa was dragged outside by the Taylor twins to the Dumpster and then the real cleaning began. Lynette and Ginger worked to clear the closets and drawers, carrying out plastic tub after tub of clothing to be washed. The plan was to take them to the local Laundromat where they could use eight washers and dryers to get the job done in as short a time as possible.

Everyone else worked on cleaning, wiping smoke from tables and chairs and from the countertop surfaces in the bathrooms. Each and every item on the bookcase was taken off and swiped clean. Mary was ordered to sit in a chair with a cup of coffee and do nothing other than supervise the job.

She didn't have to do any supervising. Everyone worked hard at each task assigned by Lynette, who seemed to be in charge, leaving Mary nothing to do but think and thank her lucky stars that she was here in Grady Gulch, a town that held so many good, caring people.

At least if Jason killed her here there would be people who would mourn for her, she thought and then cursed herself for such morbid thinking.

The work going on in the back rooms came with plenty of chatter and laughter among everyone. Brandon jokingly appointed himself the low man while Junior was his partner, cleaning the areas Brandon couldn't reach from his wheelchair.

Jeff and John Taylor began to sing "Taking Care of Business" and it wasn't long before everyone who knew the lyrics to the old song had joined in.

Mary's heart was so full at the moment there was no place for fear. She'd always seen herself as a local business owner, the woman who provided good food and good service, but it was obvious these people thought of her as much more than a waitress or just a woman who owned a place to eat.

They considered her a vital member of their community, of their lives. They thought of her as a friend. It both humbled her and awed her.

She'd never really taken the time to realize that Grady Gulch was the hometown she'd always wanted, a place of warmth and community pride and love.

She was afraid for each and every one of these people, but no matter where she went, no matter who she met, she'd be afraid. Cameron was right. It was time to take a stand against Jason here and now.

By noon Rusty was back on the grill with Junior at his side and the café was officially open for business. The smell of fresh paint drifted from the back rooms as several of the people remained back there to continue their work.

Mary manned the counter and realized toward the end of the rush hour that at some point during the afternoon the fear that had been a constant companion inside her for so long had finally vanished. Whatever happened would happen. Her dwelling on the fear didn't help and wouldn't stop it.

She poured herself a cup of hot cocoa and sat on the stool behind the counter. Her thoughts went to Cameron and the night before. He loved her. As he'd said the words she'd felt the emotion radiating from his body and shining from his eyes. She'd heard it in his voice, the softness, the want...the love.

Deep in her heart she'd always known that he loved her. For eight long years he'd sat across from her at the counter and they'd talked about life and dreams. She'd felt his love for her.

But how could she believe in that love? They hadn't dated. They'd spent precious little time alone together other than those late-night talks. All they'd really done was tumble into bed and make passionate love one time.

And she'd love to do it again...and again, but shouldn't love be about more than that? She shook her head, as if to dispel the thought. She couldn't think about Cameron right now. Hopefully Cameron had been busy all morning finding the whereabouts of Jason or at least whoever was doing his dirty work.

She was sticking here until the bitter end. She just hoped when the end came she and Matt were together and both of them were still standing.

Thomas Manning eased down into the chair across from Cameron in the interview room. He'd finally shown up at his house at noon and Ben Temple had brought him in.

"I've been wondering how long it would take before I'd finally be sitting here," he said as he shrugged off his gray tweed coat and hung it on the back of his chair.

Thomas was a thin, tall man with ordinary features and a facade of peaceful self-acceptance. He folded his hands in his lap and looked at Cameron with pale gray eyes.

"I'm assuming you want to know all about my marriage and divorce and if I'm hiding some kind of a killing rage that has made me take out that rage on the waitresses that work at the Cowboy Café," he said.

"Something like that," Cameron replied, trying to get a read on the man who appeared, on the surface, completely passive.

"My marriage was ill-fated from the beginning," Thomas said. "Before I got married, I ate most of my meals at a truck stop near my home. That's where I met Nancy who would become my wife. To be honest, I'd never much considered marriage. I was satisfied with my solitude. I liked fine wine, good books and educational television. Nancy was the exact opposite of me.

She loved tequila shots, professed that the only book she'd ever read was *How To Marry a Millionaire* and she watched the *Housewives* of anything." He frowned thoughtfully and unclasped his hands.

"So, why did you marry her?" Cameron asked.

A hint of a smile curved one corner of Thomas's thin upper lip. "I'm not so sure that I married her as she married me. She was a force like a hurricane and she'd decided I was the man who would take her away from the truck stop and into the finer things of life. She was expecting good wine, classical music and faculty parties where she could reign as queen."

"And that wasn't the case?"

Thomas's hint of a smile disappeared, leaving his features once again emotionless. "Nancy hated classical music and I didn't attend faculty parties. We co-existed for about six months before she decided to go back to work at the truck stop. I knew then that our marriage was over."

He said the words as if he were commenting that it might rain tomorrow. As far as Cameron was concerned the man's lack of passion was as disturbing as an eruption of the emotion.

"The pretense of our marriage continued for another six months or so before Nancy finally took off."

"And that didn't bother you?" Cameron asked.

Thomas shrugged. "She wasn't happy in my world and I had no intention of changing and she understood that. I'm the first to admit that I'm a selfish man, accustomed to pleasing nobody but myself. So, the easy answer to your question is no, it didn't bother me when

Nancy left me. I was perfectly satisfied to return to the way things had been before she'd come into my life."

Cameron wasn't sure if he believed Thomas's assessment of the situation or not. "What brought you to Grady Gulch?"

"My sister had driven through here one time a couple of years ago and had been charmed by the slow-moving small-town life. Last year I had enough tenure to quit my job and enough money saved to make some changes. I remembered what my sister had told me about Grady Gulch, so here I am."

"You haven't made many friends while you've been here," Cameron observed.

Thomas raised an eyebrow in apparent amusement. "I have found few dusty cowboys or cowgirls who appreciate the fine work of Shakespeare or the soul-moving music of Mozart. And as far as I'm concerned, friends are vastly overrated."

Pretentious ass, Cameron thought. "I'd like to know where you were on these nights." He listed the nights of the three murders and also the date of the fire in the café.

"On the nights those poor women were murdered I was at home in bed. On the night of the fire I was driving back from Oklahoma City in the middle of the snowstorm."

"But you arrived back here in town around midnight and the fire wasn't set until between the hours of two and three in the morning," Cameron said.

Once again Thomas's eyebrow rose. "Have you had me under surveillance? What a waste of resources," he scoffed. "Do you really believe I'm the man you're looking for?"

Cameron leaned back in his chair and eyed the man across from him with open speculation. "To be perfectly honest with you, Mr. Manning, I'm not sure what I believe about you."

"After driving several hours in a snowstorm to get home from Oklahoma City I can promise you I went directly to bed. I have no motive to hurt those waitresses or burn down the café. I enjoy the meals I take there, but certainly haven't formed any kind of a relationship with anyone there that would produce ill-feelings. You certainly have no evidence that ties me to any of this, so I'd say not only are you wasting your time here, but you're wasting mine."

There was a definite touch of arrogance in Manning's voice that set Cameron's teeth on edge. It was no wonder the man had made no friends since arriving in town. He might be able to sit in the café for an hour to eat and make nice with the waitresses, but there didn't seem to be much pleasantness beneath the surface.

Thomas stood and shrugged on his coat, carefully buttoning each and every button as Cameron sat and watched. When he was finished he looked at the lawman and offered him a faint smile. "If you have any further questions for me, I'll be more than happy to give you the phone number of my lawyer. And now I'm finished here." He turned and walked out the door.

A half an hour later, Cameron sat at his desk writing notes to himself. A knock on the door sounded and Ben came inside the small office and sank down across from him. "Nothing from the local professor?" Ben asked.

"I don't know," Cameron replied truthfully. "We certainly don't have any evidence that he had anything to do with the crimes, nor can we tie him in any way to McKnight, but there's no question the man is an odd duck."

"So, he's still a person of interest?"

Cameron went through the high points of the interview with Ben and then hesitated a moment and slowly nodded his head. "Yeah, he's still a person of interest. Something about his flat affect just seemed off to me. He talked about his wife like he was talking about a stranger he bumped into on the street. I don't know, maybe he's on some kind of medication."

"Or maybe he's just so much in love with himself there isn't room for love or passion for anyone else in his life," Ben said drily.

"In any case, he told me if I wanted to talk to him again I could get in touch with his lawyer."

"Lawyered up already?" Ben frowned. "That's a little odd."

"And Denver still hasn't delivered any paperwork to me to show that his sudden windfall is from any inheritance," Cameron said, his mind whirling. Did they have the killer in their sights or were they completely off track?

He'd talked Mary into staying here, but had he talked her into staying in a place that would wind up to be her grave?

At four, Cameron entered the café not only with Matt in tow but with Jimmy along with them, the two boys asking Mary if Matt could spend the night at Jimmy's house.

"But it's a school night," Mary protested as she looked at her son. "You know we don't usually do sleepovers on school nights."

"Mom always makes me go to bed on time on school nights, even when I have guests over," Jimmy said. "She really wants Matt to stay with me tonight. She's got a bunch of work to do at home and she tells me when I'm there by myself I'm always in her hair."

Jimmy held out his cell phone to Mary. "She said for you to call her and she'll tell you she wants Matt to spend the night with me."

"Sheriff Evans isn't some taxi service to be running you boys wherever you want to go," she said.

"I don't mind," Cameron replied, his voice brisk and businesslike.

Mary took Jimmy's cell phone and a quick call confirmed what Jimmy had said. With both boys and Jimmy's mother's pleas echoing in her ears, Mary reluctantly agreed to the plan. "Get clean clothes for school tomorrow and make sure you brush your teeth tonight before bed."

"Will you kiss Twinkie for me tonight?" Matt asked.

Mary rolled her eyes and grinned. "Don't push your luck. Go on, get out of here."

"And I'll be back here at closing to take you back to my place," Cameron said as he ushered the two boys toward the front door. "Oh, and I just heard an updated weather report. It seems there is a bit of sleet forecasted for the evening."

"I thought we were in for a warm-up," Mary said, wishing there wasn't any distance, any strain between them, but there was and she knew she'd put it there by not being able to accept what he'd offered to her with his heart.

"You know those weather guys, they don't always get it right. I'll see you later." And with that the three of them headed out the door.

Instantly what flew through Mary's mind was that without Matt at Cameron's this evening there would be no buffer. The chasm between them would be more obvious, more uncomfortable than ever.

It was around six that the last of the workers, Brandon, Jeff and John Taylor, two of her off-duty waitresses and Junior left the backrooms. "By tomorrow the paint should all be dry and you will be good to move back in," Brandon said.

They all looked happy and tired, with their faces speckled with beige paint.

"I can't tell you all how much I appreciate what you've all done for me today," Mary said, her heart once again filled to capacity. "However, I can tell you that you're all my guests for dinner. Anything and everything you want is on the house." She'd already fed them lunch, but they deserved another meal and so much more for their hard work and thoughtfulness.

They all gathered around one of the large tables in the center of the room and both Mary and Lynette took their orders, while other waitresses worked the other tables and the dinner rush. All around them people were dining and visiting with each other.

Laughter rode in the air and the warmth and friendship that filled the room once again humbled Mary. This was her place, among these hardworking, good people, not running from town to town, trying to stay one step away from a man who wanted her dead.

The sleet that Cameron had mentioned appeared just after seven, pinging against the café glass windows and shooting a restless energy through the place. People began to eat a little faster in order to get home before it got too slick outside.

By eight-thirty the last of the diners were preparing to pay up and leave and it looked like it was going to be another early closing night. She sent all of her waitresses home and then called Cameron on his cell phone and let him know that she'd be ready for him to pick her up anytime after nine.

He told her he was currently working a two-car accident and might be a few minutes late. She assured him she would be fine until he arrived.

At nine she went into the kitchen where Rusty had already shut down the grill and was seated on a stool drinking a cup of coffee. "You might as well head home, too," she said as she pulled up a stool next to him. "I've put the Closed sign on the door and locked up for the night. The sleet is accumulating on the roads and I don't expect anybody else to come in."

"You sure Cameron will be able to come and get you?" Rusty asked.

"If he doesn't I can always crash on my new sofa." She shook her head. "I still can't believe you all did that for me."

"You have no idea what you mean to the people of this town," Rusty replied.

She cocked her head and stared at him for a long moment. "Why aren't you dating? Why don't you have some nice woman in your life?"

He gave her his crooked half smile. "Who'd want to date somebody with such an ugly mug as mine?"

"Oh, Rusty, you have no idea how handsome you are. You can cook, you've got a soft heart and any woman would be proud to be with you."

"I don't know… I just don't think about it much." He took another sip of his coffee and stared off into the distance.

Mary guessed that he was probably thinking about the family he had lost in a home fire years ago. It had been an electrical fire that had taken place while Rusty was at work and it had killed his wife and son. It had also destroyed whoever Rusty had once been.

"They wouldn't want you to grieve forever," she said softly.

"I know. I'm working on it." He got up from his stool and drained his mug. "You want me to hang around until Cameron does arrive?"

"Nah, I'll be fine. I'll just lock up everything tight and maybe make myself a quick cup of hot tea. You'd better get to the cabin before you have to ice-skate yourself there."

Rusty gave her a flash of a smile. "I never was much good at skating. Oh, by the way, the kid left his cell phone here." He pointed to Junior's cell phone on the counter. "I imagine he'll be in early in the morning to get it."

"I'll just lock it up in the register," Mary replied.

"Then I guess I'll see you in the morning." He pulled on his big coat and disappeared out the back door. Mary locked up behind him and then placed a kettle on a burner to heat water for tea.

As she waited for the water to boil, she stood in the entry to the back living quarters. The new sofa was beautiful, made more so with the knowledge that her friends and customers had chipped in to buy it for her and Matt.

The walls were pristine and the smell of fresh paint permeated the air. One more night at Cameron's and then she and Matt could resume their life here. She knew Cameron wanted them to stay with him until Jason was behind bars, but she couldn't bunk in with him indefinitely. There was no indication that Cameron and his team would solve this case anytime soon.

The whistling kettle pulled her back into the kitchen where she fixed a cup of tea and carried it into the main café area. She placed Junior's cell phone on the counter near the register to lock up before she left for the night and then sat at a table in the center of the dimly lit room and looked around.

Violet Grady had not only been a member of the founding family of Grady Gulch, but she'd also been Mary's personal angel. The old woman had not only taken in Mary and Matt when Mary was destitute, but she'd also provided the means for Mary to give Matt a future.

She would dishonor Violet if she chose to run again. She would dishonor all the people who had worked here all day long today to give her back her home.

Where are you, Jason? How she wished she had the answer. How she wished Cameron and his men had some kind of clue to get her ex-husband behind bars.

She wanted this over. She wanted to be able to move back into her rooms, run her café and throw herself back into the life she'd had before murder and a monster had stolen away the joy.

She took a sip of her tea and then frowned as she heard a sound coming from one of the bathrooms. Was the women's restroom toilet running again? She set her cup down with a sigh of irritation. It had been a chronic problem over the past couple of months.

Remaining seated, she decided she'd finish her tea and then go in and jiggle the handle and if that didn't work then first thing in the morning she'd call Steve Taggart, the local plumber to come in and fix the darned thing for good.

As she sipped her tea she tried to keep her mind empty of thoughts of murder or Cameron. Both topics made her anxious in completely different ways.

Thinking about the murders and Jason created a block of ice inside her stomach where thoughts of Cameron created a pit of fiery heat.

She was too tired to entertain thoughts of either emotions. She just wanted Cameron to pick her up and take her to his place where she would withdraw into his pretty and peaceful guest bedroom until morning.

Once again she heard a strange noise, a whirring

noise that didn't belong above the soft hum of the refrigerator unit or the rhythmic faint click of the large clock that hung on a nearby wall.

Shoving her chair back she stood as she tried to identify the sound that appeared to be drawing closer. She gasped in surprise as Brandon Williams wheeled around the corner from the bathrooms.

"Brandon! Oh, my gosh, I didn't realize you were still here," she said.

He rubbed his stomach and smiled ruefully. "Apparently something didn't sit quite right with me." He looked around with a frown. "Looks like you closed the place down for the night."

"I did. It's sleeting outside, Brandon. Maybe you need to sit with me and wait until Cameron picks me up and we'll see if he can get your scooter in his trunk or something. I don't know if you can go in the scooter on the ice that is accumulating."

"That's not going to be a problem, Samantha."

Samantha?

Mary stared in horror as Brandon stood up from the scooter and pulled a long knife from the side pocket of his motorized chair. "I don't think there's going to be much of anything left here for Cameron to pick up."

Chapter 16

The traffic accident was a nightmare of whirling cherry lights, stinging sleet and rescue workers and accident victims slipping and sliding on the icy road.

This particular sharp curve just outside of town was treacherous under the best of conditions. It had been here on a rainy night that Courtney Chambers had missed the curve and flown off the ridge and into the trees below. Of course, she'd been drugged at the time by somebody who had wanted to kidnap her baby.

He shoved aside thoughts of that particular crime, glad that at least it had been solved with a happy ending and the sick woman responsible for the accident was behind bars.

He needed to focus now on the two screaming men who had been the drivers of the two cars and were now each pointing fingers at the other with blame. Wilma Simpson sat sobbing in the front passenger seat of one of the cars. She refused to leave the vehicle even to allow the emergency workers to check her for injuries. "I just want to go home," she sobbed over and over again.

Two people had already been taken from the scene, both injured but not anything life-threatening. The cars had hit almost head-on and surprisingly it had been the people in the backseat that had been injured.

Neither of them had been wearing seat belts and one's head bounced off the front headrest while the other had banged knees against the front seat. Thankfully the people in the front seat had been wearing their seat belts. It was a damned miracle that nobody had been killed.

Each driver was accusing the other of being in the wrong lane, and unfortunately both had moved their cars from the point of impact and off to the side of the road before Cameron had arrived.

The sleet and freezing temperature were only adding to the issues as he silently cursed the weatherman for missing the forecast on this band of icy mix that had moved into the area. The forecast had said a brief icy shower, but there had been nothing brief about the sleet that had been ongoing and appeared to have parked overhead.

He stalked over to one of the raging drivers and pulled him away from the other before they began to take swings at each other. Ed Ganger and Blair Simpson were both hotheads, and Cameron knew it wouldn't take much more before this escalated from a traffic accident into a brawling fistfight.

When he had Ed at a safe distance away from Blair he began a quick interview of his view of the event. Larry Brooks moved to Blair and began his own discussion with the irate man.

Cameron knew how this worked. They would both have different stories and someplace in the middle of those stories would be a semblance of the truth.

What he'd like to do was get out of the nasty weather and head to the café to pick up Mary. He'd like to be curled up on the sofa in front of a roaring blaze in the fire place at his house with her in his arms.

But it was just another one of his foolish fantasies. He couldn't leave the scene of an accident and he had a feeling the last place in the world Mary wanted to be was in his arms again.

As Adam Benson took photos of what appeared to be the point of impact between the two cars, which initially indicated that both drivers were hugging the center line, Cameron took the two driver statements with him to his car and sank into the warmth of the blowing heater.

He gave each of the statements a cursory read to make sure they had all the information needed. The reports, along with the photos they had of both cars and the road, might allow them to be able to reenact the accident to see if blame needed to be placed. At this point he considered it a weather-related accident with no specific driver to blame. They could each contact their own insurance companies and figure it all out.

He got back out of the car, grateful that both vehicles remained drivable, thus negating the need for a tow truck.

With the sleet getting more intense, he sent both drivers on their way, one heading to the hospital to check on their passengers and the other, with the sobbing Wilma, home.

All the other men who were on traffic duty left to patrol the streets while Cameron headed back to the office. He'd write up a quick report and then head to the café to pick up Mary and get her back to his place.

A half an hour later he was seated at his desk, his report written, but his thoughts drifting into painful territory. He couldn't be the son that his parents wanted. He couldn't be the man for Mary and he couldn't be the sheriff who caught the bad guy. Talk about feeling like a failure.

He tried to turn his thoughts around. He could twist and turn himself inside out and he would never be Bobby. It wasn't his fault that his father was trapped in an abyss of grief even after two years. He could only hope that with more time his father would eventually come around and realize Cameron's worth as a son… as a man.

Mary was a heartbreak that would take some time to heal. He'd entertained dreams of her for so long, and when his fantasy of making love to her had finally come true, it had been far beyond his best fantasy. But that didn't mean he was the right man for her.

He should have never gotten intimately involved with her in the first place. It would have been much easier if she'd remained just a fantasy, a vision to fill his dreams at night.

He had to figure out a way to get her out of his heart. She'd become his addictive habit...thinking about her, dreaming about her and ending almost every night of the day sitting with her across the counter at the café.

She was definitely a habit he had to break and ultimately she was a citizen of his town who he had to protect from an unknown perpetrator.

Where in the hell was Jason McKnight? And if he wasn't committing the murders himself, then who had he hired to do his dirty work? Although he'd managed to pull Denver Walton's and Thomas Manning's finances and background records based on probable cause, the judge had known that it was more of a fishing expedition and wouldn't be so lenient the next time Cameron came to him.

As far as he was concerned Denver and Thomas were his best suspects and yet there was nothing concrete to tie either of them to the crimes.

He couldn't help but feel as if he was missing something...overlooking something vital, but he'd gone over the reports a hundred times and nothing had popped out. He and his men had checked each person in town they thought the right height and weight to be the perpetrator and they'd all come up empty-handed.

He stood and grabbed his coat. Time to get Mary and get home before the roads became completely impassable. He was just about to leave his office when his cell phone rang.

"Cameron, it's me," his mother said.

"Mom, what's up?"

"Your damn fool father decided he needed to go out to the barn in the middle of this weather and he was walking back from there when he slipped and fell. I can't get him up and he's just lying out in the yard. Please, can you get out here?" There was a wild panic in his mother's voice.

"I'll be there as quickly as I can," he replied. A glance out the window let him know that the sleet still fell down from the sky.

He then dialed Mary's cell phone number and frowned when it went directly to voice mail. Maybe she had a few customers show up despite the weather and was busy serving them.

"Mary, there's an emergency out at my parents' place. It shouldn't take me too long, but I've got to get out there before I come to get you. Just sit tight, I'll be there as soon as possible," he said to her voice mail.

He'd head out to his parents', see that his father was okay and then get to the café as quickly as possible. Hopefully by then whoever had decided to stop in and eat would be finished with their meals and he and Mary could get to his house and end this long, irritating night.

"You don't look very happy to see me," Brandon said as he advanced closer to where Mary stood, still stunned and half-breathless.

No, not Brandon. Jason. In a nanosecond her brain worked to process all the physical changes that had made her not recognize the man from her nightmares.

He'd gained at least thirty pounds since the last time

she'd seen him and his brown eyes had obviously been turned blue with colored contacts. His bald head and missing eyebrows made it impossible to tell what his hair color might have been and the scars...the makeup she'd thought he'd used in an attempt to cover his scars had obviously been used to make them. He looked nothing like the man she'd run from so many years ago.

She backed up from him, aware of the knife's sharp edge gleaming in the security lights overhead. "How... How did you find me?" She finally found her voice.

"You mean after you left me half-dead on the floor in our living room?" His eyes narrowed and despite the facade of Brandon Williams, war veteran, she saw Jason McKnight's soul shining from the hatred in his miscolored eyes.

"It took me months in the hospital to recuperate from what you did to me." He took another step closer and she retreated a step back, icy terror making her entire body feel wooden and difficult to move.

"You busted my spleen, left me with a compound fracture of my leg, busted four ribs and smashed my nose." His voice was calm, the eerie calm before a storm erupted. "It was a year before I could even start to think about finding you, but in that year you never left my mind. In the past nine years you've been all I've thought about." He cocked his head and smiled, Jason's smile, not Brandon's. "I guess you didn't believe me when I told you that I'd make you pay, that I'd kill you if you ever left me."

"Jason...please," Mary started as her back hit the wall. Her gaze shot left and right, seeking something she could use as a weapon, something she could use for defense. But there was nothing.

"Jason please what? Please don't hurt you? Please don't kill you? You brought this all on yourself, Samantha. I haven't spent all the money and time of the last nine years hunting you down not to make you pay."

"Haven't you done enough?" she cried. "You've already killed three innocent women."

"And with each throat I slit I thought about you."

Trapped.

She was trapped between the wall and the man who wanted her dead, and escape appeared impossible. Her terror gripped her by the throat not just now, but also in memory, a regurgitation of the sensations of fear she'd suffered while married to the man.

She was lost in those moments of his torment, the anxiety of never knowing when an attack might come or if the next one was the one that would kill her.

At that moment the back door opened and Junior rushed in, his coat covered with a fine layer of ice. "Mary, I forgot my phone," he said and she raised a trembling finger to the phone on the counter next to the register.

"Thanks," Junior said as he grabbed the phone. It was only then he focused on Jason. "Mr. Williams…you can walk. It's like a miracle!" Junior's childish smile quickly doused as he spied the knife in the man's hand. "Mr. Williams…what are you doing with that knife?"

Before he could utter another word, Jason slammed his fist into Junior's jaw. Junior whirled around with the force of the blow, bounced off the counter and fell to the floor, not moving again.

Mary screamed her outrage. "You didn't have to hurt him. He liked you, he wouldn't have said anything if you'd just played it cool."

"I'm tired of playing it cool, besides, he's not dead, he's just unconscious. Once he's conscious and I'm finished here he can tell anyone he wants that Brandon Williams killed Mary, because Brandon Williams doesn't exist." He smiled at her with pride. "The honorable injured vet will disappear forever after tonight."

"You won't get away. They know it's you, Jason."

His smile widened, the gesture not even beginning to warm the cold of his eyes. "*Knowing* and *proving* are two different things. I have dozens of people who will swear that I never left Switzerland, that I've been there every day in my offices for the last year."

He seemed to be in no hurry to finish what he'd come here for, what he most wanted to do. "I spent a lot of money over the years trying to find you. It took seven private investigators and years before we finally hunted you down."

"Just let me go," she replied, hating the begging tone in her voice. "Like you said, nobody knows you were here. You could just walk away now and nobody would know what you'd done. Even if I told, it would be your word against mine and all of your alibi witnesses."

Just like before, she thought. She'd been afraid to tell anyone about his abuse because it would have been his word against her own, and he'd held all the power, just like he did now.

He laughed, the deep sound clenching Mary's stomach with dread. "And deny myself what I've dreamed about for all these years?" His eyes narrowed. "You've forgotten, Mary. I own you and I don't let go of what's mine."

"You beat me." She clenched her fists at her sides, remembering all the pain she'd experienced at his hands. "You choked and kicked me, you beat me black and blue."

"It wasn't my fault you couldn't figure out how to be a good wife. You had to be taught. You needed to be taught to be exactly what I want you to be and I have to say, you were a very slow learner."

She thanked the stars that Matt wasn't here now, that she'd agreed to let him spend the night with his friend. She wanted Jason to forget he had a son, to kill her and then steal away in the night and never bother anyone else here in Grady Gulch again, including Matt.

"I can kill you, go back to Switzerland and take off the makeup, grow back my hair and lose a few pounds and then I figure I have two choices. I can either play the grieving ex-husband and come back here to claim my son. Or I can tell whoever makes contact with me that you and I were divorced a long time ago and I'd rather my son stay in the town where he'd grown up, that it would be too traumatic at his age to displace him from the people he knows and loves."

As he spoke he turned the knife back and forth in his hand, the light catching the razor edge each time he turned it, but she knew he wasn't ready to use it yet.

Mary had always known the second that Jason was about to attack because his left eye twitched.

"I have a feeling your boyfriend, the sheriff, would take him on, raise the kid as his own. And every time he looked at Matt he'd think of you and what a failure he was as a sheriff. You'll haunt him until the day he dies." He shrugged his broad shoulders. "I haven't decided how to play that out yet."

Tears blurred Mary's vision as once again she looked around frantically, seeking escape and praying that the blow to Junior hadn't killed him.

The only thing she saw that might provide her any help at all was the switch to the security lights. If she could reach it before he attacked, then at least for a few seconds the place would be plunged into complete darkness and those precious seconds might allow her the time to get something to use as a weapon.

She fought back the need to vomit as her stomach clenched tighter and tighter. Where was Cameron? Shouldn't he be finished with the traffic accident and be here to pick her up?

Hearing the sleet still pelting the windows, she realized she couldn't depend on Cameron. The weather could keep him busy for some time.

And she was out of time.

With a twitch of his eye and a roar of rage, Jason lunged toward her. She had a split-second sight of the knife raised above his head when she threw herself at the switch and the café was plunged into darkness.

Chapter 17

"It's just my ankle," Cameron's dad said and muttered a curse beneath his breath as Cameron helped him to his feet. Thankfully the sleet had slowed as Cameron's mother stood beside the two men. She wore no coat, only a face of worry as she watched the two men maneuver to a standing position.

"Get inside before you freeze to death, Mom," Cameron said. "I've got him now and I'll get him inside."

As she hurried to the front door, Jim Evans leaned heavily on Cameron's shoulder. "Thanks for coming," he said gruffly.

"That's what good sons do," Cameron replied while the two began to slowly make their way toward the house. "They come when their fathers need them. Are you sure I don't need to take you to the hospital to get that ankle x-rayed?"

"Nah, I know the different between a break and a sprain. I just twisted it on the ice and went down so fast I didn't know for sure what had happened."

"You shouldn't have been out here in this weather at all," Cameron said with a touch of censure. "And don't tell me that you had to go out and check on the livestock because Bobby isn't around to do it anymore. Even Bobby would have told you it was foolish to venture out on a night like this."

"You're right." Jim shot him a quick glance. "Bobby would have told me the same thing."

Cameron helped his father up the stairs to the slippery deck and then into the living room where he deposited him into his favorite easy chair.

He knelt down and removed his father's ice-encrusted work boot, then slid off his sock and raised his jean leg up enough that he could take a look at the ankle.

It was slightly swollen, definitely sprained rather than broken in his nonprofessional opinion. "Mom, get the ice bag. Fifteen minutes with ice on and then fifteen minutes with ice off and if it's not better in the morning call your doctor and get it checked out. Hopefully by then the roads will be in better condition and if you need to get it x-rayed, you can."

Before Cameron could stand, his father's hand came to rest heavily on his right shoulder. Cameron closed his eyes and held his breath, reveling in the simple touch from a man who had scarcely even acknowledged his existence since Bobby's tragic death.

"You're a good man, Cameron," his father said softly. "I don't tell you that often enough."

Cameron's heart expanded painfully tight in his chest but before he could reply his cell phone rang. He stood and grabbed the phone from his jacket pocket.

"Evans," he said curtly, hoping this wasn't another accident call.

"Cam, it's Bev." Beverly Berlin always identified herself even though she'd been his secretary-dispatcher for the past seven years and he would have known her high-pitched, slightly breathy voice anywhere.

"What's up, Bev?"

"The oddest thing, I just got a 911 call from Junior Lempke's cell phone but he's not saying anything. The line is open but all I can hear is somebody yelling and screaming in the background."

"Did you call Lila?" Cameron asked, already heading toward the front door. Lila had given Junior's cell phone number to all the deputies and workers at the sheriff's office just in case Junior accidentally called.

It was quite possible Junior was tucked safely in his own bed at home and had accidently punched three for 911. Cameron was vaguely surprised it hadn't happened before.

"Lila is frantic," Bev continued. "She told me Junior left his cell phone at the café earlier today and despite the nasty weather he went back to get it."

Every muscle in Cameron's body froze solid as for

a moment he forgot how to breathe. Junior going to the café, not speaking on the phone, the sounds of screams and yelling in the background—Mary was in trouble. The words screamed in his head.

"Thanks, Bev," he finally managed to choke out. He hung up the phone. "I've got to go," he said to his parents.

"Go do what you do best," Jim said.

The words warmed Cameron as he raced to his car, but the warmth instantly disappeared as Bev's words rang in his ears. Normally from here he would be no more than fifteen minutes away from the café even without the use of his siren. But under these road conditions, it would take longer.

Too long.

And Mary was in trouble.

The words reverberated through his head as his hands tightened on the steering wheel and his stomach rocked with frantic fear.

Who had been screaming and if it had been Mary, then who had been making her scream? He couldn't believe that he'd misjudged Junior after the debacle in the abandoned cabin. He'd believed Junior's story about wanting a place of his own. Had he misjudged that whole situation? And yet if Junior was the killer, then why would he have dialed 911?

No, not Junior. So who?

He thought of the first victim, Candy Bailey, her throat slashed. Shirley Cook suffered the same fate, killed in her bed. Finally there was Dorothy Blake, her face chalk-white from having pretty much bled out from the slash in her throat.

Not Mary. Please not Mary. Hadn't he lost enough when Bobby had died? He'd not only lost his brother... his best friend, but had also suffered the alienation from his father.

Not Mary. He couldn't survive without her.

As the back of his car fishtailed, forcing his foot off the gas, his fear of losing Mary strangled him, threatening to stop his breath.

Too late. Was it already too late? No, he couldn't think that way. He'd lose his mind right here and now if he didn't think he had a chance.

He had to get there in time to save her. He couldn't let another murder take place, especially not Mary's murder. She might not love him in the way he'd wanted her to, but he couldn't live with her death.

Bobby's death had nearly killed him, but Mary's death would destroy him at his very core. He'd expected her to be safe in the café until he picked her up to take her home. What had gone wrong? Who was there with her and how did Junior get into the middle of it all?

Even the crumb of acknowledgment he'd just gotten from his father could do nothing to ease the restricting labor of Cameron's breathing, the slide of his wheels on the icy roads and the aching fear in his heart that no matter how fast he drove, he was already too late.

The moment the lights went out Mary fell to the floor and crawled across the back of the counter, opening doors to cabinets, but knowing that these lower cabinets contained mostly linens and aprons, napkins and official T-shirts, nothing that could be used to ward off Jason's rage or the slice of his knife.

Small sobbing sounds filled the silence and she was appalled to realize they were coming from her, the sound of terror escaping without her volition.

"Come out. Come out." Jason's voice was a singsong of anticipated pleasure. "Come on, sweet Samantha, it's time to pay your dues." The security lights came back on and a new sob escaped her as she scrabbled across the floor in an effort to get away.

He advanced toward her and she jumped up to her feet, grabbing the glass coffee carafe from a nearby coffeemaker. She wielded it before her as if it had the magical power to make Jason disappear.

But he didn't disappear, rather, he drew close enough to loom like a monster before her. In frantic desperation she threw the coffee carafe at him. It hit his shoulder and glanced off him like a fly swatted away at a picnic.

It was at that moment that all hope abandoned Mary. She would never again see that slow sexy smile curve Cameron's lips. She would never experience the wonder of his strong, warm arms around her.

And Matt. She nearly fell to her knees as she thought of the son who was her sun, her moon, her very reason to get up each morning with such happiness in her heart. She would never see him grow to be a man.

She could only hope that when her murder was investigated Jason lost custody of Matt for she knew that Cameron would stay true to his promise to her and raise Matt as his own son.

Without hope, she had no fight. Yet when Jason grabbed her by the arm and tried to force her toward him, the fight she'd thought gone returned tenfold.

She wouldn't be a helpless victim for him again. She was no longer a naive, vulnerable young woman, but rather a strong woman who had survived him once and was determined to somehow survive him again.

She flailed her arms, kicked toward his groin, anything to keep him from advancing close enough to use the knife on her throat. A white-hot pain shot across her forearm and began to bleed at the same time she managed to connect a hard kick to his thigh.

He grunted in pain and then laughed, the laughter of a man who knew he had won and it was just a matter of time before he claimed his prize.

At that moment a crash sounded from the front door. One of the large flower pots Mary kept on either side of the entrance flew through the glass, followed instantly by Cameron, his gun drawn and his eyes holding a killing rage.

In the split second of his appearance and Mary's stunned surprise, Jason grabbed her and pulled her tight against him, the edge of his knife at her throat.

A sharp sting marked the area where tip met skin and a warmth of blood trickled down her neck. She scarcely breathed, knowing that by the simple act of swallowing she could be hurt more severely.

"Put the gun down, Cameron," Jason said. "Put your gun down or I slit her throat right now."

Hesitation tempered the rage that darkened Cameron's eyes. She wanted to tell him not to listen, that if he was just patient he might be able to get off a shot that wouldn't kill her, too.

But Jason pressed the knife a little tighter against her skin and she could tell more blood seeped from the superficial wound. "Don't think I'm bluffing," Jason said.

"You know you're a dead man." Cameron laid his gun on the counter where he and Mary had sat for so many nights over the years to talk. "It doesn't matter if you kill her or not, you won't leave this building alive. I've already got deputies on their way."

"Then I guess I'd better hurry," Jason replied.

"I punched three for 911." Junior's voice came from the floor, momentarily startling Jason who eased his grasp on her. As the knife floated away from her neck, Mary slumped down and threw her weight to one side.

She hit the floor at the same time Cameron launched himself at Jason. As the two men began to grapple, Mary scooted around to where Junior had sat up, his eyes filled with the same horrifying fear that froze Mary's heart.

She placed an arm around his shoulder and watched in terror the two men fighting. Cameron appeared to have no respect for the knife Jason possessed. He threw himself at Jason and the two of them hit the floor.

Sobs began to escape her as Jason sliced Cameron's arm and then attempted to stab him in his leg. They rolled and tussled and finally Cameron sat on Jason's chest. One hand held Jason's wrist and the knife gleamed between them, the tip of it pointed at Cameron's chest. Their hands shook with their efforts to overwhelm and sweat beads popped out on Cameron's forehead as blood ran down his arm from the wound Jason had inflicted earlier.

Jason's neck muscles were taut, the amused smile that had been on his face now gone, replaced by a fierce concentration and an ugly sneer.

The knife shook violently between them and Mary's heart nearly stopped when it moved closer to Cameron's body. He was losing the battle, she thought frantically. She realized that in the scuffle that had taken place between them Jason's knife had done more damage than she'd thought.

There wasn't just the slice on his forearm that was bleeding profusely, but his jeans had darkened with blood on his upper thigh where obviously Jason had gotten beneath his defenses for a quick stab.

Cameron was losing blood, losing strength and she didn't know what to do, how to help him. Junior clung to her like a frightened baby monkey, his long arms nearly engulfing her as his heartbeat tattooed against her own.

A scream ripped from her throat as Jason won the physical battle for the knife and plunged it into Cameron's chest. Cameron listed to the side and fell to the floor beside Jason.

Jason rose to his feet, prompting Mary to untangle herself from Junior. "Dial three, Junior, and tell them we need an ambulance." Her voice sounded high-pitched, hysterical to her own ears. He couldn't be dead. Cameron couldn't be dead.

And then she spied the gun.

Cameron's gun on the countertop. She grabbed it

and pointed it at Jason, who stopped in his tracks and smiled at her, that crazy, condescending smile that had always frozen her blood.

"You don't have the guts," he said with a laugh.

In a hundred million circumstances he was right. She would never have the guts to shoot to kill a man. But with the sound of Junior's soft sobbing and the sight of Cameron's unmoving body on the floor nearby, she didn't hesitate.

She aimed and fired, the bullet exploding Jason's left knee. He screamed in pain and before he fell to the floor she squeezed off another shot, this one smashing his right knee.

He was on the floor, writhing in pain. Primal screams mixed with curses and her name, Samantha... the name of the woman she'd once been, the name of a woman she'd never be again.

She dropped the gun to the counter as Adam Benson, Ben Temple and several other deputies rushed inside. She was at Cameron's side before the others reached the counter. She threw herself to the floor next to him and grabbed his hand.

His breathing was labored and as he opened his eyes to look at her, everything else fell away. Jason's screaming, Junior's sobbing and the noise and chatter from the deputies all became white noise that didn't matter. All that mattered was Cameron and the distant sound of a siren approaching that she hoped and prayed was an ambulance.

"Help is on the way," she said, tears misting her eyes and falling down her cheeks. "You hang on, Sheriff

Evans. You hear me? You hang on because this town needs you."

His eyes fluttered closed and she thought he'd become unconscious. "Please, Cameron. Stay with us. We all need you. I need you," she whispered.

Before she could say anything more, the ambulance arrived and chaos reigned. She was grateful to see the ambulance not only load up Cameron, but also a handcuffed, still-screaming Jason.

Once they were gone, Ben Temple tried to interview her about the events of the night, but the only place Mary wanted to be was at the hospital.

As Adam interviewed Junior, Ben agreed to drive Mary to the hospital as long as she answered some questions on the ride. Mary would have agreed to sit naked in the snow if it got her to the hospital and closer to Cameron as quickly as possible.

On the way, she tried to recount everything that had happened from the moment Brandon Williams had wheeled out of the men's restroom and stood to face her until the time the deputies had shown up. Although she tried to speak clearly, coherently, her thoughts were all for Cameron. Had his chest wound been lethal? How bad was the cut on his thigh, a slash that had bled badly enough for her to see his blood soaking his jeans?

When she reached the emergency room no answers about Cameron's condition awaited her. He'd been rushed directly into surgery.

She slumped down on one of the plastic chairs to wait, knowing that she might be there for the rest of the night. Jason would never hurt another person again, but she had to know if he'd claimed one final victim before he'd gone down.

Chapter 18

Pain.

Cameron came to with a pain the likes of which he'd never known before. His chest felt as if it had been bisected and his upper left thigh was on fire. With his eyes closed he remained still, afraid to move. The constant beep of nearby machinery let him know he was in the hospital.

Mary! Her name flew through his head and he jerked up, instantly regretting his sudden move as darkness once again claimed him.

When he came to again the pain was tolerable and midafternoon sunshine flowed through the nearby window. How long had he been here? Somehow he knew it had been longer than just overnight.

Mary? He had to find out if she was okay. He fumbled to find the nurse call button and pushed it. He heard the responding ding from the nurses' station outside of his room and it took only a minute for RN Kerry Killian to scurry inside, a bright smile on her face.

"Ah, you're finally awake." She moved to his side, bringing with her the scents of antiseptic hand sanitizer and vanilla perfume.

"How long have I been here?" he asked, his throat scratchy and raw.

"Three days."

"Mary? Mary Mathis?" A frantic fear rushed through him as he stared at Kerry with the painful need to know.

"Mary is just fine. She's been here to visit you during the afternoons and evenings."

"And Jason McKnight...Brandon Williams?"

Kerry frowned. "He'll probably never walk again so he'd better hope they let him take that scooter of his to prison with him." She patted his shoulder. "And now I'm going to get the doctor and tell him you're back among the living."

Cameron relaxed back against the pillows. Mary was safe and apparently his backup team had arrived in time to take care of McKnight. Whatever physical injuries Cameron had suffered didn't matter. The bad guy was behind bars, his town was safe and most important of all Mary was okay. That's all that truly mattered.

A quick chat with the doctor let Cameron know that he'd received eighteen stitches in his thigh, and ten in his chest. He'd received a blood transfusion to replace what he'd lost and he'd also suffered a punctured lung, which was healing nicely. The doctor thought he could go home in another day or two.

It wasn't long after the doctor left that Mary stepped through the door. The sun shone bright on her blond hair and her beautiful blue eyes radiated warmth.

To Cameron's embarrassment, tears filled his eyes. Before he could swipe them away she sat in the chair next to his bed and grabbed his hand, her own eyes also misty.

"Oh, Cameron, you had me so scared," she said, laughing as they each wiped their eyes.

"I felt the same way about you. My last thought was that I was dying and there was nobody to save you." Anguish welled up inside him.

"But you did save me. You braved Jason's knife without any weapon of your own. You almost died because of me." Once again her blue eyes welled up with tears.

"I would have died for you and Matt." He hadn't meant to say the words. He hadn't meant for her to know how he ached for her love, how there were moments he wasn't sure he could breathe without seeing her face.

He cleared his voice. "Thank God, my men got there to take care of Jason."

"Actually, they didn't." She pulled her hands from his as her face paled. "You were on the floor and I thought you were dead. Junior was so traumatized he couldn't stop sobbing and there was nothing left but me, Jason and your gun on the counter."

Cameron stared at her in surprise. "You grabbed my gun? You shot Jason?"

"I wanted to shoot him through his cold, black heart, but despite what I thought I'd done years ago, I'm not a killer. I saw his power scooter and thought about the charade he'd played here for so long, the honorable vet who'd nearly given his life for his country, and had certainly given his legs for the cause. So, I shot him in his kneecap and then I shot him in his other knee."

She raised her chin, as if expecting him to chastise her, but instead, to his surprise a bubble of laughter escaped his lips. Her eyes widened and suddenly they were both laughing. It was the laughter of survival, of returning from hell, the sound of victory in the face of what might have been defeat.

As it faded away, once again she took his hand in hers. "You have your town back," she said. "The bad guy is gone and all is right in Grady Gulch."

He nodded and squeezed her hand. "And you have your life back. You'll never have to be afraid of Jason McKnight again. You're free to run your café without fear, to build your future without secrets and to find the man who can share your life with you and your son. If I can't have your love, Mary, then it's enough to know that you're happy." The words hurt but he knew they were the right ones to say.

She was silent for a long minute and then released a deep sigh. "Oh, Cameron, I've been so screwed up about all this love stuff." She released his hand and sat back in the chair. "For so many years I've been afraid to let anyone get too close for fear they'd find out that I was a murderer. Even if I could get over that fear, I had to question my judgment when it came to any man

I might choose to be with." Her face twisted in self-disgust. "I mean, look who I chose to marry."

Cameron started to speak but she stopped him by leaning forward and taking hold of his hand once again. "Then I found out Jason was alive and we fell into bed together and I told myself I couldn't be in love with you because we hadn't even dated."

His breath caught in his chest and it had nothing to do with the injury he'd suffered. It had to do with the dazzle in her eyes, a glittering that promised something wonderful about to happen.

"Every night that I turned that Open sign in the window to Closed it was with the anticipation that you were going to show up for that last cup of coffee. I loved the intimacy of sharing that time alone with you, talking about our day, our lives, our dreams. That's when I realized we've been dating almost every night for the past eight years and that's when I realized I could trust what I feel for you."

"And that is?" Once again his mouth was dry and his heart beat painfully fast. He didn't want to hope and be crushed and yet he couldn't help the hope that surged up inside him.

"I love you." She smiled, pure joy radiating from her gorgeous eyes. "I love you, Cameron Evans, and I want you in my life. I want you in my son's life forever."

For a moment he wondered if the final events in the café had altered his comprehension or maybe he was still under the influence of the anesthesia.

She frowned and loosened her grip on his hand. "Unless, maybe with everything that's happened you've changed your mind about me…about us."

"If I was capable right now I'd jump out of this bed and wrap you in my arms." He saw his dreams shining from her eyes. "Mary, it feels like I was born loving you and I'm certain that I'll die loving you."

She rose from her chair and kissed him on the forehead. "Then hurry up and get well and get out of this place so we can start building our life together."

Minutes later as he watched her leave his hospital room to deal with the dinner rush at the café, he knew he watched his future walking away and knew with equal certainty that she would be back. Their love had been strong enough to withstand secrets, a sleet storm and a serial killer. He figured together they could face anything the future might hold.

Epilogue

The café bustled with activity and the air smelled of smoked turkey and cornbread stuffing, of tangy cranberry salad and sweet potato pie. All the staff was on duty for the day when Mary provided a buffet style Thanksgiving dinner and this year she'd decided to make the meal free to anyone who lived in Grady Gulch. It was her way of saying thanks to the small town that had stood beside her during the past month.

Rusty and Junior worked side by side in the kitchen to make sure everything was ready when the doors opened in fifteen minutes. Already there was a crowd of people lining up outside, braving the cold for Mary's fare and that sense of community that the Cowboy Café offered.

Cameron, Mary and Matt busied themselves to make

sure the tables all had silverware and the water glasses were filled. The buffet itself had been set up across the counter and Cameron had already removed the stools that usually sat there and had taken them to a storage shed just outside.

The past two weeks had been crazy and wonderful. Mary and Matt had moved into Cameron's house, Rusty had officially taken over the rooms in the back of the café and even Junior had been rewarded by all the good cheer by Cameron making him an official honorary deputy for his bravery and smart thinking in punching three on his cell phone despite his head injuries.

Mary was talking to Lila, Junior's mother about allowing Junior to stay in Rusty's cabin on the weekends and Rusty had promised to supervise to make sure Junior stayed safe and sound.

Cameron was even enjoying a new relationship with his father. Although far from perfect, it was better, and Cameron was just pleased that the two of them seemed to be moving in the right direction.

Mary ran back to the kitchen to check the final details as Matt and Cameron finished outfitting the last table. When they were finished Matt touched him on the arm. "I was just wondering something," Matt said, his gaze not quite meeting Cameron's.

"And what were you wondering?" Cameron asked.

Matt gulped visibly and shifted his weight from one foot to the other, obviously nervous about something. "I was just wondering that when you and Mom get married, maybe it would be okay if I called you Dad."

Cameron hadn't thought his heart could get any

fuller, but it did as it expanded with love of this boy who had never known his real father, a boy who Cameron had called his own for a very long time. He placed a hand on Matt's shoulder. "I would be honored to have you call me Dad. You're already the son of my heart, Matt, and once your mom and I are married I intend to start the proceedings to adopt you, if that's okay with you."

Matt grinned up at him. "That's more than okay with me." He gave Cameron a quick hug. "I've got a lot of stuff to be thankful for this year," he said and then turned and headed for the kitchen.

Mary walked up to Cameron, her eyes filled with curiosity. "What was that all about?"

"He asked if after we got married he could call me Dad," Cameron replied, having to talk around the lump in his throat. He pulled her into his arms, loving the way she fit against him. "So that means at Christmas I'll officially be his dad."

She grinned up at him. "You mean by Valentine's Day."

It had been an ongoing discussion. Cameron wanted to be married by Christmas and Mary was holding out for a Valentine's Day wedding.

As he gazed down into her eyes, so filled with happiness, so full of love for him, he was vaguely aware of the front door being opened and people starting to make their way inside.

"I've got a better idea," he said impulsively. "Why don't we get a license next week and head to the nearest justice of the peace?"

"Okay," she agreed easily.

"Really?" His heart began a new beat of happiness as he thought of officially making her his bride.

She wound her arms around his neck. "I don't need the hearts and flowers of Valentine's Day or the glitter and shine of Christmas for my wedding day. All I need is you and Matt. And I've also been thinking that since Matt has shown such good responsibility with Twinkie, maybe he's ready for a little brother or sister."

He took her lips in a kiss that stole his breath away, that filled his soul with everything it had been missing. All the dreams he'd ever entertained about Mary and Matt filling his house with love and laughter were coming true.

"Now, if that's not a sight to ruin an old man's appetite," George Wilton exclaimed as he swept past them to the head of the buffet line.

They broke apart with laughter and Mary quickly left Cameron's side to take her place behind the counter where she could help serve the hungry.

Cameron sat in a chair and watched as Matt stepped up next to his mother to help. His woman. His son. Every space in his heart was filled with happiness.

His town was safe from the man who had terrorized it and next week Mary would be his wife and he'd start the adoption process where Matt was concerned.

He smiled as he saw the Benson brothers, Nick and Adam, along with their wives, Melanie and Courtney, enter the café. Melanie was in her wheelchair and Adam pushed her to a table nearby, then leaned down and kissed her on the cheek.

Cameron would always believe that the important fact he'd overlooked in attempting to find the killer of the waitresses was that he hadn't checked into Brandon Williams's background. The fact that the man had presented himself as a disabled vet had been bought hook, line and sinker by Cameron. It was a mistake he would never make again.

George Wilton slid into the chair next to Cameron, his plate heaping with a little bit of all the food that the Thanksgiving feast had to offer. "Why do you have that dopey grin on your face?" the old man asked.

Cameron widened the smile he hadn't even realized had been on his lips. "In the words of a very bright young boy, I've got a lot of stuff to be thankful for this year, George."

George huffed. "And I'm still waiting for that sexy young thing to show up in my life to rock my world."

Cameron laughed and in that moment knew that all was right in the world, or at least in the Cowboy Café in the small town of Grady Gulch, Oklahoma.

* * * * *

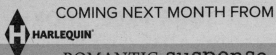

REQUEST YOUR FREE BOOKS!
2 FREE NOVELS PLUS 2 FREE GIFTS!

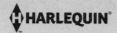

ROMANTIC suspense

Sparked by danger, fueled by passion

YES! Please send me 2 FREE Harlequin® Romantic Suspense novels and my 2 FREE gifts (gifts are worth about $10). After receiving them, if I don't wish to receive any more books, I can return the shipping statement marked "cancel." If I don't cancel, I will receive 4 brand-new novels every month and be billed just $4.74 per book in the U.S. or $5.24 per book in Canada. That's a savings of at least 14% off the cover price! It's quite a bargain! Shipping and handling is just 50¢ per book in the U.S. and 75¢ per book in Canada.* I understand that accepting the 2 free books and gifts places me under no obligation to buy anything. I can always return a shipment and cancel at any time. Even if I never buy another book, the two free books and gifts are mine to keep forever.

240/340 HDN F45N

Name	(PLEASE PRINT)	
Address		Apt. #
City	State/Prov.	Zip/Postal Code

Signature (if under 18, a parent or guardian must sign)

Mail to the **Harlequin® Reader Service:**
IN U.S.A.: P.O. Box 1867, Buffalo, NY 14240-1867
IN CANADA: P.O. Box 609, Fort Erie, Ontario L2A 5X3

Want to try two free books from another line?
Call 1-800-873-8635 or visit www.ReaderService.com.

* Terms and prices subject to change without notice. Prices do not include applicable taxes. Sales tax applicable in N.Y. Canadian residents will be charged applicable taxes. Offer not valid in Quebec. This offer is limited to one order per household. Not valid for current subscribers to Harlequin Romantic Suspense books. All orders subject to credit approval. Credit or debit balances in a customer's account(s) may be offset by any other outstanding balance owed by or to the customer. Please allow 4 to 6 weeks for delivery. Offer available while quantities last.

Your Privacy—The Harlequin® Reader Service is committed to protecting your privacy. Our Privacy Policy is available online at www.ReaderService.com or upon request from the Harlequin Reader Service.

We make a portion of our mailing list available to reputable third parties that offer products we believe may interest you. If you prefer that we not exchange your name with third parties, or if you wish to clarify or modify your communication preferences, please visit us at www.ReaderService.com/consumerschoice or write to us at Harlequin Reader Service Preference Service, P.O. Box 9062, Buffalo, NY 14269. Include your complete name and address.

Turning his back on Gabby, Trevor strode out of the living room.

The moment he did, Gabby immediately followed him.
Since the area was still crowded with people, she only managed
to catch up to him just at the front door.

Trevor spared her a look that would have frosted most people's
toes. "Where do you think you're going?" he asked.

He sounded so angry, she thought. Not that she blamed him,
but she still wished he wouldn't glare at her like that. She hadn't
put Avery in harm's way on purpose. It was a horrible accident.

"With you," she answered.

"Oh no, you're not," he cried. "You're staying here," he ordered, waving his hand around the foyer, as if a little bit of
magic was all that was needed to transform the situation.

Stubbornly, Gabby held her ground, surprising Trevor even

though he gave no indication. "You're going to need help," she insisted.

Not if it meant taking help from her, he thought.

"No, I am not," he replied tersely, being just as stubborn as she was. "I've got to find my daughter. I don't have time to babysit you."

"Nobody's asking you to. I can be a help. I *can,*" she insisted when he looked at her unconvinced. "Where are you going?" she wanted to know.

"To the rodeo."

That didn't make any sense. Unless— "You have a lead?" she asked, lowering her voice.

"I'm going to see Dylan and tell him his mother's dead," he informed her. "That's not a lead, that's a death sentence for his soul. You still want to come along?" he asked mockingly. Trevor was rather certain that his self-appointed task would make her back off.

Trevor was too direct and someone needed to soften the blow a little. Gabby figured she was elected. "Yes, I do," she replied firmly, managing to take the man completely by surprise.

**Don't miss
THE COLTON RANSOM
by Marie Ferrarella**

**Available July 2013 from
Harlequin Romantic Suspense
wherever books are sold.**

HARLEQUIN®

ROMANTIC suspense

Security genius Campbell Steele goes
undercover to out the internal threat sabotaging
Abby McBane's company. But when Abby
becomes the target, Campbell sees a greater
threat to his heart.

Look for *THE PARIS ASSIGNMENT*
next month by new
Harlequin® Romantic Suspense®
author Addison Fox.

Available wherever books and ebooks are sold.

Heart-racing romance, high-stakes suspense!

HARLEQUIN®

A Romance FOR EVERY MOOD™

Stay up-to-date on all your romance-reading news with the *Harlequin Shopping Guide,* featuring bestselling authors, exciting new miniseries, books to watch and more!

The newest issue will be delivered right to you with our compliments! There are 4 each year.

Signing up is easy.

EMAIL

ShoppingGuide@Harlequin.ca

WRITE TO US

HARLEQUIN BOOKS
Attention: Customer Service Department
P.O. Box 9057, Buffalo, NY 14269-9057

OR PHONE

1-800-873-8635 in the United States
1-888-343-9777 in Canada

Please allow 4-6 weeks for delivery of the first issue by mail.